DATE DUE

BOOKS BY FREDERICK BUSCH

FICTION

Girls (1997)
The Children in the Woods (1994)
Long Way from Home (1993)
Closing Arguments (1991)
Harry and Catherine (1990)
War Babies (1989)
Absent Friends (1989)
Sometimes I Live in the Country (1986)
Too Late American Boyhood Blues (1984)
Invisible Mending (1984)
Take This Man (1981)
Rounds (1979)
Hardwater Country (1979)
The Mutual Friend (1978)
Domestic Particulars (1976)
Manual Labor (1974)
Breathing Trouble (1973)
I Wanted a Year Without Fall (1971)

NONFICTION

When People Publish (1986)
Hawkes (1973)

INVISIBLE
MENDING

—

Invisible Mending

—

A NOVEL BY
FREDERICK BUSCH

SOUTHERN METHODIST
UNIVERSITY PRESS

Dallas

Press edition, 1997

e material from this work

Southern Methodist University Press
P.O. Box 750415
Dallas, TX 75275-0415

The author wishes to acknowledge Joachim Neugroschel for his
translation of Paul Celan's poetry appearing in italics in this novel.

LIBRARY OF CONGRESS CATALOGING IN PUBLICATION DATA

Busch, Frederick, 1941-
    Invisible mending : a novel / by Frederick Busch. —
1st Southern Methodist University Press ed.
        p.   cm.
    ISBN 0-87074-417-8 (paper)
    I. Title
PS3552.U814I5   1997
813'.54—dc21   96-29790

Cover illustration by Vige Barrie
Cover design by Tom Dawson Graphic Design
Printed in the United States of America on acid-free paper

10 9 8 7 6 5 4 3 2 1

For Nick

INVISIBLE
MENDING

—

Dusk dropped into the air like whiskey into water in a glass. I wasn't drunk, though I'd been drinking Wild Turkey for an hour or so in a bar filled with Christian alcoholics. Very few Jews are drunks, a woman named Rhona once told me. I introduced her to a man named Lefty, Jewish guy who boozed very hard and still could cope with his life, but he was exceptional, she explained, dismissing him because his life on the earth contradicted her theory. She was exceptional too. But it *did* drop down from the blankness over high bright buildings. The bar I had stood in for a while offered a bartender who'd poured the water over ice and only then poured the dark-brown whiskey, and it had filtered down through the water in oily tendrils, and then it's dusk, the day is umber and nearly night, and there you are, and there I was, standing on Fifth and 49th, and maybe thinking more about walking into all that traffic and taking my chances with the end of the world.

The taxis there come driving down Fifth Avenue with a special anger. The clots of traffic break as the lights change, and the taxis pour with an energy that's arterial. It's class warfare, and the cabbies seem to aim at the pedestrians there, threatening crushed kneecaps and jellied spleens. A snooty walker on Fifth and 49th might wear a coat that's worth a cabbie's year. *Jump!* they say in New York when a fool is perched on the edge of a high and dangerous place and threatening to dive into his audience. *Jump! Don't jump! Nah: jump, what the hell.* Standing on the curb and watching that traffic come was like standing at the edge of a high and dangerous place. Listen: sometimes in their lives people come to the edge of something. At forty years of age, in the eightieth year of the century, in the twelfth year of my marriage, in the eighth year of my child, that's where I was.

It was Christmas in Manhattan, and at dusk on Fifth the windows of the stores were bright, the clothing in them was opulent, the stores were perfumed and murmuring, and I was going to cross the street. I was not going to walk into traffic and get burst and dragged into mucus on the avenue, I think. I was going to cross the street while considering how the dusk fell down on the day, when I heard a voice. I really thought I heard the voice. I thought it called to me: "Zimmer!"

On the other hand, that's a common German-American name, and even if it had been rendered by my father, in a burst of bad choice, from the Russo-Czech Zamecnik, there were plenty of Zimmers, German and otherwise, and it hardly had to be Rhona Glinsky's voice. I was surrounded by shoulders, wing-tip shoes, long overcoats, and short mink jackets, beaver collars and woollen caps, lots of breath and jaws that popped chewing gum and, like most New Yorkers, I had little desire to raise my eyes and meet another pair of eyes—particularly, as New York has taught us, because they might be staring back. But I had heard that voice, a woman's deep hoarse voice, say my name in just that way, though not for years. I compromised and swung myself 360 degrees and stared at nothing, but made my face available to anyone who sought it. No one called me again, and that, I told myself, was that, because she wasn't there.

I did not walk into the traffic. I waited for the light and then went west, thinking how she would have laughed at the fine irony or our meeting again during Christmastime. And I thought as well that I had been thinking of her. Hadn't I heard her voice, and for no clear reason? On the Avenue of the Americas, the voice, behind me now, said, "Zimmer, will you *wait?*"

At work, sporadically for several tedious months, I had been railing at my editorial colleagues to join with me in the publication of an unnecessary, because redundant, volume of the poems of Paul Celan, the Rumanian—

Black milk of dawn we drink you at night
we drink you at noon, death is a master from Germany

—whose work, shown to me in a new translation from the German, had taken a hold on me. I should have known, I realized, that I was thinking of Rhona. Why else would I have made such a fuss about a nonprofit book of poems which already existed in adequate English? I wondered, then, on Sixth Avenue, if Andreoscu had known the poet. But Rhona, or the dream of her voice, almost twenty years after I had lived with her and Andreoscu and those crazy hunts through downtown New York, had asked me to wait.

And now, in the middle of almost everything, as the end of my boyhood and the probability of something like the end of the world began to converge, I wondered whether to turn and tell the woman, or the dream of her, and all that suddenly beckoning past, that, yes, I would.

In Manhattan at dusk, in winter, the street gleams like oil, and papers rattle at dark doorways. Footsteps near you are loud, then disappear. Everything is noticed, and then not noticeable; you are always, finally, alone. And there I was, hiding in it, a large and bold-looking man with a flattened nose—out-of-work boxer gone into well-dressed retirement, perhaps. And there I was, a man who had raged over poems in the afternoon, again, because in the morning I had swept my eight-year-old son, with his mother's cheekbones and my shoulders and my large dark eyes, out of the Lenox School and over to Hoffritz, where I had bought him a gigantic Swiss army knife because, as I had told him, "You never know. You don't. And you might need it. And I love you." And there I was, thinking of how the school had telephoned Lillian at her office, and how she had later telephoned me, and how I had finally admitted, too loudly of course, into my office phone that "Well, of course I knew it was motivated by guilt. Gee, that's terrific, Lil. You really have a handle on me and my guilt. How about, though, if I tell you I really did it—*maybe*, now—because I knew you would get pissed off and you would call me? Because I really wanted to talk to you. You know. I wanted to talk to you. It's true. No maybe."

And there I was, my recently separated wife having hung up on me, my son having looked at me with eyes that seemed bruised, and my associates, some of them intimate ones, having been estranged by my inexplicable anger about Rumanian poems in German. I was in the middle of that life and Rhona, it sounded like Rhona, had just barely finished calling, if she really had, "Will you *wait?*" She had called once before, in Greenwich Village, eighteen years ago, after a poetry reading in the Loeb Center of New York University. I was there because after quitting the M.A. program at Columbia, and after finding my level, as they say, which was as copywriter for a PR syndicate, I was trying to convince myself that I was still a man of the mind. So I went to poetry readings on 92nd Street, at Columbia, at NYU, at the long string of small bookstores that connected the various New York literary institutions uptown and down. There I was, living the life of the mind at the Loeb, listening to a recent winner of a small prize read his poems. He was funny, and a good reader, and it was half-past eight of a Thursday night, and I was not in love. I was lonely, I was hungry, I was listening to a man proclaim that he would mourn the death of a creature killed by a passing car "like a Jew, wailing, on my hands and on my knees."

The reading ended to pretty good applause, the poet was smiling and sweaty, dazed, like a lover who didn't think he'd make it to her bed, and who didn't think, once in it, that he'd make it out. "Sir? *Sir?*"

The voice belonged to Rhona Glinsky, though I didn't know it then. "Sir," she called, standing. Big shoulders, large chest, wide hips, big ass, strong legs, and everything looking, all the time, as if it were moving forward —a result, possibly, of her aggressive sharp nose and stern jaw, very dark eyes surrounded by a great deal of eye shadow. What man, leaving her, had said that her eyes were her strongest feature? How could such an intimidating woman be vulnerable to someone fool enough to undervalue her?

"Sir, don't you think that your sentimental treatment of the death of a skunk by the side of the Cross Bronx

7

Expressway is a trivialization of what people *do* mourn for 'like a Jew'? Or 'like Jews'? I forget which. Thank you."

She sat down to the moaning of poets and poetry lovers, some hisses, and the total bewilderment of the poet. "Death is trivial?" he said, looking around, though still smiling, for support. He got it. They clapped.

She stood up again, in the slanting cool hall, surrounded by disbelievers. "When it's a rodent's death, compared to that of the children in wars, yes. I do. When you think of the Six Million, I do."

The poor poet. He said, "What, I killed them in Poland or something by writing a poem? I can't write about death without your permission?"

What made me cry out? Doubtless, it was my need to live the life of the mind. If you did what I did for a living, you would cry too. "Maybe it's the difference between art and propaganda you're talking about. Ma'am."

She wheeled, directed those eyes at me, and she said, "You don't have to call me ma'am. Unless you'd like me to call you sir. And all art is a form of propaganda."

I was pretty sure there was something to reply, but I was embarrassed to have ridiculed her, and the hall was really alive by then, the poet slipping into a casual cross with thorn-garland and palm-nails, wailing and walking back and forth, declaiming, the angry woman with bold eyes crying her objections back at him, and others in the small audience letting slip their hoots and hollers. So I left, heading across the lounge for the street and a walk in the park in October, some pizza and some beer and a visit to the Eighth Street Bookstore.

Rhona caught me half a block away. "Will you wait?" She spoke firmly, I stammered; she offered to pay for half of the pizza, I said yes with too much gratitude. And there we were.

Rhona had changed her life a few times, she told me. Like most women and men who lived in New York during the sixties, she did life-changing of the sort you associate with repapering the living room, or altering a hairstyle, or moving from one vaguely beneficent group to another—from Friends of Polyps, chaired by a Bakuninite marine biologist, to The Red and the Black, an interracial Trotskyite chess club. Rhona was the daughter of a man who had lived through a year in Birkenau. Rhona was the daughter of a man who had sold submersible pump motors to the Coast Guard during the Second World War. In consequence, she had grown up well-to-do and brooding and fat; in consequence, she now was thinner, scornful of money she didn't earn, and broodier. She had changed her life in high school by becoming a Jewish zealot and, in her senior year, by sleeping with a boy whose ambition was to kill Arabs of any nationality and persuasion for the sake of peace on earth and an Israeli hegemony extending from Taiwan to Detroit. She had changed her life again at Barnard by becoming artistic, short-haired, more or less slender, and a student of Oriental philosophies. Her understanding of these was limited to what Gary Snyder and Philip Whalen had told her after a reading at Columbia.

At the New School in 1960 she met a man who wore a black leather jacket that creaked, yellowish-brown boots with high heels, careless flannel shirts with expensive turtlenecks under them, and blue jeans with ironed-in creases; he carried a briefcase made of thick leather with American Indian magic signs tooled around the strap. She later saw the briefcase advertised in *The New Yorker*, the boots at Abercrombie & Fitch, the turtlenecks in the L. L. Bean catalogue, the jacket at Hunting World, and his watch strap—it was two and one-half inches across and supported a Rolex—at Mark Cross. He was a pi-

oneer, an authority at Queens College on herbs and
chemicals that galvanized the consciousness; he gave
courses on how they provided bright vision in a world
become murky, especially to undergradutes with enough
money, and a high disregard for what was called Mental
Health. He was seven years older than Rhona. He practiced no religion, but was the son of a Conservative
rabbi. He permitted her to type some of his manuscripts,
and then tired of her impatience with his interest in
being interviewed by anyone, but especially by women
from college newspapers. Rhona entered my life with
Jewish skunks and thick-crusted pizza two weeks after
his book, *The Defeat of Sorrow*, was reviewed gloriously
in the *Herald Tribune* with, as Rhona put it, "self-serving
majesty" by a professor at Brandeis. The author was now
loving someone thinner (Rhona had started to eat sugar
buns and ladyfingers when she detected his boredom
with her boredom), and Rhona had recently changed
her life again. "For the last time," she told me omi-
nously.

Rhona was a librarian now. She had accepted some of
her father's submersible money, and had traveled to
Michigan, where she had earned her master's in library
science and had decided to return to New York to work
at a public library, and to listen to her Jewish heart. This,
she told me over chianti poured from (what else?) a *fi-
asco*, meant *Jewish* heart, not merely the muscle hung
crookedly among the ribs of Jews. "Life among the
goyim taught me some things," she said of Ann Arbor.
"The blacks are right, first of all. You are either an
enemy or a friend. Part of the problem, or part of the
solution. You've heard that? Also" —thumping on her
drum of a chest with enough resonance to move me back
in my seat—"I do not subscribe to the ancient fooleries

of an often misguided people. Read the laws." I nodded, as if it were an order. "Women are unclean during the menstrual period, that sort of primitive gobbledygook. You understand? I reject the prejudices of a bronze-age tribe. What I accept is I-am-I, that force in history. And the savage unpredictability of fate. I accept that. Being a Jew is living *in* history, with an interventionist Lord. I accept *that*."

Rhona's favorite library work was in serials, and I thought of her, as she told me things, locked each day in a room with flaking newspapers and magazines, the covers of which curled and the spines of which had lost their staples. There she sat, doubtless on a high three-legged wooden stool, cataloguing old magazines and hunting for sour news.

She paid for her own pizza. We discussed Isaac Babel. He had said a Jew on a horse was not a Jew, she told me. I agreed, thinking the remark was about Cossack self-hatred. Rhona corrected me. I didn't much care. I walked her to the West Fourth Street subway stop. We shook hands goodbye, first trading phone numbers—Rhona's idea—and we said we'd stay in touch.

Crazy? Of course. As crazy as half the girls I'd been at high school with, and some of the women at college, and many of the people with whom I shared toilets and typewriters at work. Crazy Jewish female: what else is new to a boy from Brooklyn? But her eyes remained—that pathetic effort to look like a vamp. The body, I confess, also remained: sad because while the breast jutted and the shoulders hung back, and there was stalk in her walk, you could also tell that what she wanted to do was fold her arms across her chest, and curl her legs together, keep the knees high before her as she sat, and be seen perhaps a little less. And the early spectrum of commitment, zealotry, faith—I could not have named it, and I'm not certain that I could today if I had to—this too remained, but as hint or warning more than comprehended fact: the arc of conviction, with the needle wobbling between Jewish skunks at poetry readings and I-am-I over pizza with an obvious non- or semi- (how could she tell yet?) believer. I vowed to not be enchanted.

So I went to work the next day, and I didn't think of menstruating Jewesses or crucified poets at the Loeb. I went to my desk at American Synopsis, and getting there was in itself the usual adventure. Past the blind black singer on 42nd and Broadway, past the pimps and pushers drinking beer and eating hot dogs at 9 A.M. in the bar with no front wall. Up in the slow elevator. Along a shabby corridor lined by offices that never were open. Into the four rooms comprising American Synopsis, run by Maxwell Ollub for the glorification of man and his slower-moving products.

That's what he told the staff—Mel, the drunk from Texas who, in his forty-fifth year, sold space in Max Ollub's "magazine"; Laraine, who weighed in at (conservatively) 245, and who talked loud and long about love in its coarser aspects ("I'm telling you, I'm so sore I can't *move!*") and who always wore the New York fashions first, despite her size; Howard, who wore the same blue suit every day, and who looked like Laraine, but who didn't seem to have a life outside the office, much less one with sex in it. Those were the sales personnel, who occupied the room off Max's. On the other side of Max's office, in two connecting rooms, were the underpaid high school kids and autistic women who stuffed envelopes and ran the mimeo machine. And in the last room were the writers—Len, from Glens Falls, who had come to New York as a chorus boy and who had learned to talk deep, smoke too much, and call himself Managing Editor; Grover, who wanted to get a Ph.D. in medieval lit but couldn't afford to; Janie, who commuted from New Jersey, who was married to what sounded like an artichoke, and who was the best writer in the shop; and I, Zimmer, disappointed scholar and composer of snappy synopses.

Max or one of the sales people would get hold of a sad, failing public relations hack from one of the larger firms. This person was almost always a man, was almost always overdressed and undertalented, and almost always drank too much for lunch while making the mistake of thinking that he, and what he did, mattered. Let's say that X, a PR man, needed to promote peanuts for the Georgia Peanut Council. Let's say he'd circulated recipes for peanut brittle to the radio stations, had paid a bum to wear a peanut suit and walk up and down Sixth Avenue, and had begged a TV "personality" on a local show in New Jersey to say he'd heard that peanuts were good for people with recent surgery. He'd have a few hundred left in his budget, and he wouldn't know how to spend it. How do you make peanuts glamorous? Ask Maxwell Ollub of American Synopsis, Inc. He'd watch X drink, Max would, and he'd let his lower lip droop above his chinless neck and he'd nearly drool while rubbing his crew cut. But he'd get the order. He'd dash into the writers' room and say, "By tomorrow morning! Four versions! Peanuts! Here's the poop." Setting down in a flurry of anxious triumph some Peanut Council information sheets, Max would disappear, leaving us to compose on the run. Grover would do, say, Peanuts in Viking History, while Janie would do Nuts Through the Ages, and Len would look at books while getting us to do the work; I'd take The History and Mystery of Peanuts. Each synopsis, short and punchy, would go something like this:

> Think the peanut's a nut? Wrong there! Wonder how it's connected to American Emancipation? Greater sexual energy? The exotic cooking of distant India? Ever wonder how the salt is made to stick to each and every nut? Read on!

The synopses would, of course, summarize articles that didn't exist. Whatever Max sold a synopsis for, we'd have to write, and instantly. And then, four times a year, we'd put together a catalogue of synopses ("I'm in magazine publishing, I was known to say casually) and send it to every smalltown paper in the country. When they ticked off on their postage-paid card which articles and illustrations they wanted, the Hispanic-Americans and silent women would mail them their mimeographed stories, complete with cartoons, drawings, or photos. And that's why, in little papers all over America, there appear articles on peanuts, clean floors, tourism in Des Moines, and the virtues of cotton. And in each article, planted at least three times, usually with such skill that part-time editors can't cut them out without rewriting the feature, there appear references to products or other clients—those who paid American Synopsis enough to pay us enough to climb the IRT steps to 42nd Street and Seventh every day.

The week after Rhona and I met, my college roommate's father died. The roommate, Benny DiLorenzo, and I had seen little of each other since college. Some months after graduation, while I was losing my grip on matters at Columbia, he had married Joanne. And a year after that, his father died and he invited me to the funeral. In college, while Benny played inspired football for the varsity squad, he was in love with Margerie, a pretty Jewish girl from Brooklyn. Benny was not Jewish, and though Margerie loved him, her father did not. That was why he set detectives on him—friends, from the local precinct, who beat Benny up. That was why he locked his daughter in the house. That was why the girl, finally kept by force from seeing Benny, grew fat and crazy, developed a glandular condition, swelled about the neck and chin, and helped drive Benny somewhat crazy too. Margerie survived, and she grew healthy enough to marry a Jewish man in business. Benny survived, and Joanne, who had loved him for years and who'd been willing to provide him with affection during each interdiction Benny and Margerie suffered, waited long enough, again, and then married him. I remember Joanne, short and thin and buck-toothed, telling me just before the marriage that she cleaned between the tiles of her bathroom with a toothbrush. I never forgot that advice, and I never took it.

So there came the call from Joanne, no reference to tiles or toothbrushes, but the word that Benny's father had died, and they thought I might wish to attend a high mass on a dark winding street in a part of Brooklyn I didn't know. So there I was, lost and panicking, sweaty, among brownstones and barber shops, huffing and closer to a run than a walk, late for my former roommate's father's mass. I crossed a street, turned a corner, knew that I could never find my way back to the subway, that I'd be forever lost. And there it was: a tall narrow church, blackened by grime, with undistinguished doors of great tallness, and I was late, and suddenly the doors sprang out at me, and there came the weepers, the dumpy women in dark clothes with their bleached hair, and there were the men with narrow mustaches, and there were the children, pale and yawning, and two policemen, signs of honor and corruption, and they all passed me without noticing as they went to the hearse and the black limousines. My roommate, out of sight, my old friend, was on his way to the graveyard without me, and here I was, failing him. My knees grew weak, and I felt that I was falling to the sidewalk in a cloud of corrupted funeral lilies and the pollen that made my nose itch and my eyes water. I was shaky and lost and I saw the little priest trailing the procession, swinging his censer, god-gas surrounding it, and the barbarity of it, the final fact that this was *mass* for a person who was *dead*, and that on top of physical death, ritual mass, and the panic of being lost in eastern Brooklyn, I had committed grave social blunderings by missing all the Latin parts, this struck me like a heavy hand. I slid backward and almost went down. I was weeping at last, between sneezes, and I felt that I was stranded in a nation whose language I would never learn.

The cops, however, after watching the limousines follow the hearse, lit up cigarettes. Two remaining mourners unfastened their ties. No one spoke, but the air of the street had somehow loosened, and breathing was a simpler business. I leaned against the iron banister of the church steps. A ten-year-old Chevrolet pulled up, and a tall Italian boy with a low forehead emerged to lope up the steps. The car pulled away. Then a black Lincoln parked, and my roommate and his wife and mother got out. "Here we go," a young mourner said to the police, "this is the big one." A policeman shrugged, they both put their cigarettes out, and I had to learn to mourn the death of strangers all over again. I have doubted my sincerity, in the presence of corpses, ever since. And the spirits I most feared, from that time on, were my own.

I first met Lillian at Babe Ruth's locker. We were in Cooperstown, in central New York, about 200 miles from the City. She was at the Mary Imogene Bassett Hospital there, watching her aunt die of unnamed cancers. I was visiting a jerk whose parents' home had promised relief from Manhattan in August. For a break from differing slow deaths, each one, we would learn, typical of us—my version had to do with mild discomforts, while hers could be verified in the actual world—Lillian and I had come our separate ways to the Baseball Hall of Fame.

Upstairs they had the turnstile through which I had walked into Ebbets Field, off Bedford Avenue. There were souvenirs of the Polo Grounds, where Sal Maglie had snarled, and where Willie Mays had been young on behalf of men like my father (and, all of a sudden, as old in my eyes as my father had become). There were recordings of the crowd noises from big-city ballparks— guys crying out about hot dogs and beer, the murmuring static of men and women connected to the players on the field by tension: everyone in ballparks, whether eagerly or sleepily, was always *waiting*. The hall was hot on the top floor, and the small exhibits—tiny gloves, and stubby bats, and little creased shoes—were surrounded by sweaty people, most of whom cared, as much as I was finding that I really did, about all that evidence of serious play.

There she was. I was wondering whether I had come just to return from the alien hugeness of Cooperstown's lawns and high houses to the roar (recorded) and turnstile (transplanted) of New York City's stadiums. I was concluding that, indeed, I had. And there she was. Tall and lean and big of shoulder and crowned with gold hair, she stood at Babe Ruth's Yankee Stadium locker, and she cried. For opposite the red locker was a television monitor on the wall. Over and over and over, without stopping, it showed a very short film loop about the great Bambino's life. Many of us, I noticed, stood to watch it again and again—as if hoping that, *this* time, after the perky speeded-up waddlings around the Stadium's diamond, after the fine heavy double-breasted coat, after the eager posings with crippled kids, after the smiles and the long cars and, again, the tiny mincing steps, as of a great bull with dainty feet, he might *not* be suddenly dead, and the film ending. Always, as if its producers also agreed, the film would jump from darkness and into the story of the Babe again. She was leaning against his locker. She was crying into white gloves. I hadn't seen white gloves on a woman in summer since my last Deborah Kerr film. I hadn't seen Rhona for several years. And I was certain that I understood this large, exotic creature's suffering and needs. Was not I of the Babe's own city?

I didn't have a handkerchief to offer her, and I wouldn't have known what to say if I had. Before my thoughts went beyond hurling her to the floor of the Baseball Hall of Fame and saying "Hi" in smooth tones, my body had moved me to the locker and to her, and I'd said, in all my wit and wisdom, "I see that you're crying—"

From behind her gloves came a sound, something like "Dooooooooop!" She made it again, after looking through her white cotton fingers, and as I watched her mouth I understood that she was laughing at me. Which was fine, because she wasn't moving away. Her eyes were red and quite ugly. Her nose was running and her skin was blotched. My stomach kicked, and I was off: Zimmer, in love with one more stranger. She sniffed, blew her nose in her own handkerchief, and looked at me so hard I thought that we might have met, that she might be bearing a memory of grudge or, worse, long boredom. But she said, "If you buy me a drink, I'll buy one for you."

I wanted to ask her to wait. I wanted her to wait at the Babe's locker while I ran to telephone one or two people from the publishing house where I worked. I wanted to say to them, "I am completely in love. It is very much like a terrific movie. She's waiting for me near Babe Ruth's dirty towel and cracked black cleats."

Instead, I did as she instructed—it promptly became something of a habit—and we bought each other drinks at a fancy bar the name of which had something to do with one of the infield positions. It might have been the Short Stop Bar, but I don't remember, because I was studying the texture of the dried skin along the top of her lower lip, and the tan along the barely visible knob of her left collarbone, and the length and strength of her fingers. She told me about her aunt, and how certain she was that her aunt would soon die. She told me about her father, who sat beside her bed and wept without sobbing or wiping his face, who only held his sister's hand and said, to anyone who came to check a chart or swab the bathroom, "Thank you, thank you very much." She told me about her apprenticeship with Bache & Co., and what it was like to be a woman in what men kept telling her was basically a man's world. "I own *three* man-tailored suits in tones of blue, for Christ's sake," she said.

I told her that I only owned one.

"But you're in publishing," she said. "Artistic occupations can wear anything."

"Is that a truth?"

"Guaranteed," she said. "I bet on . . . what—Wednesdays? I bet on one day a week, and I bet it's mostly the same *day* every week, you go in wearing a tweed jacket and jeans and desert boots. Or a navy-blue wool shirt with a red wool tie and a heavy jacket with elbow patches. Or just a crewneck and khakis. Am I right?"

I have mentioned that the movies were on my mind, and they were, to the point were I seemed to have lifted her hand to my lips and was kissing it. She nearly tore me out of our banquette at the Short Stop by not only not taking her hand away, but by quite directly opening her fingers so she could touch the tip of one to the outside of my lip. I think my pulse spiked twenty points.

Had she smoked, I would have lit cigarettes for us without getting smoke in my eyes. Had we both been boozers, I'd have ordered a fourth round with a masterful gesture. But we were college-educated thinkers-aloud —sometimes described as *intellectuals* by people who really didn't like us—and so I talked. I talked and talked, and told Lillian about the work I did, and the work I didn't do, and what sort of apartment I had on the corner of Cherry Lane and Commerce Street in Greenwich Village, and what my parents were up to, and what I ate for lunch, and how, when I had worked for a magazine about schools, in Greenwich, Connecticut, I had eaten every day at a bowling alley and yet never had hurled a bowling ball in anger in my life, and I watched her watch me, and I watched her lips for boredom, her eyes for fatigue, and I kept on seeing that this woman, at the ultimate least, did not mind that I was a one-hundred-percent Zimmer.

We agreed at last that she had to return to the hospital, and I to the home of my chum. We agreed that we would meet again the next day. I said, as we slid from the booth, "But when do we move in together. In town. When do we get married?"

She looked over her shoulder and said, "Don't push me, buddy." She was nearly smiling, but she wasn't. And she scared the hell out of me.

I felt two and a half feet tall. I felt as though I were looking up from the floor of the Short Stop Bar to this great golden creature who had something to do with bearer bonds for one of the West's great counting houses. I felt as though my voice were only a squeak. But I said it: "Lillian. Forgive me. I'm afraid I meant it, though."

This time she turned. This time she did smile. "I know," she said. "Isn't it scary? Isn't it *fun?*"

I moved toward her, because this was the time for the kiss. I was betting with myself that her lips would be cool.

She said—and I was two point five feet high again— "But let's *not* push me too hard anyway. All right?"

I would have said all right to surgery without anesthesia. I settled for a peck on the cheek, and the odor of her skin, which was a compound of sunshine and mild sweat and powder and something dark that made me think of bed. The door closed behind her as I rounded third and dug for home to pay the bill and get to the street just to see her go down toward the hospital. But I missed her. And I had to settle for standing on the sun-flooded sidewalk, impeding the progress of dozens of tourists while I grinned with triumph because I was the man who had just invented life.

When Sam, my son, our son, was asleep, his long dark lashes made him look delicate—no: vulnerable, I think. I think it was also his posture in sleep—arms thrown open, legs wide and stretched full-length, as if he were about to receive something, or as if he were endangered by something in the dark and he didn't know it. His eyelids and lashes often moved as he slept, and I looked at him and sometimes understood how much life teemed inside his skin. Sometimes I held his wrist as he slept, or lightly touched him on the cool forehead. He was often difficult to hug, for he would shy from me at emotional moments. I got him, though, during lightning storms and in airports, and of course while he slept. I suppose that even early on I was trying to keep him.

Not that Lillian was cruel. She was brilliant, she was tall and blonde and lanky, of course I had called her Snow Queen and Ice Maiden when we had fought early in our marriage, and she had fought well. But she rarely was cruel and almost never about Sam. Lillian made enough to pay me an allowance. But we had no official arrangement; she lived in the West 79th Street apartment with Sam, and I lived at the Tudor Hotel, that pitstop for pilots; we shared some bills, but otherwise didn't talk much about money. We talked about love and the death of love. She wondered if ours had died. I claimed that it was tired. She worked as an investment counselor. I went to work as a publisher. I often sniveled, and sometimes she did too. I saw pretty much of Sam, but I wanted all of him, everything, and Lillian too, and I think she was beginning to believe me. One night early in the separation, over sausage at La Louisiana, Lillian, her blond hair coiled behind her head and held up by magic, her bold cheekbones bright because she wore little makeup, said, "Do you see other women?"

I didn't gag. But I swallowed without chewing—a waste of Cajun cooking. I shook my head and I stared.

She laughed, showing teeth and rice and her long tongue. "No," she said. "No, I'm not dating."

I strove for hauteur. "No, I'm not, either," I said, patting my silky napkin on dry lips.

She laughed and shook her head and pointed, until I took note of the paisley necktie with which I'd wiped my mouth.

"The tie that binds," I told her and the waiter behind her. Smirking, he moved on.

"Do I get any rights of forbidding in this insanity of ours?" she asked.

"Lil, you get anything, I think. What is a rite of forbidding?"

"Can I forbid you to date other women?"

I sighed. The waiter still watched me, so I smiled a Latin roué's smile on a separated Slovak-Jewish husband's face, and I said, "Yes. And you too—well, you know. Men. Yes?"

"Yes I only like men? Or yes I agree not to see people socially?"

"Just say yes, Lil."

"But you're not supposed to tell me what to do."

"But you just told *me*."

"I asked you."

"Can I *ask* you?"

"No."

"Lil—"

"I won't date. All right? Can we stop arguing now?"

We were each forty. We were married. We were arguing about not arguing about dating people. It wasn't easy, but it wasn't over either. Ease, I told myself then, had always been significantly overrated. So, probably, had I. But I hadn't been easy. Perhaps I'd discovered a new virtue in myself. Perhaps it was like my other virtues so-called, or honesties, or fat-mouthed moral stances: forced upon me until I owned up to them, as in the case of my Jew Shoes.

When my father went to City College in 1930 at night for accounting, he sold shoes during the day. He hated selling shoes, but he wanted to be an accountant, so he kneeled beneath chafed red thighs, and fat-bubbles squeezed over stocking edges, and maps made of runs, and he pushed pumps over hammertoes and bunions, tied oxfords onto ankles heavy with bone. My father knew shoes. He took us to Florsheim for school shoes until their prices rose. Then we went to Thom McAn on Avenue J, where he helped me destroy my wardrobe for a year by convincing me, in junior high school, to buy brown tasseled loafers instead of black—little knowing, dear person, that brown shoes were fag shoes, while black was the color worn by men. This was particularly true if you wore a powder-blue suit with patch pockets, as I did: brown tasseled loafers which clopped on the sidewalk like horses' hooves under the narrow (though not, alas, pegged) cuffs of a woollen suit in skiest blue. *Fag!* But he wouldn't let his boy look like a ruffian, or too old, so it was bright brown, and I clopped in shame.

This was particularly true of Jewish holidays, or Holy Days—it depended on whose mother talked to you about them. To Mrs. Habbisch, across the street, it was Holy Days. To my mother, a high school teacher near Coney Island, it was the day she had to teach while I, doing what my friends did, took a holiday. To my mother, it was a babysitting problem. When I was cute and small and bright, she could take me to high school and the big Italian girls would hold my fingers and let me sit beside them at their desks; now I was thirteen and sullen, I wore my dark hair in a Vaselined pompadour of intricate pattern at least five inches above my pimpled forehead. I stayed home with my friends, and we walked the streets.

My mother worried because I was on the loose, unsupervised. My father worried because I was hanging

around with a bunch of posturing adolescents while pro-
fessing a faith he'd rejected. Many of the neighbors liked
it less. Our section of Brooklyn, called Midwood, ran
like a seam of Christianity for two miles at least between
the newer-money neighborhoods (Avenue M, say) to the
oldest shady streets of huge houses; once, it all had been
dark and cool and elegant, two miles of wicker, and Vic-
torian oak, and blue-haired ladies in white-and-black
polka dots and bosoms like the prows of ships. Such were
the ladies who taught us at P.S. 152, and such were the
remaining ladies who looked from behind the pure white
lacework of their curtains to feel embattled by the little
Jewboys in their suits, parading on the Semites' Holy
Days. Now, there were Greeks on the street (they lived
next door, and ran a concession at Coney Island), there
were Italians (the Tortoreses, whose daughters became
the two most beautiful women in the Northeast). Then
there was my family, the Zimmers, who, though we
didn't sacrifice gentile children in our cellar, didn't have
—with a cross on top—a church. The rest were new,
had followed us as if we were blockbusters, and they all
—light-haired and boisterous like the Habbisches, small
and sly like the Inmans, smart and private like the Fin-
kels—were Jews.

And all of them, because they wanted the kids out of
the houses while they fasted, or cheated on fasts, or just
because it was as good as the Easter Parade and why not
—all sent their kids to march along the street in bright
suits with narrow cuffs, and of course with tasseled loafers, one pair of which, that year, were brown.

The girls always stayed where their parents did. Billy
Inman didn't, and Mo Moscowitz, Stevie Finkel, Al
Habbisch—a year older, and the first of us to produce
semen through the modern miracle of friction—and I,

clumsy Zimmer in browns and powder blues: we walked
and wheeled all the schoolless day, up and down the
street, talking of girls and food and school and, finally,
religion. It was 1952, the sky was clear, the leaves were
crisp, and I was slowly flying in formation with my
friends, when one of them—probably Mo: in those days,
he hated me for being the less fat of us two—asked me
what shul I went to.

None, I said, blushing.

Where, then, did I receive instruction for my bar-
mitzvah?

Noplace.

How, then, would I become a man?

By moving along from thirteen to fourteen, I guessed.
We don't believe in all that stuff, I told them, waving my
young hand at the ritual, at the parents' intolerable expense, at the relatives' gifts of money that could, if properly managed, finance a college education—at what, in
short, they had consecrated the last twelve months of
their lives to.

So why, if I was no better than a *Christian*, was I
walking with my friends instead of sitting in school with
the gentiles? Why was I wearing my powder-blue suit?
Why those *fruity* brown shoes?

That's really all. It was, simply, the first time and, in a
way, the hardest time, I'd been notified that I was not a
Jew. By Jews. I felt the circle open, felt myself hurtle
out, and heard the circle snap closed behind me. I was
ethnically on my own. That night, I discussed the afternoon, and my parents offered me Hebrew lessons and
bar-mitzvah preparations. They wouldn't spend as much
as Allie Habbisch's parents, I knew (I resented this at
once), but they would spend. I wasn't touched, then; I
was merely lazy: I didn't want to study *any*thing, espe-

26

cially a language where you had to bow and rock all the time, and which was closer to Chinese than felt comfortable. So I thanked them and said no, and I remained, though friendly with my childhood chums, excluded by this new social note to which they gave serious overtones. And it was only years later that I realized how much my father—son of an anarchist who had actually once spat on a rabbi—offered to surrender so that I could become superstitious like my friends. I didn't know he was proud of me, and I'm sorry that his pride was for the wrong reasons. I just didn't want to have to learn anything.

But here I am, at the only college in America to accept me, in my freshman year, surrounded by Lutherans: literally *surrounded.* I'm on my way to dinner, wearing the prescribed coat and tie, and freshman beanie, remembering to salute the statue of the Founder by removing my hat, and I'm wearing my canoe moccasins, worn mostly because I grew up with a father who changed into them on Saturday morning and wore them until Sunday night. I'm scuffing along, thinking of xylem and phloem for a botany test, when I notice, near the low wooden dining hall, that I'm surrounded by people I will later identify as Phi Taus. They will become ministers or heads of family florist businesses.

"Hey, Frosh!" calls Stretch. Stretch was recruited by our basketball coach, a man of consummate dimness and cruelty, sight unseen: an alumnus telephoned with news of a seven-foot basketball player, and Coach recruited him by phone. Stretch *was* seven feet tall. Unfortunately, he fell down a good deal because he possessed the nervous system of a man three feet shorter. He was ultimately stationed beneath the offensive basket, during emergencies and routs, and we sent four men back on defense. He played a total of eighty-eight minutes, and he distinguished himself by never changing his expression in four years.

Stretch called me, and I saw that nineteen or twenty upperclassmen had me trapped, as was their wont and right. I did what I was told: called them "sir," recited the Fight Song, sang the Alma Mater, listed the fifteen salient achievements of the college's Founder. And then Stretch, as the thought which had begun ten minutes before finally trudged its way through the synapses to his fingers, pointed: "Whatcha wearing, there, frosh? *Jew* Shoes?"

And then, as they say, I knew. I had forgotten to be a freshman Jew. I had forgotten to make much of the fact that my roommate, a Jew from Brooklyn, had told me— that there were exactly four percent Jews in the new freshman class. I thought that I could ignore inconveniences like religion, even if we were required to go to chapel every day. And I had forgotten that I was different—one of the distinctions Rhona later wanted me to know: Jews are Jews because cast out.

I told Stretch to eat his face. He fought to make his arms work, reached down, seized me, spun me, passed me along to the jock beside him, who spun me back, and so around, a little orbiting Jewboy, shaken and spun and then released, in laughter, for the evening meal. "Stamp your Jew Shoes before you go to dinner, now!" Stretch instructed me.

I still wear canoe moccasins, and sometimes to the office. I bought a pair for Sam when he was six. I accept that I'm not what others wish me to be, and that I'm less attractive for the acceptance. I call such inwardness strength, though Rhona called it Jewishness, and Lillian named it the stubbornness of a fool. All of us could be correct to some degree, though we ought to reckon with Sam who, upon receiving canoe moccasins, had the wisdom to ask me, "When do we get the *canoe?*"

"Jew canoe?" Rhona might ask, speaking over my shoulder two days before Christmas and eighteen years after we'd met.

"No," I would answer, if I turned to speak. And the question was whether I should. Or should I continue walking toward the rest of my life, which included a distant Sam, a more distant wife, and too many decisions I would need to make? Now, I had to decide whether to turn. "No. Jew?" I might joke in reply, if I turned.

*T*here I was, then, in the shapeless Sixties, in a small room filled with the noise of typewriters, and the deadline, like a descending ceiling in a horror film, pressing ever lower as the day wore on. I was pretty well crouched by the time I figured what to say on behalf of an outfit that groomed tycoons. My synopsis (hence, the unwritten story it summarized) was *Capitalists—Communists—or Criminals?* It went like this:

> Would you be surprised to find out that your teenage son or daughter favored *government control* of the nation's basic industries? In a recent survey, *more than half* of the teenagers questioned were *opposed* to free enterprise . . . 84% considered patriotism *unnecessary* . . . 40% could name *no advantages* of capitalism over communism! Yet these are to be the businessmen of tomorrow! What is behind the teenage rebellion? Why do they adopt these frightening attitudes? What is being done

about the explosive problem of teenage un-
employment? How have businessmen joined
in the crusade to educate our youth? What are
the best ways to keep adolescents out of trouble? All the answers in a story that's your business to read.

It was one of my better jobs—"rebellion," "explosive,"
"crusade," and, of course, "communism": little bombs
for the rural readers of packaged stories. What made me
roll the fresh paper in, I cannot say; what made me write
a shorter synopsis, but one closer to my heart, I need
not say:

Would you be surprised to learn that your
teenage daughter makes love to her *gerbils?*
That your preadolescent son wears his *mother's underwear?* That in a recent survey, only
16% of those taking the test could read?
That the same 16% were the only ones who
didn't masturbate with cream cheese? That *no*
woman in America has telephoned me to plead
her unconditional love? That my life tastes
more and more like my socks? Total truth, in a
story you'll want to devour.

No sooner had I pulled the paper from the machine and
torn it into eighths, did the writers'-room telephone ring
and my managing editor—chorus boy in striped shirt
and Brooks tie, a filtered Kool in his characterless face
(with strong fingers, you could have molded the putty of
his features into Dagwood), smoke making his right eye
tear behind his glasses—call, "Zimmer, telephone, and
make it quick, please." He always told us to make it quick
so that we'd remember on whose desk the phone was. It

31

was hard to forget, since you had to sit on the edge of his desk and feel his eyes on your flanks.

"This is Rhona Glinsky," her very low voice said. She was nearly whispering.

"Yes," I said heartily, for the sake of the office. "Sure. Nice to hear from you again."

"The one at the Loeb?"

"Yes, I recall that one."

"You're in a crowded room?"

"Certainly am. Surely am."

"I'm in the hallway at the library. Listen. I saw a Nazi today."

"Fine," I said. "Fine. Excellent."

"You understand? A fascist who killed Jews in maybe Poland? He's still here."

"Yes," I sang, "splendid. That's really grand. Thanks so much for bothering to tell me."

"You're done at five o'clock, as in most offices? You'll come downtown and tell me what you think? You'll help?"

"Ah, which?"

"Which question?"

"Sure enough."

"All. What else? All."

"Ah."

"Come."

She hung up. The "Come" had been tinged with a disgust I had not heard in a woman's voice since I had confessed to a graduate student at Columbia that I had thought of inserting nearly any part of myself between her legs. The student, it turned out, had been thinking of either an article on Wallace Stevens or a roast beef sandwich at the West End Cafe. I turned the phone around, simpered at my managing editor, called goodnight to the staff, announced that my Commie-copy was on my desk, snatched my wrinkled dark-brown corduroy jacket from the coat rack, and headed for 14th Street.

It's a strange neighborhood down there—last vestiges of prosperity left behind on 13th Street on the West Side. It's a meeting of east and west at Union Square, where on one side of the little park you're east, near Klein's. Union Square Park itself, now a haven for salesmen of exotic drugs, was in those days merely an idyll for bums and boozers. I had to walk across the park, which is slightly raised above the street, like a moral lesson for prospective degenerates. Strange shapes coiled in the shadows, old black men gargled with synthetic wine wrapped in brown bags, two male hookers leered, while taxis, as darkness fell, speeded up to pass the park. It was a September night with an October wind, and I kept wishing that I'd brought along a raincoat, or a sweater, or a gun.

A block up 14th, I found the small public library branch where Rhona worked. It was in a building which flanked the library doors with shops: milliners, candy, shoe, cardboard-box. The doors were heavy wood frames around glass, and I pushed on brass bars to enter what I'd nearly forgotten. For in graduate school, the library had been a nasty place of metal stairs and darkened stacks and hostile guards who fingered brief-bags. This, though, was more like the library of my child-hood, and I remembered being a boy—I wanted to be a boy again—who walked to 12th Street and Avenue J in Brooklyn, then up a flight of wooden stairs into the old library that creaked as I walked across the floors toward war and science fiction stories, and that smelled of bees-wax polish, and that seemed to be sealed away from the world.

As I entered, my glasses fogged up. I peered over them at golden oak tables, six or seven in the right-hand side of the room, the high golden checkout counter running down the left, the shelves of books in waist-high stacks between those areas and along the windowless walls. The lights burned yellow, there were the smells of steam heat and even beeswax, I thought. I sighed for old mysteries.

I used to take out stories about how Red Randall or Dave Dawson or Lucky Terrell was killing Germans or Japanese for the Allied cause. I wanted to see such books again, but Rhona by then—taller than I'd remembered, leaner at the hip, more fiercely handsome, more strangely flustered—was pushing against me, hands at my chest, with an intimacy I didn't understand but which I did enjoy. She shook my hand, as we left, but she still pushed. It was 1961, and we were chasing Nazis.

She wore a long sweater with a belt around the middle, and her figure flattered woven wool. She had chosen the clothes, so she knew; she then had chosen to walk and stand as though she didn't know. The combination was attractive and frightening: she quested for truth (dead Jews, live Nazis, living Covenant) and yet she lied about the prow her breasts made through the air we shared. She was dangerous. She stood close to me, I felt her leg push against mine, and she whispered in breath she had scented with peppermint Life Savers, "Here he comes. Stand back there with me. Watch!"

We walked into 14th Street, and we crouched across the hood of an illegally parked car as the old man walked into the street lights. "Rhona," I whispered, "why are we hiding? He's *blind*."

"Oh," she said. "Habit."

In his flapping old brown suit and brown checked shirt and dark-brown tie—someone mousey, I thought, laid his clothing out each day—and with his cordovan shoes scraping their leather heels and soles, with his thin white cane groping before him like a finger feeling for bugs on the back of a basement shelf in the dark, he made a neat left turn and headed for the subway.

"Come on," she said.

"Rhona, he's an old man. He's blind, for godsakes. He wears a white straw hat! You don't wear white after Labor Day, Rhona! Let's have dinner. Let's go to bed." She looked up at that one; she'd been speculating, I thought.

"Nazis go blind," she said, pulling my hand with both of hers as she moved slowly behind the old man. "Nazis get old, they go blind, they wear straw hats. Often, before they do, they murder Jews. I will not ignore this."

I liked the way she held my hand, so I went with her, through the Latin crowds and toward the subway. But he made another turn before he got there, and soon he was leading us toward Irving Place, which was once probably charming, and which in the right light can remind you of Greenwich Village, and which near 14th Street hosts a few business practices in which pointy weapons are considered useful. It was getting dark. In the darkness, you lose patience and courage, manners too.

"Shit, Rhona, dammit. What the hell's a blind man doing in a library?"

"That is exactly the question I would like to ask him. If he's blind, why come on in for several hours every now and then to sit and *stare*? Or seem to stare? I think he's pretending to be blind. He watches us when we sit at the circulation desk, when we shelve. He looks at our legs. Brr. Disgusting."

"But not your tried-and-true Nazi tactic."

"Zimmer: you're a Jew."

"I was born a Jew."

"Then you're a Jew. If he's a Nazi you want to catch him. If you trust me, you'll believe he's a Nazi. I read about them. I look at their pictures. You know, the immigration let them in so *easily* after the war! Better a Jew-killer than a communist, was their instruction from the State Department. So half of the Rumanian Iron Guard are in this country disguised as Catholic priests and blind old men."

"I thought you said he was from Poland."

"Poland, Austria, France, Rumania, what's the difference? They beat up Jews and deported them to die in the camps. You want to split hairs?"

The old man's cane rang along the iron railings of a fence, and he stopped at the fence's gate, outside the cellar entrance to a brownstone. We hadn't yet stopped, and we were close to him, arguing in whispers about the provenance of sightless Nazis. His face swiveled, his nose came up, he seemed to sniff us. "*Ah,*" he said, or something like it, and he panicked; I don't know how else to describe it. He crossed the street in front of traffic —nobody honked a horn, they just missed him by an inch and gave him the finger—and then, with his cane like an antenna before him, he headed back toward 14th.

"He knows we're here," Rhona said.

"He probably thinks we're going to roll him."

"He probably knows we're Jews," she said, as the blind old Nazi led Rhona, and Rhona led me.

It didn't occur to me until much later to ask her how she had remembered where I worked, and why she'd thought to telephone me, and why she needed me, of all the men she knew, to help her track the Rumanian or

Polish fiend down dark streets. I assumed, at the time, that she loved me, or thought I was worth some attention. I was glad to be valued. I was not, however, glad to be chasing old men.

The old guy was tall for a blind man. Stop to think: how many blind men over six feet have you seen? This was a tall blind man, and thinking of all those six-footers in the SS helped give some weight to Rhona's crazy suspicions. He seemed to know his way about the subway station remarkably well—or he was, in fact, faking blindness. Maybe he thought we were Mossad agents. He could *be* a Nazi, I kept telling myself. Hell, *I* could be a Nazi. Anyway, he was tall, he didn't slouch or rock, and he didn't flinch when the train, shoving fetid air ahead of it like stale breath coming up a dark throat, rocked and hissed to a stop. He avoided passengers with skill, and of course he was lucky, if blind, in that he didn't have to see the pigeon-gray platform floors littered with papers and dotted with trodden gum, nor the steel girders which were clammy to the touch, nor the awful ads for the Barbie-doll Miss Subways contest. He unerringly made for an open, unobstructed door. He could be pretending blindness, I thought, and if he was a member of the Iron Guard, and if Rhona was right, then he was no Nazi, officially, but he surely was a killer to the bone, and he *had* helped break the windows of Jewish merchants' shops, and break the bones of Jewish merchants, and perhaps send people on cattlecar rides. The bastard. I almost said something loud and cruel, then, as I realized how far into folly—probable folly—I could be tempted by Rhona and her dream: a religion which proved its wisdoms through verifiable deaths. It was a cult of the corpse-count, I thought. And I was co-opted by lust and maybe more. I was a vulgar, second-rate

Sonderkommando. Rhona's hand was sweating in mine, but neither of us tried to break our grasp. We were united in pursuit, and frightened by it, I suspect—I surely was. But passengers slept while standing at the porcelain center poles, looked past us while swaying at hand-straps, and you could have sworn, in that roar and clatter and communal fatigue, that the world was an ordinary place.

At 34th, he got out. He seemed to know 34th Street awfully well too. All in brown, handsome and tall, his face very white around his dark glasses and beneath the brim of his unseasonable straw hat, he swung his cane grimly and with enough of a grip for me to guess that he wasn't weak, and wasn't all that old, perhaps in his late fifties. He made his way up the stairs and directly into Macy's, open late for Thursday-night shoppers. Macy's smelled of sweat and cologne on the first floor, and of some sort of roasting meat. I nearly drooled as we followed him past handbags, under bright cold light, toward the escalator. His head swiveled frequently. He didn't forget that he might be followed, and he kept moving once he stepped—without the hesitation of the totally blind, who might time the escalator by the touch of a cane—onto the metal stairs. He went past other passengers, around them, up to the second floor and unerringly around to move and glide and ride, evading us. Rhona and I touched one another a lot, and I cannot tell whether it was sex or history which drove me on. But I truly did doubt his blindness, and I wanted us to stay close. Near the fourth floor, a heavy black woman stepped aside to help him step past her and he sniffed, his head swiveled with the nose up, and I swear I heard him, I swear it, mutter, "*Schvartzeh.*" And that did it for me. No doubt, the Iron Guard had picked up the finer points of racial nomination from their tutors in Berlin, and no doubt he *could* smell a Jew or Negro at some distance, and Rhona was right. I didn't know what we'd do about it, but I thought that somehow if we stayed near him and worked together, Rhona and I would conclude beneath the same blanket. And he could have been a Nazi. I do not think this is what is meant by historical determinism, but I didn't wish to argue, just then, with the forces in my life.

At the sixth floor, he got off and went past a mound of heavy cloth and a department that was being remodeled by late-working carpenters who smoked a lot and swore in high voices. He headed for a room labeled MEN, and I stopped, grasping her forearm, which felt heavily muscled even beneath the sleeve of her sweater. "He's taking a pee," I said.

"Or putting on a disguise."

"Okay," I said. "If an old guy comes out, and he's not blind, but he's carrying—no. Rhona, he doesn't have anything with him to change into."

"Sewed into the lining of the jacket. Eric Ambler. A Russian spy working against the fascists suggested it."

"What if just a blind man comes out?"

"Go see."

"Me?"

"Would they let *me* in?"

"They don't have guards in men's rooms, you'd probably make it."

"Zimmer."

So I went, strode into the men's room of Macy's, its noise of toilets and running faucets, and looked for feet under stalls. I found one set of shoes and crouched, blushing, to look: loafers (untasseled)—not our man. And then I saw him at the end of the row of urinals, his

39

face covered with sweat (which I hadn't seen in the subway), his large penis standing semi-erect, maybe with fear, as he stood pissing with great force, and some relief, I imagine, partly into the urinal and partly against the white-tiled Macy's wall. He spattered his clothes. I felt great shame. I held my breath, stood with my ass halfway into a sink at the opposite wall; the old man, true fascist, didn't wash his hands when he was done. He caned his way out. I counted to ten by twos, then followed, seizing Rhona and pulling her behind a large square pillar.

"Rhona, there's a problem. He's circumcised."

"You never heard of doing it for health?"

"Not at his age."

"I mean when he was *young*, stupid. Or what if he comes originally from an Arab country? Morocco, or someplace. Lots of Nazis in Africa, you know. Lots of French fascists."

"Rhona, his—you'll have to excuse me—his cock throws me into grave doubt."

"I didn't think you'd be the kind of man to be thrown into doubt by your enemy's penis."

"That's a category of a kind of man?"

"Come on."

We three went, along the sixth floor, directly and unerringly to a nearly inaccessible down escalator, and by jumping off in blind slow motion at the third floor, and moving in crowds, he lost us. We stood in front of the escalator, the people moved around us, two rocks in a stream, and I tried to console Rhona without showing my relief. "Listen, circumcision's not a bad disguise," I told her.

"Depends on who's wearing it," she said, looking me in the eye.

But did that *happen?* In such a farcical tone? To a man whose life seems now, to him and others, to be somber and stuffy—the heavy worst of Bruckner's music, say. Did I believe in such events, I wonder. And, if I did, I wonder how I forced myself to do so. Perspective, the age has taught to people of my age: perspective, relativity. It depends on how you see it, sure, which makes for Nazis in the woodwork and Mengele come to Bedford Hills from Auschwitz (*New York Post*). It all depends on how you see things.

"I, myself, saw my first Nazi on DeKalb Avenue," I told Rhona some days later. "He was my dentist." I am ashamed to admit that before and after our visits to his office (where I would tear out pinups as quietly as possible, while holding his *Esquires* close to my chest in the usually empty waiting room) I often, but only to myself, accused my mother of collaboration. "Little shitty kid," Rhona said.

His name was Dreibach, he was gaunt, never shaved well enough to keep his white bristles from showing, had a breath as sweet as cloves—fabricated from cloves, in fact—and was completely bald. He was middle-aged, middle height, middle weight, and in all ways unmemorable, except for the roll of fat at the back of his neck, which made him look like what the comic books called Krauts, and except for his delight in causing me great pain, which makes him to this day extreme in the ease with which I can summon him to mind.

How old was I? Six, seven, eight—the age, whatever it was, when a kid needs lots of assurance (that stage, at which I can still find myself, is apparently an elastic one). What I got from Dr. Dreibach, called Andrew by my mother, was pain. I figured it was pretty close to the interrogation methods of Nazis in their SS questioning-chambers, those rooms of bloodied walls and gut-littered flooring. (*Men at War* Comics.)

He would stand by my right hand which, like my left, gripped the arm of the torture-chair with enough force to crush small stones. He would probe my mouth with cold steel implements, while breathing cloves at me. And each time he deftly found a way to probe the nerve, make me jangle, jab a gum so it was sore for weeks, he would say, "Ah. Not brushing, are you? Not using dental . . . ah . . . floss. Not, ah, flossing the way I told you to."

And my mother, standing behind me, sometimes to my left where I could see her, but more usually out of sight, would echo him: "Not brushing? *Again* with not brushing? Andrew, how bad this time?"

And he would tell her, "Bad enough. Maybe, ah, worse than that."

And she would echo, "*Again* with worse than ever. You see? You must *brush!*"

Before I could remind her of her duties as the parent of a sufferer, Andrew Dreibach, who had never smiled from the day of his birth, had shoved cotton into my cheeks and gums, had started his dreadful machines, and with no anesthetic—he reminded my mother, each time: "It hurts them more than it helps"—he would drill and drill and drill, as tears ran down my face, as I lost all dignity by moaning wordless sounds, as the pain like a high metal bell above my nose would finally make me gag and push the drill with my lips, and he would have to stop and rescue the drill, saying, "Don't *move,* please."

My mother, behind me, a gentle hand on each shoulder to help, would then say, "I know it hurts, darling, but you did this to yourself. Well, maybe next time you'll brush."

I would then cross my arms on my chest, hold my elbows, and pant. Before I could catch my breath, he would begin again. My mother never made him stop. And going home on the BMT from DeKalb Avenue, she would remind me, "You brush better, you know, this wouldn't happen." Tall and elegant, my mother in her blue gloves which matched her navy-blue dress and blue pumps, me in corduroys and sneakers, and my mouth feeling larger than her handbag (also navy-blue), she would speak at me, her breath redolent with Juicy Fruit gum from the bulbous penny dispensers fastened to the girders that supported the station's roof: "It doesn't *have* to hurt so much."

"I don't like Dr. Dreibach," I once told her.

"Nonsense. We've gone to him for years."

I couldn't refute her logic. Belief is belief. If it hurts someone else, you can always hold their shoulders and tell them of their guilt. My mother had faith in her physicians. There was a chiropodist—in those days, you went to one if you had made your way to the middle class—and he had a little practice over an office-supply store on Kings Highway, near the Kingsway, the movie palace we went to in high school because it was too large for the ushers to catch you necking with your girlfriend. We went to a chiropodist named Aronson, whom we had to call Doctor. He would kneel before us and rub chalky substances into my feet, and file my calluses with emery cloth or something like it; he would soak me, rub me, grind me with small wheels on motorized drills, he would file me and peel me. At the end, my feet were smooth, and this fact was a considerable source of satisfaction to him and to my mother. At the postoperative consultation he would tell my mother, "He walks heavy on his heels. Very heavy."

"*Very* heavy," my mother would reply. "You're telling

me? I'm the one who pays his shoemaker bills. This is the boy who *invented* very heavy on his heels."

"Did you ever try to walk lighter on your heels?" Dr. Aronson would ask me.

"I really never did," I would admit, an admission I willingly gave because it didn't mean drilling in my mouth.

Dr. Aronson, whose face was long and blue with beard, and whose eyes always seemed so sad about the condition of our soles, looked at my mother and beseeched her, "He should walk lighter, if he can."

"Can you walk lighter?" my mother would ask me.

"I can try," I said.

"He'll try," she told Dr. Aronson.

"Listen," he said, "trying is . . ." and then he ran out of advice, in his little office that smelled of feet and soapy water and a certain staleness that clung to his yellow metal cabinets. "So try," he finished, having run the spectrum of his medicine.

"You hear this?" my mother checked.

I nodded. And the doctor, seeing that I'd heard, smiled a weary smile. My mother paid him as she paid other doctors, willingly, but she was far from inept in her own medical practice. There was the case, for example, of Christmas morning. I was then a traitor, according to friends who had recently been told in detail of the Holocaust; I betrayed the many dead whose sacrifice had somehow gotten me from Europe, in various bloodstreams, to the U.S.A. I betrayed the living and the dead by coming downstairs to the Christmas tree my parents decorated each year. They even put a five-pointed star on the top. On the bottom, on the floor, arrayed like the produce of an especially gentile garden, were the goods which annually flowed, with real love, from this inverted cornucopia: Shaw's *Pygmalion* one year; one year, before Shaw, a plastic replica of the goy Flash Gordon's gun; there were implements of make-believe war, there were clothes sold by Jews and stitched by Catholics and finally worn by me, the treacherous amphibian who waddled on the Christian sands and swam in the blood of the Jews. I thought Christmas trees were simply what one had, and of course there were kids in school with me whose parents raised them in the same perfidy—the disenchantment of the Jews with their origins, later translated by my smarter colleagues (especially the readers of Walter Lippmann, and the actual anti-Semites) into Jewish anti-Semitism. It seems simpler to wonder, sometimes, how one adheres to a faith that punishes so much.

But there I was: it was Christmastime, and I had wonderful loot, and I wandered around the corner to see how the kids on 17th Street were doing—Howie Balaban, whose father owned a kosher butcher shop (Howie liked to hurt people with his hands); the Goldstern kids, whose grandfather was reputed to have invented the egg cream (they liked to hurt me, in particular, with their hands). One of the twin brothers got angry with me for not liking his sailor hat, and he rejected the notion I had proposed: that kids of eleven were too old for sailor hats. He chased me home, flailing a hammer, and shortly before I made it through the hedges and behind the neighboring garage into my own yard, he connected, taking some skin off my scalp. I ran upstairs, howling something about imminent death and great suffering. My mother, ever the quick thinker in emergencies, hit me as hard as she could on the jaw, so that I wouldn't feel the pain, and then she poured a large bottle of iodine over my bloody head.

45

My mother broke the little finger of her right hand. She permanently stained my shirt with iodine. She missed the little cut and bruise on the back of my head, and my father washed it out that night, since my mother wasn't speaking to me and since her hand was immobilized. But she had practiced medicine. Our dentist would have been proud of her. "For a Christmas tree," Rhona said, "you all deserved worse."

My mother had a friend who worked for the Margaret Sanger Clinic in New York; among their friends from the Thirties were sculptors, pianists, teachers of the arts and sciences, out-of-work agents provocateurs, and a professor suspected of turning six of their friends in to a City College committee on internal menace and the Red Threat (he confessed in 1957, and half of their crowd forgave him, thus ending the Thirties for those of them, including my parents, who didn't).

I recall their Friday-night dinners, the highballs in the living room, talk of *Peter Pan* and Maurice Evans and the martyrdom of Chaplin. Chief among the friends was the woman who worked for Sanger. She influenced my mother considerably, and once my mother practiced some birth control counseling on me.

It was the night before I was to leave for college. I was one of three students from my high school who were not attending an Ivy League or Big Ten school. I was a source of shame and amusement to my friends. I had been admitted to a little college in Pennsylvania, run by the Lutheran church, because they detected "possibility" in me and because my parents had not requested financial aid. (I think they were considered potential millionaires because they were Jews; for this assumption, the college received four years of big talk from them, and a $5 donation.) There I was, scared, whistling a lot, in love with my parents, grateful, guilty, loaded for loss.

My mother called me into the kitchen. She was in her blue jeans phase, wearing men's baggy Levi's with backless high-heeled white shoes and a silk shirt, with bags beneath her eyes, but pretty and worried-looking. Her mouth was tough. When I'd sat at our kitchen table, as she was making her lunch to take to the high school where she taught—what else?—Home Economics, she talked. She was pretty clear about what she had in mind, as she said, with her back to me, "If you get a girl pregnant in college" (and here, of course, I thought she might tell me exactly how I could go about doing so) "I will take the girl in and help her to raise her child, and I will never let you come here again. Is that clear?"

That was pretty clear. So I said yes. I waited for the rest.

"And now," she said, "your father has something to tell you."

So I rose from the table, having partaken of my mother's medicine—I thought for years that medicine was what didn't feel good but you didn't die from it—and went into our small living room, where my father sat on the dark bench of the upright piano, leaning against it, I imagine, for support. One hand struck something sharp over and over. Perhaps the sound comforted him. It reminded me of the dentist's office, although we were surrounded by pictures painted by some of their friends, and photos of Einstein and Mt. Everest, and a large black-and-white of me, holding a book and looking adorable.

My father, tall and handsome, prematurely bald, possessed of a fine broad nose and strong chin, looking like the Riis Park lifeguard he once was, played a few renditions of something sharp. He looked studiously away from me. He said, "When you're in college, it might . . . I thought you might find it useful to know." Here it comes, I thought. If I'm going to be disowned, I will at least know how to *get* disowned. I recall, also, that I simultaneously wished that he wouldn't talk about such things, while reminding myself that it's either hear it now, or learn by trial and possibly humiliating error. He went on, after doing the little something sharp on the piano: "You'll find, when you're in college, that if you get hungry, and you buy a candy bar for a nickel, instead of a hamburger for a quarter, you'll have a lot more money left at the end of the month." His face burned crimson. Mine did too, probably. We solemnly nodded.

Everything being relative, why not? I said something to that effect one night to Lillian.

It was late, Sam was asleep, and the apartment was dark because Lillian, on the big old sagging sofa, wearing pants and slippers and one of my flannel shirts, was sleeping too. I was walking from the windows in our living room, which looked over the West Side of New York, to the bookshelves, which fairly exploded with books I hadn't read, and where I couldn't find anything now that I wanted to read. I was distressed by the green of our carpet and fatigued by the prints we'd framed years before. My back itched, and I couldn't reach it, so I leaned against the doorway that went to our dining room and I rubbed my back against the wall, scraping up and down like a sour-tempered bear.

The rasping woke Lillian. I'd wanted it to. She said, "I fell asleep."

"That's why you wake up so early," I said. In the big plaid shirt, with her hair tumbled down, she looked like a girl. She looked little. I regretted a lot. "If you went to bed later, you could *sleep* later."

She lay back and covered her face with both hands. Through her fingers she said, "I wake up because I have insomnia. I fall asleep because I'm tired."

"And you get out of bed and come in here to sleep."

"And that wakes you up. And you feel abandoned."

"No. Yes."

"Yes."

"Lil, it feels like you're leaving me when you do that."

"I'm just getting some *sleep*."

"Well, everything's relative, huh?"

"Or paranoid."

"Thank you."

"Well, Jesus God. You see traitors at the office when people argue with you. You tell your authors they're disloyal when they bitch for money, which authors always do. You give me this *incredible* shit when I can't sleep, like it's my fault. You know, I have business troubles too. I have problems too. I'm a person too."

"I'm sorry I'm making you unhappy."

"I know you are. So what, though. What kind of good does that do me? I'm crying. I feel terrible. I want a divorce."

"Excuse me?"

"I don't think I'm kidding," she said.

I didn't, either. My stomach disappeared, or all feeling vanished from the center of my body. Blood, electrical pulses, all the wash of all the chemicals I produced, were centered in my head. My sinuses sang little pig noises, and the muscles in my neck and shoulders squeezed. In the front of my head there was a feeling of great weight, and my vision broke into hundreds of small bright dots; I could see, but not really. If I had told her I was blind, she'd have thought I meant it metaphorically—all things being relative—and I suddenly didn't want her to have such an admission in her arsenal. Because, I realized, she was persuading herself that she meant it.

"You don't love me anymore?" I made the mistake of asking that as, with my back still pressed against the doorway, I slid to sit on the floor.

She thought, I guess, that I was burlesquing, somehow turning the moment in my chosen direction, for she said, "You're too old to talk that way about it. When somebody has lung cancer and dies, what—you say, 'Doesn't his *heart* work anymore?' "

She mimicked me, she added a touch of baby's lisp, and I was not only lost, but enraged. Worse, I was frightened to show my rage—impotent is a word that comes to mind—because I feared her decision. It was one-way politics that night. I had no power, she had it all. Because I wanted her to not leave me.

I wanted her to not leave me alone.

I knew enough to know that I would have to decide which I felt. So I sat in a bubble of blindness and spasming muscles, I rubbed my head and hated how reduced I was, and instructed myself to think—not feel, but think about Lillian, whom I'd loved, and really, and for a long time—and I waited, at her mercy, on the floor.

It was my sense of direction, I thought, after a while. It was because in New York, my hometown, I still got lost, made turns up wrong streets, and couldn't tell you east from west unless the sunset were labeled and the street I walked went one-way. So I had come to depend on Lillian for such simple matters as knowing which way to physically go. My tall, fair, midwestern shiksa tycoon, trundling her burly Hebrew down his own boulevards: I was afraid of getting *lost*. And I was wondering whether I needed Lil specifically, or just a lusty Girl Scout, when she cleared her throat and blew her nose. My aplomb

disappeared—I wanted Lil, I wanted Lil, I wanted Lil—
and she said, "You've been acting irrational. Fine. Go
ahead. You've been alienating your associates. Okay.
But you've been very edgy with Sam. You know this.
Words won't make it not . . . won't fucking *erase* it, I
mean. Dammit. And you haven't forgiven me for anything. You never forget *any*thing. And you know what
you've been accusing me of?"

She was crying again, and I hated her sorrow. I hated
mine too. And I was thinking about Sam. "You know
what you're not forgiving me for?" she said. "Working
hard. Working late last week, two nights. Falling asleep
early. Waking up—the insomnia thing. And *leaving your
bed*. That's what it really is. It's about the *bed*. That no-
joke joke you made at breakfast to Sam? 'Soon we'll have
to make a bedroom for mommy so she can sleep.' Laying
that shit on a little boy. But you know *why*, Mister Zimmer? Because you've been leaving your *own* bed. When
I'm *in* it. Understand? If you were impotent, or a jackoff
artist, or a queer, I wouldn't be so worried. If you loved
another *woman*, I could understand it. But *you*. You
fucking *bastard*. You love *me*. I know it. I'll be humiliated, I'll be *dead*, if I'm wrong, but I'm not. I'm not. You
love me. You even need me. And you're working very
hard at staying away from me. It could go on *forever!*
That's why I think I want a divorce. See? I have to save
myself from something, sometime, don't I? So I should
start now, shouldn't I? Don't you think?"

What I thought was how, years before, in the air, hag-
gard with taxis and airports and the terrible taking off
toward Phoenix, sorrowful of leaving Sam with Lillian's
parents, and pleased to be alone, but also emptying of
joy because our mutual solitude was aimed at duty to my
parents, not unencumbered fun, there we were. We

flew, drank coffee, read papers, got groggy, and we flew. And because we were pretty much all right at that time of our life together, and because I always told my wife too much or too little, but never what was merely useful or pleasant to know, I went on at some length about Rhona.

Lil had heard it all in summary. Parts she had learned without much delight and in great detail. She was always wary when I spoke of Rhona. She was usually annoyed, she had told me once, because I spoke of my time with Rhona in such absorbed tones. "You sound like a drunk who talks about when he swore off," she had said. "Or like a Marxist who still has this teensy weensy little hope that *this* time, *maybe*, he could keep believing in it."

Maybe I was lusting after Lillian. And maybe I was just the kind of permanent child who had to tell his every intimacy—a continuing traitor to the silence in which certain instants might, if buried with dignity, have some silent life. I told her of Rhona, her body a V of loin and thigh.

Lillian sat away from my whisper. She shook her head.

"Isn't that sad?" I asked.

"No. Sad? Of course not. No."

"Lil," I said, "She wasn't *that* interested in sex. No: I mean that she wasn't interested *only* in sex."

"Well, of course not," Lillian said. "She was after your *soul*." Lillian smiled her wide wonderful smile. I felt happy that she was enjoying me. "She was buying your soul, she was buying *back* your assimilated soul. With her body. It's not that different from the usual Jewish Princess pact, is it?" Lillian smiled again, then stopped. She leaned toward me and put her hand on my thigh. I spread my legs. She said. "And you're all balls."

We dropped uncomfortably through eddies of heat

and the ebbings of fuel-soaked air, and wherever I looked, no matter what I tried to see, the air in columns of shimmer and vertical flow made my vision turn back upon itself in defeat. Nothing looked like anything except the overcooked soup they called air there. Everyone was brown and everyone's lips and jowls and eyelids and cheek pouches appeared to be stretched and then dried into place on top of the bones, like *papier maché* on cardboard and sticks.

In the taxi I said to Lillian, "This is a city full of mummies."

"And daddies."

"Not funny. You're nervous?"

"Why should seeing your parents make me nervous? Didn't I once hold a snake in high school science?"

And a few streets later I tried it again—for it was an image hard won, and I refused to lose it to mere life: "I meant, they all look so *brown* here. And dried-up. They all have those creases in the corners of their eyes and next to their mouths. It looks like thread."

"Everyone from the east always says very cleverly that everyone from the west looks like a mummy. I deal with these east-and-west interchanges every day. I was here, once. Well, I was almost here. Actually. Actually, I ended up having a miscarriage on a New Jersey airport bus."

"Oh my god," I said. "Oh my god, Lil. You've been thinking about that all the way *here*. You were going to Houston, weren't you? You were flying to Houston. Oh my god, I'm sorry. I think I wanted to suppress that."

"Fortunately, you were able to."

"I'm sorry."

"No sweat," she said. "And they do look like mummies, anyway. Even if everyone says it."

"Just no sweat, Lil?"

Actually, there was sweat, and it lay along her upper lip and above the bridge of her nose. She saw me looking at it, and she wiped with a tissue, leaving little screwed crumbs of paper on her brow. I picked at them. "This is very much like monkeys," she said. "The way they groom each other. Although it's possible *mummies* groom each other too. They, well maybe they pick the bandage lint out of each oth—"

I kissed her clumsily and sweatily and of course unsatisfactorily.

"We could," she said, sitting back so that I couldn't easily reach her, "try picking each other's *lice* once the party loses momentum. Which it is bound to do pretty promptly, if your mother has retained both her charm and her affection for your goy wife."

"I keep telling you, she's a liberal, they're both liberals. They are old-fashioned Roosevelt liberals."

"I know," Lil said. "I work with some. Remember? They moved out of the City because of blacks and Puerto Ricans. And they moved out of Westchester because of blacks and Puerto Ricans. And they've been chased into Putnam County by the rising mongrel tide. And now they're all considering the big move—either into upper Dutchess County, if they can swing a quarter of a million for the right-sized house in the proper school district, or they're waiting for promotion and a major tip on the market so they can move directly to Fairfield County, Connecticut, and the appropriate skin tones. I know about liberals. My father's one. He only mentions *Jew* every seven minutes when we talk or visit. He used to say it every thirty seconds. He tells me he's *proud* of my Mister Jewboy the publisher."

I changed my body-type for eleven seconds so that I

could reach into the corner of the cab and kiss her cheek. She patted my knee as I did, and that made me grateful. "So how do you feel about seeing my parents?" I asked her. She snorted a fake laugh and I snorted back to tell her that I understood, which perhaps I almost did. And there we were, a couple of big strong horses from the chill northeast, crouching in the back of a cab that drove over streets I felt certain were bubbling in the dry heat as we snorted our way to the great anniversary and reunion and trial.

All the little cousins who could be there had come. One or two as big as my father and me stood above them and looked about like large slow herbivores in a meadow. Lillian stood out and above as well. She seemed to glow with heat and nerves and tension in the small cold living room of my parents' well-guarded and very expensive air-conditioned condominium. On the mantel above a phony fireplace—it held wood, possibly sculpted plastic, but I was reluctant to find out—were the photos of my childhood: me in striped polo shirts and me in the powder-blue suit; me in shorts at Camp Nock-A-Mixon, where I had lasted five weeks; me in my college cap and gown, virtually collapsing in upon my own face because of the dense gravity of my self-regard; and me with Madeleine at college—this last one unknown to me, and unremembered. I assumed that my mother, the liberal, had put it out to remind my blonde and Protestant wife that once a Jewish girl with tits out to *here* had worshipped Captain Delight for eighteen months.

My father and I had once again exchanged our embraces and, saying to each other, "So?," had then gone on to talk about the numbers in our lives: his work as a consultant, my adventures in costing out the publication of books on unpopular subjects. This was before I had joined with Abromowitz, and before so much else, but after I knew enough of publishing to earn my keep. We spoke again of Sam, and of our cruelties in having invited Lillian's parents to use our apartment for a weekend of theater in exchange for sitting with Sam and checking on his regular sitter. We returned to a few more numbers, and then, donning casualness as though it were a suit of clothes, slid on to what had clearly become an issue: "Mother was so disappointed that Sammy couldn't be here," my father said.

"We thought he's so young, the excitement, the confusion—"

"Of course," my father said.

"You know, Dad."

"Naturally." Then, looking about, and apparently finding no rescue, he said, "But Mother—well, she was awfully disappointed."

"Next time," I said. "He'll be older," I instructed him. "He'll be older next time."

"*We* might not," my father said immediately, showing me his teeth. Clearly, I had stumbled into a retirement joke that thrived in the compound of their condo.

I went for another drink. I circled around toward Lil, who was sitting in a chair I remembered from my boyhood. I kept waiting to be struck with melancholy and remorse because I had grown away from the home in which such furniture had once been customary. It didn't come, and it occurred to me that I was either an adult now, and such failures to feel guilty were one of maturity's rewards, or—this seemed more plausible, because more fraught with self-punishment—I was growing to be an unfeeling man. I stood beside my seated wife, and I felt her, to prove feelings—at the back of her neck, along her bare strong arms, on the side of her warm face.

She turned just enough to touch my fingers with her lips and softly kiss them. I remember thinking: This is what I've been growing up for. This is why you do it. And then my mother flowed over, chubbier, and brown as a walnut and—suddenly this had happened—nearly as wrinkled, and followed by two or three dark relatives and friends who all looked like members of other nut families. One, with a moonface and a liverish complexion, reminded me of a heavy pecan. Another, a middle-aged man who perhaps did business with my parents, was cleanshaven and burned to a smooth red-brown, and he made me think of a gargantuan hazelnut. My mother, in her long bold Indian dress, was enjoying her gin and tonic; it seemed to be one of many in that afternoon's long line of refreshments.

She insisted upon hugging me again, and kissing me again, and, after introducing me to Pecan and Hazelnut, she told them loudly, "This is my daughter-in-law, Lillian. I have told you about her."

That sounded as dangerous to me as to Lil. I felt her go tight.

"Their son, our Sammy," my mother said, "had to stay home. Lillian thought it was better that way."

"Actually," I said. Lil squeezed my hand to shut me up.

Pecan said, "Actually?"

"To be sure," I said, with whatever dignity I could find.

My mother said, "We were talking about South African gold. I thought that Lillian could advise us."

"Good investment right now," Lil said, a little automatically. "You might want to think just *gold*, not Krugerrands, if you're not in the money market regularly."

"But Africa's so *interesting*," my mother said.

Lillian said, coldly but not combatively, "I've never been there."

"No, I haven't either," my mother said. "But I've always loved the idea of the mingling of races there—black Africans and white Africans and Indians and—other Asians, of course. And—"

Lillian was still holding my hand. "Actually," she said, in absolutely the same tones I had used when saying the word a moment before. "Actually, Tessie—" My mother stood a little straighter, and her lips jerked. She looked at me. Lil had always called her Mother, dutifully and with no pleasure.

My mother said, "Yes? Dear?"

"Actually, South Africa and Rhodesia are doing a good deal to *prevent* the mingling of the races, black and white and colored. They call anyone of Asian or mixed blood colored."

"Really?" my mother said. She smiled a sort of smile. I thought of mummies and thread. "I had heard of *apartheid* someplace before. Actually. I meant mingling in a more, oh . . ."

"As a metaphor for the continent?" I begged. "Fine metaphor."

"As a metaphor for the life of the continent," my mother said, in grudging acceptance.

Lil was squeezing my hand so hard it hurt. I knew she was trying not to laugh. I was too. I was also, however, trying at the same time not to whimper and shriek. The impossible distances between them—you could measure them out in units called Zimmers, I think—had changed the climate of the room; emotional winds were whistling, and a sour cold front had settled upon us. Guests had ever so slightly, in response to the changing environment, turned their bodies so as to see us more clearly, and had lowered their voices in order to catch my mother's and Lil's. I waited for it.

"A changing world, isn't it?" Lil said. "Black nations excluding whites and coloreds just as the whites have done. Office buildings near where game preserves used to be, and that retirement condominium for whites only on the edge of Botswanaland." I could see only the top of her head, and was really afraid to see her expression, for I knew I'd start to guffaw. But I didn't need to see anything to recall how ignorant she was of African politics or geography, specializing as she did in domestic investments, and relying on the office's experts when she needed foreign information. I also knew, therefore, that she was lying about office buildings near game preserves, and of course about the retirement condo near Botswanaland.

My mother said loftily, "I would like to see the countries of Africa for myself. I have always felt that the continent is a—a metaphor for the way we all should be living here and in Europe. All the races together, you know." She looked at Lil as though Lil were last night's food. "I had always hoped," my mother said, looking back at Pecan and Hazelnut and the other guests beyond, "that my son might marry an African woman."

Lillian squeezed my hand so hard—her hands were large, and they were an athlete's fingers that crushed upon mine—I nearly gasped. Someone back near the bar did gasp, and I was grateful for their incredulity. My dear father, as caught by surprise as I was, said, "Did you? We never discussed that. Well, Lillian. Are you prepared to put on blackface, or must I be satisfied with a middle-western beauty?" He walked through some guests and pushed by Hazelnut, and bent over to kiss Lil on the front of the head.

In the hotel that night, Lillian told me, "I finally found out where your little Old World gallantries come from."

But before we could be there, in the hum of air conditioning, exhausted on the bed, drinking sodas because we were so thirsty, we had to be, respectively, standing and sitting in Hadassah West with my mother in a quiet rage of longing and dissatisfaction, my wife shocked into silence.

Pecan said, "Tessie, you're such a dreamer."

And Lillian pulled the trigger at last, as her wits and voice returned, by saying softly, "Tessie, what you haven't realized is that right now, I am all the Africa you're going to get."

So the fabled Nazi was lost to us in all of our preposterousness, in our monumental mutual desire to be fooled by dreams of murder and love. Rhona held my arm as if something important had been decided. And I felt, in the noise and congestion of Macy's, the erotic shame of a boy on a date with a girl who is known to put out in gratitude, and who probably doesn't understand that she is grateful for the date, and that her thanks degrade her in the eyes of the boy who will degrade himself by accepting what she simplemindedly, and predictably, will give. And I couldn't understand why this clever person in this very exciting skin would need a large square-shaped person with glasses, and not much vocational future, to help her pursue a blind, frightened man who peed on the wall and didn't wash his hands. I felt that if she delivered up the gratitude I sensed behind her grip on my arm, I would be making careless love on the bony backs of the dead. Since when has a lumpy mattress stopped that selfish piston-and-spurt?

We walked in the dreamy, gassy blur of New York in

early evening, headed downtown, sauntering, held—I by her arm and the body I brushed, she by something I still failed to see—and we were often silent, with rather more ease than I'd expected. When we spoke it was at first about work. I learned that the least of a librarian's job involves the stamping of cards or shelving of books. I told her how I wrote small fictions for smalltown papers. We discussed graduate school; she had liked hers, I'd been daily defeated by mine. Then, at the Flatiron Building, a triangular monument of sorts, and always worth staring at (especially when you ask tough questions), I said, "Rhona, how did you know for sure he was a Nazi?"

And the word pulled her breast onto my bicep, placed her hands around my wrist and hand. I stepped into something suspicious of texture, I slid a bit but kept our proximity. "Fascist," Rhona said, in a voice grown husky. "The Iron Guard. In Rumania."

"Rumania. Right. How did you know?"

"Well, of course you can't ever know for certain unless you have the photograph right there in front of you. But I'm still very, very sure. I have looked at so *many* pictures." She was chattering, she was lively, she was glad: I was near to her heart. "Of the camps, of the survivors. Of those *swine* who strutted in the streets while the little people were beaten and terrified and disgraced. *Murdered!* I have seen his picture someplace. He was an officer. I know it. I'm *right*, Zimmer. If my mother were there, in Macy's or the library, she'd have smelled him out."

"Your mother was there? Wait, you told me that."

"My mother, for almost a year, was in Birkenau. For eight months. No one she loved died there with her because her father died from his heart attack when they arrested him. Her mother had died many years before. And her little brother who would have been my uncle, they took him away and she never saw him again. He was blond, she said. Maybe they let him live. Maybe he's a politician in West Germany, sending machine guns to Brazil, part of the Economic Miracle. She weighed less than seventy pounds when she was rescued. She's very proud of that number. We grew up remembering it."

"Do you hate this or love it, Rhona?"

She looked up as if I'd pinched her. And why was I asking such questions on 23rd Street, when clearly we were going to walk downtown to her apartment and reward me for having been born with balls and a high broad brow that could wrinkle, at will, in great sympathy?

"My sister moved away from home when she was seventeen," Rhona said. "To Michigan, where there are cousins. In Ann Arbor, Michigan, you know it? She works in a dress shop in Michigan. She sells to rich college girls with perfect figures what they need for having sex with large blond boys who play football. That's her life, and I don't blame her. She couldn't live with my mother. Neither could I. Only, I believed it all, and Edith, my sister, didn't want to remember it. Much less believe it. Me? I look ten years older"—she waited for me to demur, but I was listening, so she went on—"I talk twenty years older, and what I'm worrying about started longer ago than that. I don't love it. But that doesn't matter, does it?"

Finally, I did say, truthfully, "You don't look twenty years older, Rhona."

"Well," she said.

I was still wondering what it was that did matter when

we reached her apartment on 12th Street, a two-room furnished dump, which in a couple of years could qualify for slum, though she kept it clean and had pictures on the wall and a lot of books. I sat on a hairy chair with wide wooden arms while Rhona brewed tea that smelled like a funeral home. She put music on, Mahler, songs about dead babies, and I became fairly certain, sitting over an ancient maroon carpet, surrounded by stark white walls and a reproduced abstract expressionist, that I would not be seducing Rhona. I was relieved. I couldn't imagine how to begin. She was, for all the lushness of her body, the aggressiveness of her face, somehow without sex. No: she had hormones, and that was clear; but it was also clear that she spoke harshly to them. There was something clerical about Rhona. That was it: I felt as though I were sipping herbal tea in the headquarters of a religious order dedicated to suffering and, one day, God willing, blood-revenge. What was waiting to emerge was not primarily sex. First would come rage. Anything else would have to wait its turn. And of course I wondered at whom the rage would really be directed. I also wondered if I wanted any more to do with Rhona and her cause. It might have been at this point, a chilly night after following a fascist to the men's room at Macy's, that the guilt began.

"Are you aware," Rhona said over the soft singing, "that there is a movement afoot among certain Jews to pursue converts?"

I dutifully told her that I was not aware of such a movement. This is a hot date, I also told myself. *Kindertotenlieder*, an apartment that was brown from its furniture to its very air, and a young lady with terrific tits who wants to talk about movements afoot among zealots.

"Intermarriage," she said solemnly. "Also just lapsing,

and the death of the old ones. The number of Jews who worship is diminishing. There will soon be an effort to increase this number."

I wondered why she sometimes talked so like my immigrant grandmother, this daughter of Barnard and student of library science. I raised my brows in lieu of a lie about my interest in this subject.

"The argument will be that even Abraham was a convert. Of sorts. You knew this?"

"I didn't, Rhona."

"He began as Abram. Just as Sarah was Sarai. He began in Ur, in Babylonia. Only after he received God's command did he build a temple at Bethel. In Canaan—Palestine. You know. *Then* began the nonsense with Hagar having his child Ishmael, all that unfairness to the darker peoples. It still goes on among us Jews, believe me. So, in a way, he's a convert. After he sees the vision of God, *then* he circumcises Isaac that his wife has when she's about ninety-nine. *Then* he's a Jew. You see? A convert."

"Meanwhile, it's the Joseph and Mary story with a different twist, right? Instead of Joseph watching his wife get laid by the Lord, it's Abraham watching Sarah get knocked up by heavenly magic. Instead of Jesus, we've got little Isaac the Ikie, who his old man is *perfectly* willing to slice up and roast up and offer to the Big Magic over Genesis. *Really.*"

"You're angry at God?"

Quite without knowing I'd say it, I set my cup down on that dismal dark rug and said, "Rhona, I have to leave. I've got a date." I meant appointment—though I had none.

"Date?" She meant dalliance.

"I've got this date, yeah." I wanted her to think whatever she thought. But I wanted no more ringing defenses of anyone's—Abraham's or Isaac's or Rhona's—faith.

"Well," she said, "You've got a date, go ahead. Fine. Wait. Why don't you—where is it? Yes. Here, will you take this and look at it and tell me what you think?"

It looked like a children's book, and I didn't read the cover until I was on 14th Street and walking. It said *I never saw another butterfly*. On the subway, and then at home, I knew how much trouble I was in.

Home was a loft on Varick Street, a neighborhood where precision machinery was made, from where quarter-inch drills were shipped, and where, in a very small shop, egg rolls were manufactured by a man named Lefty for the Chinese restaurants of the East Coast, and maybe the world. Lefty was a joke; he had only one arm, his right. He worked with two black women, presumably neither of them Chinese, and together, in vats and great aluminum cauldrons, they made raw egg rolls of dough and partly cooked shrimp shipped up from the Gulf of Mexico in formaldehyde (more difficult for Food and Drug inspectors to smell the rot), and then sent them out to be frozen and packed by an outfit on West Street, under the elevated highway. Lefty was tall and paunchy, always wore white shirts, starched collar, a gold-chain cufflink, no tie, khaki trousers, bedroom slippers, no socks. His eyes were sad, over big pouches, his face was always clean-shaven and scrubbed-looking. His big nose was unsurprisingly red, and the blue-red-orange broken veins around it were no shock either: all day, in a white china coffee mug, ice cubes floating serenely, Laird's applejack sat by his side. He drank Jersey Lightning from the time he arrived from Purchase, around eight in the morning, until he lurched into his Caddy to drive home after dark. The women, Loretta and Piggy, were shiny blue-black, intense of expression, related by birth and by marriage to distant cousins, and were the sober control Lefty needed as he wove through his days. They propped him up and checked the products out and made him talk sanely on the phone. They were also the principal owners, though Lefty didn't like admitting that he'd sold them a major share of the business when pony racing left him in hock. Some mornings, as the only residential tenant on the block, I would descend with majesty to drink a little coffee with Lefty while the day started. We were friendly; Lefty liked advising me about the profit-and-loss of civilized life. After coffee, I would take the train uptown and would arrive five minutes late for work: my declaration of independence.

I thought of Lefty, not Rhona, right away that night, as I lay in the loft I illegally lived in—the block was zoned against residences—surrounded by some boyhood furniture and the remains of a plumbing-fixtures company that had been there before me. I thought of Lefty, a Jew "within reason," as he said it; he had told me a story of the camps. Moishe and his friends are in Auschwitz, before they used gas for killing. Guards back a truck to their shed, and twenty-nine starving, sick men are loaded on. Each knows he's to be taken to the woods west of Krakow, under the mists off the Carpathians, and get shot backwards into a trench he'd help to dig. The SS man in charge of their firing squad, a kindly fellow, asks whether anyone wants a blindfold. Moishe's friend, Lev, raises his hand. Moishe jabs him with his elbow: "No!" he whispers to Lev. "Don't make trouble!" When I read the book, I thought of Lefty and his ptomaine shrimp, and his ability to tell that joke.

The book was a collection of drawings and poems from Terezin concentration camp. Between 1942 and 1944,

15,000 children went through what was publicly referred to as "a model camp." The gentlemen who ran it called it a "ghetto." It was a showcase for the Red Cross and other interested bystanders. It actually served as a way station to Oswiecim and other places, in Czechoslovakia and out, where the children at long last died.

The first page of the book was a child's traced hand. It was the hand, I would say, of an eight-year-old; he or she had drawn a hole in the center of the hand. There were pictures of walls, of barred windows, of children in boxes, in pails—all drawn by the kids—and there were children in bandages, numbered bunks with mounds on them, a mother waving goodbye, little people in railroad cars, and a poem which said

I'd like to go away alone
Where there are other, nicer people,
Somewhere into the far unknown,
There where no one kills another

—and of course it was the artlessness which seized me: the simple praying (they were children of language) which making such poems undoubtedly was. I hurled the book aside.

In the morning, I was downstairs at the egg roll factory early, waiting for Lefty. Piggy was there, winking at Loretta over a story she'd been telling. "All right?" she said, pouring me some coffee.

"Yeah," I told her, and that was usually our sole exchange. She had a son at Union College, and she didn't have much use for a man like me, who had wasted his B.A. by going to a job that paid him so badly that he needed to sleep in a loft above an egg roll factory.

"Good for you," she told me, and then went back to waving her hands and talking to Loretta, who smiled at me, yawned, and nodded to the rhythms of Piggy's tale. I sipped the coffee, smelled the sour salt smell of leftover rotten shrimp, and thought about the last lines on each page of the book Rhona had lent me. *Anonymous* appeared under many of the poems, and that was bad enough, such disappearance; but the name *Mif* and 1944 were somehow worse—it was a nickname your mommy would know, except they would eventually take her away from you and leave you all alone and then kill you.

Lefty came in, white shirt, cufflink, khakis and slippers, his battered face. He accepted coffee from his colleagues, poured a little applejack into it, sat down beside me at a kitchen chair near the shrimp vats, and said, "Who stole your wallet?"

"You ever hear of Terezin?"

He shook his head. "It's a camp?"

I nodded.

"You hear the name, you can tell it's a camp. Where?"

"Czechoslovakia. Near Prague. It was a ghetto camp for the ones they'd kill. A lot of kids were there, you know, with their families. I read this book last night." My voice actually broke, and I tried to imagine what someone like Rhona's mother would say about this new sentimentality of mine—something like "Mount it on your Christmas tree," I thought. Not fair, but also not surprising. I told Lefty, "This book had pictures these kids made. And a lot of poems. It said about one hundred kids came back from the camp. Out of—"

"Yeah, sure. Thousands, huh?"

"Fifteen thousand, Lefty!"

He drank some coffee and applejack, and he said, "You know the one about the two old Jewish ladies? They meet on the street?"

I gave up. I shook my head.

"One says to the other, 'Pearl, a long time, blah, blah, how's the family?'

" 'My daughter is pregnant by a Japanese sea cook.'

" 'Oh, I didn't know. Your son?'

" 'My son, he's a robber in jail for life now. Just happened.'

" 'Sol, your husband, anyway.'

" 'Sol, I have to report to you, died last night. The heart.'

"Long pause. And then the old lady says, 'Listen, Pearl. As long as you got your healt'.' " He looked at me and smiled with his broken face. His teeth were even and white, and their condition always surprised me. "You hear that, kid? Keep breathing. Go to work. Do good."

There I went, and there I was, telephones ringing, coffee climbing back up my throat at me, the typewriter shaking under my hands as if I were trying to hurt it, when all I was doing was the fugue and variations on Rat Facts and Fancies for, of course, a poison manufacturer:

> Though rats have seldom won any popularity polls, they were respected symbols of wisdom in ancient Egypt—because they always chose the best bread! During the Middle Ages, Irish villages with a rodent problem tried *rhyming* the rats to death! But there's more truth than poetry in the fact that America's rat population —estimated at 100 million—does a billion dollars' worth of damage each year! Fortunately, science is fighting back with new weapons, like a chemical product which is deadly to rats but harmless to pets and livestock. Yet in some parts of the world, people are not allowed to kill rats! Know whether rats *really* leave a sink-

ing ship? How rats are said to have changed Western history? Fascinating facts, plus useful tips on ending a ratty problem.

All I had ahead of me now was finding out whether there were indeed 100 million rats in the world, and whether rats leave sinking ships (who wouldn't, I wondered) and whether rats did, by spreading black-plague fleas, change the Western world. A nasty day's work. I needed a reference librarian. Then Grover answered Len's phone (Len was out, sick in bed with a cold or a friend) and he announced, in the tones of disgust with which he addressed us each, and the office, and his job, and most of the world, "For you." I knew it was Rhona.

It wasn't. It was the rat-poison client's secretary, phoning to say that her boss had a photograph of a rat if I needed it. I told her I kept a real rat in my top drawer, and no thanks. But I understood, as I stared at Rat Facts and Fancies, that I had, indeed, wanted Rhona to call. And I knew, too, that Rhona was going to see me again, and that I was not going back only because of lust or curiosity, but very possibly out of guilt—a bad reason for going anywhere except to prison. I spent the rest of the morning working on matters of guilt, and on the influence of rats on Western history. That afternoon, I skipped guilt and settled on fatigue and boredom as my central topics, permitting myself a subtle deviation to my new interest—thwacked, in an assignment folder, onto my desk, by Max—which was going to be a synopsis on vision. Thus far, it was Ten Ways to Care for Your Eyes. It was brought to the world by a manufacturer of decongestant eyedrops, and it began with quite possibly the worst sentence ever written outside graduate school: "You may see your way clear for a longer period of time,

if you take some foresighted advice from eye experts."
Hello. I am writing synopses of nothing, on behalf of the
military-industrial complex and a man who drools a lot.
I am befriended by Lefty, who has only a right arm and
who manufactures egg rolls made of shrimp packed in
formaldehyde. Also, there is Rhona: she hunts blind Ru-
manian Jew-killers in Macy's. Are you listening?

"For you," Grover said, as if I'd troubled him once too
often.

"You don't mind?" I asked him. He blushed.

Rhona said, "Hello, it's Rhona."

"I know," I said.

"How could you know?"

"Because of the book. Because I was thinking about
you. Never mind. Because."

"Oh," she said, and there was sex in her voice.

"I'll meet you after work, if that's all right, Rhona."
There was no sex in mine, I think; only business. Dead
Jewish babies and monsters with straw hats. "I'll meet
you at the library, if that's all right."

"Oh," she said. "Yes. Surely. Goodbye."

I had made someone happy. All you need is a few
thousand dead kids and empyrean journalism such as
"Never rub your eye when you get something in it." *Are*
you listening?

Life had been asking me questions too, from time to
time. For years, in fact, the question had been phrased
in this fashion: Her tits or my brains—which had outraged them the most?

She was beautiful and a freshman, her nose was long
and curved, her breasts were heavy, and her thighs were
long-muscled, smooth, and round as saplings. She was
tall and bosomed, then. On a small, rigorously Christian
campus in the late 1950s, she looked like a lingerie ad in

the magazine section of the Sunday *Times*. She was Jewish—to a lot of the students, and to many of her teachers, she was a "Jewess." The blond and crew-cut ATOs, rich and drunk, with a better brand of acne than the Phi Taus, skinny pre-theo majors with deviant modes of sex without penetration, even the TKEs, who read Hermann Hesse and clapped to Peter, Paul and Mary and who wanted to teach English or be drunk forever or both, but in a gentle way, and who permitted Jews to join because they needed Negroes for their sense of generosity and didn't have any on campus—even they, and of course the pre-gynecology/obstetrics majors in Phi Ep, the all-Jewish fraternity, all agreed: Madeleine was to be fucked, and by one of them, with no prejudicial attention paid to race, creed, country of origin, or color of clergyman's eyes.

Unfortunately for all, Madeleine chose me: a junior with an A average who wrote poems about dying; who was stocky and therefore useful for touch football and the occasional barroom fight (I was so frightened of being a coward that I distinguished myself by tearing telephones off walls to use as weapons, by waving beer bottles as clubs); who wore black chino trousers and black scuffed boots, black socks and sweat-blackened boxer shorts, black sweaters and black rings beneath the eyes—all that study, all that writing of poems about the Bomb and something named Death—I was the one she chose. But I *was* smart, and I let myself be chased and chosen. She was a generous person, and she wanted to be bright, and I did my best to be decent, and I loved the body she gave me so unreservedly. I loved the person who lived in that body, finally. They hated me for that, brains or boobs or both, and a tax was exacted on a Saturday night a year after her arrival on campus.

I was weaving home across the Quadrangle to my dormitory, drunk on vodka, some of which was in the bottle thrust through the cummerbund of my tuxedo like a rake's sword. We had been celebrating some aspect of spring at a formal dance, and then we'd celebrated some aspect of her body, then mine, and then eternal love. And post-coital hungers had driven me to the five-cent candy machine under the dormitory's Gothic arches, where I was plugging money in, getting Baby Ruths back and stuffing them into my drunken mouth and, incidentally, taking my father's advice.

From far across a campus lawn that ran to the arch came a hoot and then a cry: "Fat fucking Jew cocksucker, you finished fucking your Jew whore bitch?"

I have to confess this. Knowing that it was either my brains or her breasts, I was touched at once, and galvanized, by the word "fat." He'd insulted me! It was merest vanity, I think, that drove me.

When I told her so, Rhona kissed my arm—available, bare—and she said, "You're also noble, though. You *want* to be. You're *gallant*, is the word. Even if you have a chunky build. You're chunkily gallant, Zimmer."

I whipped the vodka bottle from my cummerbund, extended it like a sword, cried my challenge back, and I saw him appear and appear and appear: Les Ruggink, six feet tall and looking six feet three, driving like a lineman. He sneered curtly, and pounded the living shit out of me on the Quad of a mid-May night. He did it, he told me, because I was "a fucking Jew bastard drop dead and get the fuck back to where you belong." He did it, he told me, because I was friendly with a "Jew handjob fuckernut." I didn't know what a fuckernut was, and I didn't care. For in this second round of insults—one eye was closed, and the blood from my nose absolutely poured around us—it became clear to me that the man who had called me fat could now call me whipped. I would *not* be humiliated. And, though I don't know how, I simply reversed things; and even now that means a little to me, I confessed to Rhona. She snorted the snort about men behaving like boys. One minute, in the blood and darkness, he was kneeling on my body. In another, I was kneeling on his shoulders. I held a handful of his fine fair hair. I was going to slam it down onto the pavement of the walk we'd rolled on, and then I lost it all—my knees slid, my hands lost their hold, and I thought that I'd throw up. So I stood and extended my palm in an interethnic handshake, saying, "We shouldn't be doing this to each other."

He ignored my right hand, then stuck up his left, and then got up without my help. Still holding his left aloft, exchanging palm and five fingers for one finger, the pan-religious international Fuck You, he said, "Left hand for niggers and Jews," and he walked away. I went into the dorm to tremble a while, and wash at bloodstains, and tell whoever might listen that I'd been beaten for a Jew, and had fought for being Jewish. I knew that I'd be understood. But didn't I lie? Wasn't it either my brains or her tits I fought about? Rhona nodded emphatically. I was trying to make her see something about the un-Jewishness of her new lover, but she wasn't over-whelmed by my logic. And even if it was my circumcised penis or what Moses did from the bulrushes on, didn't I fight for pride and then, at last, against whole humilia-tion? And if *that* is being Jewish, then I might have served coffee in the bunker in Berlin. "*You* can't serve anyone, Zimmer. You know that," Rhona said.

I wanted to give her that story as an admission, a gift. When I did, she took it as something trivial—a trinket, a token—and maybe she was right. That afternoon, though, and on Rhona's behalf, before our third meeting, I walked from the office to Scribner's on 5th, and I bought a book. I carried it with me downtown and, after we had met, very shyly, nodding, shaking hands, grimly discussing which restaurant we'd go to, and after we had made the outrageous decision to venture to Luchow's, I handed her the book and started to walk while she unwrapped it. It was *I Marry You*, by John Ciardi, and I liked it because it contained these lines:

> *Men marry what they need. I marry you,*
> *morning by morning, day by day, night by night,*
> *and every marriage makes this marriage new.*

I had owned a copy since 1958, when I was too young to marry, but old enough to be sentimental about the notion without losing sight of the possibility that it contained either brilliance I should know or nonsense I should cure; I'd never decided which. I loved the idea of loving someone that much, and of being loved that way. I now presented it with much embarrassment to Rhona, this new goad and astringent in my life, with whom I trudged to Luchow's because I'd heard it was fancy, and because she had made me read of dying Jews.

The menu didn't frighten me, because I had a credit card issued by American Synopsis, in order that its writers be able to take PR men to lunch and tell them what Max boasted most of, that we were Phi Beta Kappa. And my shabby sportcoat, Rhona's turtleneck sweater and plaid tweed skirt, didn't bother me, even when I saw the bare arms of the women around us, the tight unwrinkled business suits of the men. No, what bothered me was that I had forgotten the country of origin! Here we were, with a fat little string quartet playing songs of old Vienna, and here was all this good German wine on the menu, and even the Puerto Rican busboy seemed to have a German accent. Zimmer, the master of time and place.

Rhona knew this, and she leaned across our little table —after one look at us, the maitre d' had put us beside the hole leading to the center of the earth into which they dumped the garbage, or so it smelled in our dark corner—and she said, "It's all right. Germany used to have Jews in it. It once was a very cultured nation. It's all right. They're mostly Americans here, and a lot of them are Jews from Yorkville."

I wanted, despite my guilt and confusion, to ask why one couldn't eat in a restaurant not sanctified by persecuted people. But while I might have thought I knew her well enough to have a crush of sorts on her, and to be stimulated in uncertain ways, I knew that moral theology would have to wait. So I nodded, asked if she would like a drink, waved aside as if I owned bonds her worries about cost and her offer of dutch treat (*Deutsche* treat?), and ordered brandy alexanders. These, in case you cannot remember your adolescence, are a nauseous compound when you drink too many, and then have dark beer with your sauteed veal dinner and a lingonberry torte, cooked at your table and dripping preserves, followed by a cognac and a peculiarly long walk among little tables to the street. What I mean to say is that we staggered along 14th Street that night, and we didn't talk about the dead. I told Rhona of the time that my roommate and I, leaving college out of spiritual exhaustion, had been arrested for driving 90 on the Pennsylvania Turnpike; of how, once, after being overstimulated by a college production of *The Tempest*, I lay down in the middle of a two-lane road, playing catch in the dark with

FREDERICK BUSCH

my empty wine jug, and proclaiming to the world that I could not be killed; of how I had written poems in college, and had even participated in a reading of poetry before the annual dinner of the Lions Club of Emmaus, Pa.

Rhona told me of Barnard days and nights, and then she listed for me the famous female writers, mostly poets, who had been at school with her; she told me of the girl she had known who spent twelve hours a day quietly drunk at the West End Cafe and who nevertheless earned a B.A., and of the girl who played tennis all spring and nevertheless earned her M.A., and of her sister in Ann Arbor, who on a dare had played Russian roulette with a Russian—this last was simply intolerable, and we sat down on 14th Street, our backs against a tailor shop—Invisible Mending, the window said—and we whooped for lies and silly truth and mostly for the relief which the ease of our laughter gave us, and then we stood to shuffle and sway and dance away to her bilious apartment.

Inside, having turned on lights, Rhona presented her back to me for the removal of her coat. I took it off. She remained against me, and I placed my hands on her stomach; she winced as if one of us were burning, the other ice cold. This was not true. Neither of us was cold. And all that was said thereafter was this, from Rhona: "In the morning, we'll call in and say we're sick. We'll stay home together. Yes?" First we had to get home and, leaving the foyer lights on, and leaving some clothes on the floor, we did.

I am speaking of something more important, in a way, than how our bodies fitted and slid on her sheets. On the other hand, it is possible that there's not much of more importance, if we're speaking of human beings on

78

the earth and how they march along to death together. So I should say that her skin was smooth, except for her elbows, which were roughened, she said, by allergies to certain fibers in cloth. I should say that she smelled of talcum powder and a heavy perfume I didn't much like —she later told me it was Russia Leather—but which, in her neck and under her arms, which were stubbly, smelled musky and provocative. I should say that her legs were a little too short to be exquisite, if one lives with tape measures and calipers, but were muscular and were long enough to go around my waist. I should say that neither of us was an expert at the making of love, but that both of us were randy and energetic, and neither of us was selfish enough to deny the other hard work, and lots of happy noise. We made love three times, we woke gluey of mouth and rancid of breath, and neither of us seemed disturbed, and then we dropped off into deepest sleep—that state in which, as in coma or panic or death, you do not take any care about your appearance—and we woke together, late, in Rhona's bed, in something like love, and with hours ahead of us which even from the muffled darkness of my sleep I had looked forward to the way you'd wait for Christmas Day.

We cooked half a dozen eggs. When I asked for bacon, she turned from her chore—scraping the frozen orange juice from the can—and she said, "I'm not kosher, stupid. Bacon doesn't make me faint or call the cops." She threw a can of juice at me, inaccurately, and made a face of burlesqued fear: "Quick! Get me the Emergency Squad! There's a man here menacing me with *bacon!*" We choreographed with some grace my drift toward the toilet and hers into the farthest room. We reversed courses later, and I lingered at the front door in trousers, sockless feet, whistling so she could splash. We walked around, we hugged, we kissed, and then we brushed our teeth together—total intimacy: gargling and thick spitting in unison—and then we kissed some more, and went back to bed.

Waking, we took a shower together. I waited for us to commit marvelous perversions, for I had read about the taking of showers together, but all we did was wash one another's back, and sudsily cup loins, and kiss under warm water. We dressed and went out, determined to hold hands before the weary world. No one noticed, of course. But we kissed in the street as she led us, though in a clever design (it was a seven-block tetrahedron, I think), toward the library. Seeing that the history of the persecution of the Jews was about to intervene, I brought up the Jewish regard for women, like a sort of counterargument, with my usual violent subtlety: "Even in shul they treat them like scum, the Orthodox, don't they? Do they let them pray as equals?"

"Jews don't 'pray' in shul, Zimmer. It isn't that highfalutin. They talk to their Lord and they discuss with him what they said behind his back, in confidence, to other human souls the day before"—and with that in my ears, I saw him, coming from the corner, with a heavy book beneath his arm.

"Tell me he's blind," Rhona said.

"Maybe someone reads to him."

"It's also possible," Rhona said, "that he sits in a chair and looks at pictures of old Rumania."

"Rhona, who in *hell* looks at pictures of old Rumania?"

"Old Rumanians," she said, most seriously.

I giggled, and the giggles sputtered into long laughs and she punched me in the sportcoat, but not before the tall old man, still in his brown suit, but this time with a white shirt and yellow tie, lifted his nose, sniffed for danger, turned his face toward us. "Swine," he cried in a croaking ragged voice. "Swine."

Rhona turned from him. She put her face where she'd just put her fist. My hand came up to cup the back of her head and to protect her from the man we'd been, as far as I was concerned, persecuting. I loved it that she was so frightened of being found out. But then I realized that she was frightened because, as far as *she* was concerned, he had been persecuting her, or hers, others, who were gassed, and dead, and crazy in Astoria in old apartments near synagogues. And suddenly, my hand around her as if she were my child—it is easier to believe in what you patronize, isn't it?—I did assume that I was protecting this sturdy young woman with eyeliner stains on her face, and from a history of oppression. I turned, so that I stood between her and the blind man. She peeped around me when I had stood still for too long, forcing her face into my tweed. Looking between my elbow and my side, she said, "He's gone. He went inside."

"It's all right."

"Yes."

"It is."

"Yes. But what should we do about him?"

"Rhona, we could stay away from him."

"We could also report him to the Immigration. You're not supposed to come into America if you used to be a Nazi and you lied about it."

"You know who puts the rockets into space, Rhona? A lot of Nazis in Florida. Right near the leather-faced Hadassah ladies on vacation. They mingle, I imagine, near the same cabanas."

She shivered. She meant it. "Don't be a ghoul, Zimmer."

"Let's leave him be, then."

"When did he ever leave *me* be?"

I had known she would say something like that, and I was nodding by the time *be* snapped out, summarizing five or six thousand years of oppression by the polytheists and the adherents of that running dog of zealotry and self-sacrifice, Jesus. Want to know why Jesus *actually* let himself be immersed by John? How the rock of the tomb was really *lifted*, not rolled? Who Jesus *truly* had in mind when he punished the money-changers? All the facts, in a story that will nail you in place. We went back to Rhona's apartment, and I knew that we'd drink tea, and maybe even hug, but that last night's abandon, and this morning's, was vitiated.

In truth, we were no sooner in the foyer with its scrap of napless rug and scuffed parquet, than did Rhona tug on my belt and say, "Come with me."

"What?"

"Don't talk," she said.

"I won't."

"I won't let you," she said, balancing herself near the old iron bed as she rolled a stocking down.

"But *why?*"

"Because," that brilliant woman said, "you have a terrific squat little ass. And because I will *not* have you thinking of me as some sexless Jewish avenger." She sat naked on her bed, she closed her eyes, she fell backwards, did a shove-and-grunt of some sort, and there she was, on the sheets and waving before me: buttocks, crotch, thighs and calves, all supported by her strong hands, and there was no face, her voice came up and over the V which hung before me: "Come and get me, Zimmer, I'm all cunt."

82

Which returns me to Lillian, who was a happy woman in bed, crying out, "I love it!" during love. I'd grown used to that, I thought, but apparently I hadn't.

We were done and sweaty, and apparently I hadn't at all, because I said, "You *do* love it."

"When I let myself," Lillian said. "When we do it enough to just be doing it, you know? And not waiting to see who wants to do which, and who should say something to the other—you know," she said gently.

"I'm so sorry we're like that," I said. "I always thought I was this great sex fiend."

"You were. Before we got married. Remember? Marathons, you'd call them, when we'd spend the weekend together. Sometimes it still happens, we relax enough to go crazy. Not go crazy. I don't know. We relax sometimes."

I kissed her cool shoulder and pushed my nose against her, sniffing. "Ah," I said. And then, because apparently I had not grown used to it, I said, "When we make love, and you shake your head back and forth, you know what you say?"

Her body didn't stiffen, but her throat muscles tightened as she said, "No, what?"

"You say, 'I love it.' "

"Oh, yeah? Do I say it all the time?"

"Pretty much."

"Well. What do you think?" Her voice was wary now.

"I guess I sometimes wonder whether you love *me* doing it with you, or just *it* by itself."

"You know, you're a romantic fool. A complete idiot baby arrested-development Jew moron baby."

"You think I'm not showing very much wisdom about this, Lil?"

"There's only one batch of men," she said, "who need to be mothered while fucked. Guess who?"

I slid my face along her chest until I was over her nipple. I pounced, I sucked, she squealed, we played and we even enjoyed ourselves, and we didn't forget what we'd said.

Saying it had worsened it, somehow. Now we had to contend with conscious matters, not only with what our bodies told us in silence; we had to live with statements, now, about how separate we were, and therefore we had to respond to them, by making other statements. Once, at the office, during the Tuesday editorial meetings, one of our junior editors, Walter Stottner, proposed with some vigor a book I had suggested we decline. It was by a homosexual and dealt with his adjustments, public and private, to his sexuality. I had admired the prose, and some descriptions of family turmoil, but had thought the book neither memoir nor novel, and finally insubstantial. Stottner, who might have had homosexual leanings, was exercising his right to argue for a manuscript he liked. I tuned in and out as he spoke, for I was thinking of Lillian while the six of us sat in our managing partner's dusty office, drinking coffee at a harvest table on which were scattered heavy ash trays from famous resorts. On the pastel-blue wall was a skewed wide triangular shape, made by a novelist on whose book of short fiction we'd refused to advance more than $3,000; he had thrown an ash tray; he then had accepted the advance; the book sold 2,500 copies of which 1,075 were eventually returned. And Stottner said, ". . . the essential separateness in these people's lives. What *moves* me so—"

"Wally," I interrupted, "is this author suggesting that they're . . . what would you call them? Separatists—"

"They're Canadian political types," the managing partner, Abromowitz, said.

"Don't forget the Basques," sang Sally. She was our

editorial future, I thought, so I smiled though I felt vertigo in spite of sitting down.

"No," I said, "really. Does the author say that isolated people are homosexuals?"

Stottner shook his head. He had a hefty high permanent wave, and he couldn't keep his fingers away from the curls. "Not at all," he said. "I *do* think he's suggesting that being a homosexual means living and seeing a life in which people are essentially alone."

"Doomed to be alone," I said.

Sally said, "Are you having a horrible morning, Mr. Zimmer?"

"Just plain alone is bad enough," Stottner said.

"It's a terrific metaphor," I said.

Abromowitz asked, "For what, though?"

I was enough of a publisher to agree that the book might not pay out, and we went on to consider a first novel about eagles. Everyone waited, I thought, to see whether I'd find a terrific metaphor in eagles. I winked at Sally, who blushed, and I tucked my hands beneath my armpits and flapped my wings while sitting in place, I flapped and flapped and flapped.

So there we were, Lillian and I and Sam, and it was 1980. The house published a lovely reminiscence by a middle-aged Flemish woman about how, when she was a girl, her family sheltered a fleeing family of Jews. *Time* reviewed it, and a man in Skokie, Illinois, recognized the author, and the sheltered family (his own) and the New York *Daily News* arranged a reunion in our grimy downtown offices, and there were pictures in the paper of Daddy, I explained to Sam, because I'd edited the book.

Sam was in our shaggy, disheveled living room, pounding a baseball repeatedly into the glove we'd given him for his birthday. Standing in a welter of Sunday papers, he said, "Do you think George Brett saw the picture, Daddy?"

I said, "Nope."

"How about Dave Winfield?"

"The Yanks are in town," Lil said. She was still a rabid Yankee fan and wore an official Yankees hat (she'd seen the ad for it in *Sporting News*) when she jogged.

"Well," I said. "Well. Maybe yes, Sam. He probably looks at the papers when he has time."

"So you're famous," Sam said. "If Dave Winfield sees you, you're famous."

I seized his lean waist and pulled the long body—already growing hard and gristly—and squeezed him to me. The arm of the Mission Oak rocker was between us, and Sam called, "*Ow!*"

"I'm a dummy," I said. "I'm sorry. Forgive me? I'm sorry. I was sneaking in a little loving, is all."

"Don't sneak it," Lillian said from behind the sports section. She was warming up for a day of televised athletics.

"Okay," I said. In my jeans and moccasins and torn mud-colored sweater I rose to announce to our family: "I love you, Sam. I love you, Lillian." I was red and sweaty, for some reason, and I was breathing pretty hard. Lillian rattled the sports section and looked at Sam. He looked at her, made an exaggerated shrug, and said, "See you, guys," as he walked to his room.

Lillian looked at me and raised the newspaper again. From behind it she said, "Sweetheart, we don't *give* medals for that. Not right away. Do it all the time, all the good ways, and then—"

I didn't know what to do, so I sat down and raised my own screen of papers. I heard hers rattle, and I knew that she was looking, across the room, from outside her papers at mine. I stayed as still as I could for some time.

It reminded me of our wedding day, the way I held my body. On that day, my knees were trembling, and my chest was heaving, and I felt as though I clenched my entire *skin* in order to remain upright and not fall over onto Lillian, beside me in Professor Stiefader's study. He was a former teacher to whom marriage between Christian and Jew was as important as the Gospel according to Mark. He was German, and this was not surprising. Every other person at my old college, from the registrar to the skinny woman behind the counter at the student union who fried the dogmeat hamburgers, was German. So it seemed to me. The girl I had loved there, as Arthur Miller was said to love Marilyn Monroe and *her* body while peering at the world through glasses just like mine, was German too; her father had an accent like a bad guy in a 1940s movie. So did Stiefader, and so, probably, did Marilyn Monroe's father, if we but knew.

My parents had never accepted my explanation for my being married without them, nor had they believed that Lillian's parents were present only because I'd been unable to keep them away. My explanation, to be sure, was astonishing to them; when my mother, tears in her eyes and an unmodulated drift in her voice, had later asked, "Why?" I had replied with this: "Well, *because*, Mom." This she deemed unacceptable, and I could hardly blame her. And I hardly believed it myself: *Because.*

What I hadn't said was: Because I needed the long slow train ride, in no one's company but my own. Because I felt like my own family, Lillian's in-laws-to-be. Because, I mean, I felt as though I were losing Zimmer to these alien beings with their golden hair and delicate cheekbones and with no hint of eastern Europe in their light eyes, creamy skin, long arms. Because I could not understand, suddenly, how I, the only Zimmer I had lived with this long, could be merging my blood and sperm and my former pretty-baby's being with these people of the wide plateaus and long prairies. Because I was scared, as never had I been before, to lose what I suddenly, for only the second time in my life—the first had been when I was beaten at school for my Jew Shoes— had fully realized I carried: not Jewishness, I think, but the freight of all those squat and un-Americanized, Yiddish- and German- and Russian-speaking passengers in steerage on the foul dark boats that had come with sickening lurches to the harbor of New York. Because, in short, I knew that my life would change. Because I was becoming an American. Because my country frightened me. Because it was a great place, immense and eddying out from people, and a man could become lost in it. Because I saw myself, dark dwarf for all my size, disappearing in a great golden field of grain; because, on closer inspection of my waking nightmare, the sheaves were people and the gold their hair, and I was submerged in a nation of Lillian's people. And because, while mourning the loss of the-Zimmer-I-had-been, I could not spare the feeling—hadn't the requisite generosities —for my suddenly dark, suddenly exotic, suddenly, dammit, embarrassing mother and father. Because I owed them those feelings, I would probably have given them, during the ride, and during the service, and during the flashing of the Cross, and after. And because, therefore, our day of marriage would have been the first of many days of combat between in-laws, and precisely the sort of civil war my more-or-less civil ceremony had been designed to forestall.

So: *Because*, I said to them.

Lil and I got married during the year of Richard Nixon's wage-and-price freeze. Nixon was with me in 1971, as he had been with me in college and before. I had debated on him as potential president on behalf of the Young Democrats, and I had later played and replayed a recording of his Checkers speech. Lillian, whose father was, like her, an expert on money, and whose mother, like her, took men and money seriously, was outraged. I had insisted on coming by train, and alone, to the Lehigh Valley Station, because that was how I had always come to college after vacations; now, after a sizable vacation, during which, I thought smugly, I had done a little growing up—"But not enough, surely!" I could hear Lil scolding me—I was coming back to school for my wedding. And Lillian, meeting me at the station, while her parents recovered in their motel from the cross-country drive, middle-west to middle-east, Lillian was nagging me about Richard Nixon!

"New Economic Policy," she said. "It's Democratic Party policy, and his hand's forced because we are doing an inflationary spiral like you haven't *seen*."

"Our cost of paper's doubled," I offered hopefully.

But she wasn't mollified by that kind of participation. Lil was, like me, quite terrified. When frightened, I either talked about books or withdrew into heavy dreadful silences; when frightened, Lillian spoke of the dangers that danced upon the air and in our very bodies, insufficiently noted or acted upon. So there I was, on my wedding day, hearing about the effects of the Vietnam War on the international monetary system. Lillian was telling me about the Bretton Woods Conference of 1944, and European revaluation, and the gold standard, and I, on the day of my marriage, was thinking of Rhona Glinsky. She and Lillian scolded existence in similar ways, I realized. It only made me smile to think so.

I was to call her father Dad. When we met, that's what I did. He was fractionally taller than I was. He seemed, I thought, to be stooping, or to look as if he stooped, so as to emphasize the difference in our heights. I slumped my shoulders to make him happy, and I called him Dad. He told me how pleased he was that we would have a nondenominational service. I said ditto. Lil's mother, whom—surprise!—I was instructed to call Mom, I called Mom. She was shorter than I was. And she was terribly concerned that my parents weren't there. I told her that

I'd neglected to tell them any more than that I was going to marry a woman they one day would meet. "But why, dear?" Mom said.

"Because I didn't want anybody hating anybody at the last minute and queering things."

"Queering?" Mom said.

"Messing them up," Lil told her.

"He didn't really mean, ah, *queer*," Mom said.

Dad said "Nah." But he looked at me intently.

Lillian laughed so hard, she dribbled a Manhattan onto the dark dress she wore in the cocktail lounge of their motel.

Mom said, "Well, as long as your parents, and we *ought* to meet them just as *soon* as we can, dear. Your parents mustn't think it has to do with, you know, *religion*."

"Think what has to do with religion?" I asked Mom, batting my big brown eyes.

"Oh!" she squealed. "Why, why, *any*thing."

"Oh," I answered, as if we all were speaking the same tongue. And in fact we were. "Oh. Well, of course not," I told her.

"Well, *there*," she said.

And, well: there. For there we were, in Stiefader's country house, a dozen miles from the campus, and in his cellar. Upstairs, his wife and children thumped and bumped, prepared the living room for our emergence as man and wife. Downstairs, in his cellar study, its walls hung with anthropological trophies—it seemed to me that every primitive people of the earth had given something to my teacher's ecumenical embrace—we were waiting for him to begin. I have to confess that little of the ceremony remains with me. Lil always complained because no one thought to take a picture of us. I have only pictures of us in my mind, no more than one instant of multiple images, smooth action; the rest is a photo album made and kept by the utterly scared.

There we are:

Lil and Zimmer before the Reverend Stiefader. Alongside are Mom and Dad. She is crying into stubby white gloves. If you study Zimmer's face, it is possible to read regret for the absence of his parents. If you study Zimmer's history, you can read his mother's refusal to speak to him, or to his new wife, for one calendar month.

Stiefader beaming, his red face aglow and dripping sweat onto the collar that bites his chubby neck. Lillian in yellow gossamer material, Zimmer in his heavy winter suit of dark flannel. Stiefader reading from the Good News According to Matthew, and Stiefader actually flushed with real joy.

The open mouth of Mom, as Stiefader is saying words like "Christian" and "Jew." A quotation from John Donne's sermons now opening up Dad's strong mouth. The perfection of expensive dentures visible, still, to the mind's eye.

Zimmer unable to look at the woman he marries. Zimmer agape and weak of knee, looking into the third button of the Reverend Stiefader's black suit.

And then there is the one slow-motion moment of multiple images as Stiefader actually winks at Zimmer, and then with dreadful amusement, twitching and smiling and blinking and reddening, the minister makes the high and wide and unapologetic sign of the Cross as he brings the service to its close.

He hugged my shoulders at the end of the afternoon, and he whispered to me, "I couldn't resist to offer you the mercy of the Cross. Just in case, you understand? Think of it as an insurance policy. Think of me as an eschatological insurance salesman. You never will know when you will need a little extra help, hm?"

One day in college, the word had gone out (it was a small campus, and if the word merely crawled or sidled, we all got it): Stiefader was holding a special meeting. This in itself was not sufficient to draw the student body; we cut his classes in religion and religious philosophy just as we cut everyone else's classes. Though we did attend when he taught Old Testament, because he then breathed fire. First of all, when he said Abraham, he wasn't talking about a biblical character; he was mentioning an intimate by first name. When he thundered on behalf of the Hebrew prophets, in spite of his being a Lutheran pastor in the countryside somewhere, he sweated down his wide face, his eyes opened hugely behind his gold-rimmed glasses, and he meant what the Bible said: salvation! damnation! pay *attention!* But the reason we attended this meeting was because it was said to have to do with Jews.

On our rural Lutheran campus of 1,000 students, most of the city kids were from Philadelphia and New York and Passaic, and were (1) pre-med (2) Jewish (3) alert to the confusing fact that the world was made up of more than Lutherans and those the Lutherans hadn't yet converted. They attended the special meeting because they were rarely addressed, as subject or object, without embarrassment or opprobrium. And they liked the attention. The other kids attended because of Jews the way you'd attend a meeting entitled Bloodletting for Lithuanian Copts Converted to Rosicrucianism. Once, a short, chestless girl who wore pink a lot and whose curled blonde hair hung in greasy tubes, and whose contact lenses blinded her and whose skin was spotted, and whose rubber bands for her braces were always gluey with food fog, this girl said to me at a party given by ATO—they let Jews in toward the end, and the Brothers peed in the ice bucket of the tapped keg, side by side with Jewish guys, to show that we were all a part of the family of man—this girl got drunk enough to actually touch my hair, forward of the ears, asking, "Do you really . . . *have* anything there?" Horns. Horns. And she and her friends came to the meeting on account of Jews.

I had told her yes, by the way, but that they were soft because of spring molt, and then I had gone back to peeing on the keg with my fellowmen.

It was wonderful theater, and also wonderful confession. Stiefader wore immense academic robes which seemed to swell up until they threatened to rise from his shoulders and devour his head. In red wool and red silk and red velvet, he looked like a Hans Holbein painting. He looked like Hans Holbein. In the hot afternoon, in the fug and funk of a sealed lecture hall, he took the regalia off and stood before us, hatless now, and gownless, in shabby shiny gabardine pants and a sweated-through tee-shirt. He looked at us, winked at his favorite students (girls, always; preferably Jewish girls) and he began: "Today, it has been announced, agents of the Israeli secret service, living in Argentina for months, made final a plan they had carefully prepared. They secreted from that country, which has a large proportion of Nazis and Nazi sympathizers in the government, a man named Adolf Eichmann, a colonel in Hitler's SS, and the man who was responsible for the implementation of what was called The Final Solution. I, as a German, though now an American citizen, and as a man of the cloth nevertheless drafted, you would call it—conscripted—by the Nazis, into the SS as interpreter—I salute this just event."

Tears ran down his face. What impressed me so much, then, was that his eyes ran, his lips were wet with saliva, his nose flooded his upper lip, his face was beaded with sweat, his undershirt turned pink as his skin showed through, and yet his voice never broke or even shook: a true preacher, Stiefader. And he preached.

He told us of babies torn from screaming mothers' arms and kicked into formations which were marched off to the gas. He told of men and women shaking hands goodbye, and kissing perfunctorily, then walking to the sealed trucks which throbbed as gas poured into the back and they knew it, they had to know it. He catalogued the heaps of teeth and rugs of skin, he told of shoes saved and house keys, pitiably saved by the homeless, until keys and those who had turned them were melted down. He told of records kept. Nazis especially, but Germans in general, kept records of everything, he said, and murders too—because records, simply, were to be kept. He made in the air above and around us the wails of the dying, he presented over and over the images of babies with spilled brains, of stuffed animals dying in the fires with the people who had stuffed them, and of the mass graves, and of Eichmann, for reasons Stiefader could not, almost would not, understand, making each day's slaughter a little more efficient.

Some of us cried, and some of us covered our ears, and most of us listened, and I got mad. I always did, I always do—it was brilliant, it was horrible, it was *control*. I don't want to be controlled. Even for the memory of such dead strangers, I would not be overwhelmed. Peeping infant ego, or whatever it is: I don't want to be swallowed up by anything. Licked a little, sure. But not eaten up.

So when we left the room, Stiefader alone with his horror at the podium, having told us that he did approve, and that we must too, a contravention of international law—the world must not be allowed to forget! he had cried—and the students commented on his lecture with "Fucking A, man!" and "Jee-sus!" and "You *believe* this?" and "Aw-w-*right!*", I went back to my room and I wrote my column, "Zimmer-ing," for the college paper.

Mad as hell, I instructed a waiting campus that, sure, it was tough what Eichmann had done, but now about all those Negro people in witchy strange places like *Florida*, who stood in the backs of buses, and didn't get to vote, and had to use different toilets because of the bigot white man KKK fascist.

I cranked up several thousand words like that. I knew that I was supposed, by good people like Stiefader, and fools like the girl who sought horns, to feel my Jewishness keenly. The self-appointed steward of Jewishness will say, as ever: A good opportunity for your Jewish anti-Semitism to assert itself; you were embarrassed and ashamed, so you proclaimed your separateness from your people and even from their Holocaust. And maybe

I did. I wrote, in essence, this: Yes they killed Jews. But killing Jews' killers doesn't help these darker Jews down South. I was later to learn that I had probably inhaled some fifties *Zeitgeist*. For such perverse, tangential reasoning was filling the *New Republic* and the *Partisan Review*. Reputations were being made by older Jewish kids who demanded that attention be turned from awful public spectacles and directed at *them*. And that is, more or less, what happened to me. For there were dozens of phone calls reported, and letters received by administrators at the school. It seems that "Zimmer-ing" was picked up by some wire service and syndicated without my knowing it. I was news: how today's Jewish youth feels about the Eichmann kidnapping. From my little German-Lutheran campus, I was singlehandedly helping to throw Israel, and the ghosts of the Holocaust, into American disregard. Well, the calls from Southern colleges, and from midwestern fraternal organizations, began to come in. And, magically, they came more and more to Phi Ep, the Jewish fraternity on campus. So there I was: the girl in pink would call me Jew, and so would my Southern "readers"; thus I was a Jew. The Jews who knew me as Jew, reading "Zimmer-ing," must, more than likely, have found me desperately deficient, if not anti-Semitic, and they thought of me as traitor, maybe goy. So that's what I was: the Nazi or the Jew, depending on who cast the vote.

I was a loudmouth. Stiefader was a brave man. And when he was taken by force to be an interpreter, he did what he could from within the uniform. Six men were captured in a basement in France, he'd told us, and his detachment was sent to interrogate. He quickly learned they were Jews, and he knew they were dead. He screamed at them to take their pants down. And I can see them, pissing and knowing how soon they'd die, standing bare-assed in some cellar in a French village, surrounded by soldiers and this screaming man. One by one, he'd told the special student meeting, though he told it with great delicacy, he picked up each Jew's penis and dangled it for his *oberst* to see, and then he spat. A Moslem circumcision, he said, slapping the fear-shortened cock against the doomed Jew's leg. These eastern dogs always cut it *left*, you see? He spat again, the *oberst* nodded because he didn't know, and the men were placed in a factory instead of a death camp. And the man who years later would marry me, beaming and sweaty while I chattered and shook, to the pale still Lillian, had stood before students and taught them how Jews could be Moslems, and how a traitor to German policy could be a savior to those condemned, and a grace note in his country's savage decline, and how you aren't necessarily what you're named.

But Rhona and I, a few years later, were lovers. We named ourselves, officially, lovers. One morning on Varick Street, before I left for work, I told my landlord and confidant, Lefty, that "I have a lover," and Piggy giggled into her palm. Lefty, with his busted veins, and with one arm up to the elbow in terrible small shrimp, paused to say, "That's all right, kid."

Rhona and I were lovers, and at night, when I was without her, to celebrate our love I read Anne Frank's diary and Bruno Bettelheim, Primo Levi's *If This Is a Man*, about Auschwitz, *Smoke Over Birkenau*, books about Buchenwald and Treblinka, books in which the predominant word for titles was *Dead*, or *Death*, with *Ashes* running a close second, and in all of them the same initial disbelief, and the same unwillingness to waken each day, and gray clouds hanging low above them, and the smell of their burning, and typhoid, and the dying, and the children lost, lost, and the need to not forget. We spent weekends together often, but weeknights, late, at the start, we spent apart because Rhona believed in her job—reference tools, catalogues, indexes, lists: she was good at finding things, not the least the dead and those who killed them—and she did not wish to arrive at her work too tired to function. So our raptures were disciplined after a short while, and in between the good-to-terrific love we made two or three nights a week (and sometimes, to tell the truth, oftener, standing up in the hall and even in the bathroom once, and on the floor), punctuating these outbursts were the books she took from the library and from her own shelves so that I, if I were to stay a Jew-manqué, could at least become a conscious one.

That was the plan. She would fuck me into submission. She would educate me. She would also find considerable pleasure in my person, I decided, and that might wreck her plans; I suspected she truly hadn't intended to love me until I woke to the nature of the world: A Jew's God in charge of all Creation, Nazis underfoot and slithering into our lives, and a history of merciless dyings. Rhona had wanted to save me while saving the Jews. This she worked at. Alas, she found herself also working to save herself—from one lapsed living Jew for whose conversion she could not use blackmail. She wouldn't withhold herself, and therefore couldn't threaten to, and so she had to love me and hope. There was tension for us, to say the least, in being lovers. But that's what we were.

We also, doubtless, were fools. And we were surely persistent. We followed the poor blind man in his brown suit all over his neighborhood, and all over New York.

We went to the delicatessen with him when he bought a quarter-pound of Nova Scotia cheap, because shaved from the fatty part. We watched the man behind the counter, a crook, lean hard on the scale. We hid behind salamis hung from hooks, and yet the blind man's nose swung up, his eyebrows rose above the black glasses, and he hurried from the store. Sometimes there was a woman too. She looked like our victim. We saw them in the library at dusk, emerging with books Rhona had charged out to him—some of them the same books I had read at night. Rhona had no explanation for this; she likened his interest, at last, to that of the actor who reads his press clippings. After a while, we followed his sister (or so we presumed her to be), and she did some shopping and came home. Thus, five nights of those weeks after we made love, and two Saturdays, we were mild persecutors. The old man interested me. Rhona excited me. I followed the one to follow the other. I lied my acquiescence in that folly for the sake of her foolish love. And I studied death for a life with her, and I either was a generous man, or a preposterously selfish one. And I must confess that I probably received far more than I gave. On Sundays, we went to museums and movies, walked, read the papers together, performed invigorations of sex in Rhona's apartment and in my loft. I recall her having asked, as I first showed her my loft, "Is this Lefty person peddling his egg rolls as kosher? Can you find out for me?" When I refused, calling her a Jewish vigilante, she sulked before she laughed at herself. But she didn't wholly mean the laugh, and I knew it.

I think she sensed an end to things too. She laughed at herself more, lectured me less, hectored the world in newly diminished tones, and on our third Sunday together, she took me on several subway trains to Queens, where her mother now lived in misery and where her father, always by her mother's side, was nevertheless a mere visitor.

The borough of Queens will always be for me a dry run for the post-Atomic age: it is what our world will look like by the time we power our generators with burning bones, and eat frozen fingers instead of ice cream bars on sticks. The wind always blows colder in Queens, the streets are more carelessly labeled, so that you lose your way more easily; the numbers on apartment buildings are hidden so that you walk past your destination a minimum of three times before you know to enter; the lock never works; the buses there don't run; you wait for an hour for every train; the people don't speak English, only arcane European dialects unrelated to the Romance languages; there is no friendship in Queens, there are no open shops, no bathrooms you can get to, and no policeman within twenty miles if you should happen to be dying of coronary insufficiency. That's where Rhona took me. Where else would her mother keep house?

The building smelled of old food—such buildings are designed, by architects and contractors, to retain the smell of food: they use a certain plaster which incorporates cabbage, and sometimes the odor of bowels, into the very walls. The building was dark because a computer saw to it that only forty percent of the lights worked at any one time. And the building was noisy in mysterious ways: there was a faint babble, as of children in a mild distress, although I was certain no one in the building was under the age of 59. When we walked up four flights, gusting out breath, heaving it in, we were accompanied by an insistent trickling sound. Doubtless, somebody on a seventh-floor stairwell was urinating at us. I did not inquire. While we walked, I heard the broken elevator whine into action. The moment was not auspicious.

Nor did it improve when Rhona rang the apartment bell and her father opened the door to raise his brows, smile a little smile, and admit us. He was shorter than Rhona, he had little hands and feet, he wore a tie and a clean white shirt under a weed-green cardigan. He held a newspaper, perhaps for protection, folded in the New York subway fold—it was a sixteenth of its normal width, arranged so that one could hang on a strap and read one column at a time without provoking one's neighbors. His face had Rhona's sharp nose, but on a rounder head and with a shorter neck. Because he didn't wear eyeliner, his eyes were small and looked lighter. His voice, when he finally said, "So?," was husky, as if he had a cold.

In the dark small hallway, outside a darkened living room, Rhona said to Mr. Glinksy, "And Ma?"

He shrugged, moving his neck like a buzzard's, and he said, "Ask me about something else."

I expected him to offer me a celery tonic, but he returned from the kitchen, while we fought our way around the coffee table and into the yellow brocaded sofa, and he virtually slapped a large tumbler of ice and blended whiskey into my hand. "You'll take a highball?" he said.

I smiled. He looked down at me. He looked over to Rhona, to whom he hadn't brought whiskey. He looked at her legs. He nodded.

"So," he said.

"Yes?" This came from the entrance to the living room. It was spoken by a woman who, though taller than he, was short. She had stumpy legs, and she wore an ugly purple dress, a lot of clanking metal on her neck and on her arms, and she seemed to be going bald. Her hairline was as far back as any I've seen on a woman who hasn't lost her hair. Mrs. Glinsky wore purple orthopedic shoes which made her look as though she had no toes, or very little left of them. Her eyes were ringed in black, though not from makeup, as in Rhona's case; this was a woman who didn't sleep. I thought of what I'd been reading during my own mildly wakeful nights. Her sleeves were long, so my search for a tattoo was fruitless. She saw my eyes move, though, and she put her hands behind her back. "How do you do," she said. "I am the mother of the bride."

At the last word, I must have panicked visibly, because she started to laugh at me in a kind way, and Mr. Glinksy, apparently delighted with her pleasure, laughed even harder than she. Rhona was not amused, but I really didn't care; anything which smoothed my stay there, in something like a foreign country, was more than acceptable to me. Rhona finally finagled a drink for herself, and Mr. and Mrs. Glinsky poured Cherry Heering into little glass thimbles, and we all sat in the living room which they kept so dark we might have been sitting outside at night. We peered at one another, and into Mrs. Glinsky's past, and made swallowing noises.

"You're in magazine work," Mrs. Glinsky told me. Rhona moved uncomfortably, as if the air about her didn't fit right—she knew I'd know that she and her mother had conferred about me on the phone. She also knew I knew that conferring with her mother was not a habit. And I suspect she suspected that I was hearing her voice emerge from a black receiver to say to this woman with black-circled eyes, "I have a lover, Ma."

"I am," I said. "It's not much of a magazine. It's actually more of a rag. Pretty shabby, really, public relations stuff."

"So how is it you're so proud of your work?" Mr. Glinsky said, smiling. His grin told me: Here we are all family.

"You don't hurt anybody with your work?" Mrs. Glinsky asked.

Mostly me, I decided. I shook my head no.

"So," Mrs. Glinsky said in her brittle almost-high voice. It was the voice of someone who kept careful control because the loss of control meant the loss of much more. When she spoke there was much at stake, and I didn't know what. "So, tell me. You're a Jewish boy."

"I was born one."

Mr. Glinsky smiled because he hoped I was a jester. Mrs. Glinsky knew, however, that I'd dodged. Rhona said, "He's one of the assimilated. He had Christmas trees when he was a boy."

Mr. Glinsky did not stand to take back my highball. But he didn't offer me more ice, and his grin this time was tentative. "Christmas trees are nice things," Mrs. Glinsky said smoothly. "They are symmetrical and they smell sweet. Children will find under them handsome toys. This is all supposing, of course, that real trees are as symmetrical as the trees in children's story books, and that the parents have money enough to provide the presents. And of course—"

I honestly didn't know what she'd say next. Rhona did, apparently, for she interrupted with a noise, a kind of throat-clearing sneeze which ended with the bottom of her tumbler striking the table harshly.

Mrs. Glinsky stared. She nodded. She said, "You would wish me not to continue, miss?"

"It is *allowed* to have Christmas trees," Rhona said. I was wholly confused now. She was offering me, but not trusting them with me. She was tossing me to them as bait, but defending me too. It did not occur to me at that moment that a child could so effortlessly love and hate a parent, or her history, at once.

"In that case, since you have such pardon me *faith* in them, you should ask yourself why you told your mother such a thing in the first place," her mother announced. "When you know how she feels."

Mr. Glinsky said, "A Jew is not a bigot."

"Sometimes," Mrs. Glinsky said, "it would be wise for a Jew to try being one a little bit. It couldn't hurt that much, I think, since there seem to be so many bigots who survive it. Hmh?"

"Actually, we stole the trees from neighborhood Christians," I said.

"This is not true," little Mr. Glinsky said.

"Yes." I was desperate. I was laughing but desperate. "On Christmas eve, while the gentile children slept, the Jewish kids would sneak into their houses through the cellarway—see, they always left the cellar door open to bring in the Christmas bike, you know, some big gift, from the garage at midnight before they went to bed. So we'd get in there, me and my friends, and we'd lift the whole tree up, tinsel and all, and we'd carry it out to the yard of this empty house on 18th Street, that was our block. When we had enough, we'd make a bonfire and we'd burn them all."

"Zimmer is being a fool," Rhona said, "because you were giving him a hard time. He was embarrassed." She had so *many* loyalties.

"If that's the case," Mrs. Glinsky said, "I apologize for a hard time. You have to understand: I *am* a bigot."

"Let us say that my wife is persuaded," Mr. Glinsky said, smiling like a master of ceremonies.

"I wait for them to turn on us again," she said.

"May it be a long wait," Mr. Glinsky said. "Forever. At least."

I had expected something like this. What did surprise me was Rhona's failure to tell her mother of our Irving Place Nazi, and after meeting Mrs. Glinsky I was further surprised: she was not quite the coiled spring I'd expected, and I imagined she might be able to tolerate— might greet with pleasure—the news Rhona bore, like a new pregnancy, invisible and invigorating. But that Rhona said nothing suggested to me how in turn invisible Mrs. Glinsky's wounds were. Certainly her jumpiness, the obvious difficulty with which she slept, her feeling of being unwell, these were clear. But I had seen survivors in my neighborhood sit, elbow on oilcloth, hand on tea glass, eyes fixed on lemon pips and the past, frozen, for hours on a winter afternoon. I had heard one weep aloud in the subway because we were stuck and starting to sweat: the low bubbling moan of saliva on the lips, and the eyes unclosable because *it* was on its way from someplace secret, and the body shaking, and then going rigid, and the long fall to the floor. I had seen the tattoo on the wrist and had understood everything. Or, as Mrs. Glinsky might tell me, I had recognized everything, but hadn't acknowledged any of it in my so-called soul: those Christmas trees, those years of perfidy, my failure to regret them.

And because of the hot stuck subway car, or because of a childhood I'd enjoyed and which seemed under assault, or because I truly didn't understand—I hope so— I said, suddenly, softly, "Why should we know who we are only because of the dead?"

"Excuse me?" Mr. Glinsky said, setting the cordial glass down and leaning forward for a ripping good phil-

osophical discussion: the children in the temple questioning the elders.

But Mrs. Glinsky knew. "Perhaps," she said with especial gentleness and modulation, "perhaps we know
from the *manner* of their dying. As well as the fact of
their death. Hmh?"

"Is Judaism a religion of death, then?" Oh, I can *hear*
it. The sorter-out of Hebrew truths getting down to business in Queens. You could count on one finger the times
I had been in a synagogue, unless you also count the
two services out-of-doors, which I was forced to attend
at Boy Scout Camp, when I was eleven and a half. I'd
chosen the kosher division of Scout Camp because I'd
heard the food was better. The chicken was served raw,
with feathers on it; we had to stand in the rain with
rabbis who wore shorts and ponchos and sheath knives;
I had to endure the humiliation of admitting to the con-
gregation that I didn't know the prayer I was asked to
lead. And here I was, telling a survivor of the camps, this
tortured bitter woman who *knew*, some salient wisdom
about the way she chose to worship and hate. But I was
a teller. Oh, boy. And I told: "Because what confuses
me, Mrs. Glinsky, is here we have the Christians worshipping a dead God on a cross, and that's not supposed
to be for the Jews. But then what I hear is we're supposed
to be Jews and love Jews, and hate all the rest, on account of the horror of the dead in the Holocaust. Isn't
that loving death, not, ah, gee dash dee?" Three fingers
of religion, please. No ice.

But there was ice: it was on the air, and it frosted the
walls of the lungs and hung, all cutting crystals, on the
throat and tongue. It was coming from Mrs. Glinsky's
shadowed eyes and from her wounded heart. It was thick
on Mr. Glinsky's face: I had injured his wife, and I would

not be forgiven. I smiled at him, foolishly, and I wanted to tell him how superb he seemed to be, just then: a regular little hero with his size six feet.

"The gee dash dee is for writing it down, shmuck," Rhona said. "For the Orthodox. You can *say* it, anyone can, all you want. It's about graven images. Tell her about the guy."

"Rhona, let's go home and come back when I haven't hurt your mother's feelings."

"My mother's feelings are always hurt. Aren't they, Ma?"

And then I understood the other side of it: that because I could be offensive, given my past, I'd been serving sufficiently as Rhona's weapon. I would tantalize them by being a nice Jewish boy whom Rhona slept with; they would need to make me more of a functioning Jew for her honor's sake, or their own. And, on the other hand, I would reveal to them—Christmas trees, my big loud mouth—that I was something special in that I was incorrigible, given their terms, and more of an insult to the Jews than Rhona usually trafficked with. "Nice going," I said.

"In that sense," Mr. Glinsky said with desperate rationality, "they *should* be hurt, darling. *Feel* hurt. Shouldn't they?"

And Rhona said, "Yes."

And Mrs. Glinsky said, "I apologize for casting a pall over this occasion." She stood as if to leave, and that was to be my signal to dismiss myself.

"Tell her," Rhona said.

"Perhaps you should tell nothing more today?" Mr. Glinsky suggested. "We'll all get together in time and have a nice chat. Today, I think maybe this is it. Hah?"

"*Tell!*"

We were all standing, and I saw how little of Mrs. Glinsky's body was left. Under the clothing, there were sticks with skin to pad them, and ribs you could play, as in a Disney cartoon, instead of a xylophone, and the neck was blood vessels and nearly transparent skin, and under it was her pulse, making the skin bulge as if she carried a fist in her chest which opened and closed. I wanted to look at her legs, to see how thin they were, but I didn't for fear of being caught; it would be like feeling up a corpse, checking her legs for heft. She saw me looking at her. She didn't care. She said nothing, went out of the living room, then returned, to peep around the corner almost coyly and say, "Rhona, you'll call us sometime?" Then she was gone.

Mr. Glinsky said, "You should know your people better—not that I would tell you how to think. But put it this way. I'll remind you. Question: How can you tell when a Jew is happy? Answer: When he hangs himself, he taps his toes and kicks his heels."

Rhona muttered, "Jews don't kill themselves, Daddy."

"Tell me," he said. Then, louder: "We could call such footwork maybe transports of delight? Hah? Hmh?"

Mr. Glinsky shook my hand as if he didn't mind, hugged Rhona, wished us the best of good days, and was already walking up the hallway to the bedroom she lay in while I went down the stairs with Rhona and out to the fierceness of Queens.

She did not berate me. She did not reflect on what had happened. Not all that much *had* happened, actually. And for the length of the walk to the subway, she didn't speak at all. She looked up when a big jet went over, and she watched the taxis go past, dodged two kids on roller skates, looked into the window of a shut-down bar which was made of pink stucco and which had a picture outside of a woman taking off a huge brassiere. We walked up the metal stairs to the elevated train without speaking, and without speaking Rhona paid my fare.

In the train at last, almost alone in the car, sitting with our heads down, looking at the floor and seeing dirt, gum, bugs, we said nothing. Then she took my hand. She didn't squeeze it, but she held it. Check one: (1) She berated me for not maddening her mother by telling her of the fascist. (2) She took me to task for challenging her mother's right to live in dread. (3) She told me I was a swine for being smug about anyone's notion of gee dash dee, and anyone's sense of the past. Well, *wrong*. She leaned over and kissed me under the left ear. She whispered into it, "Where should we eat tonight?"

We three had gone to the Central Park Zoo, and there Sam had held a helium-filled balloon and had not let it go. I'd admired his self-control: for a boy, not sailing a craft against gravity, when it pulls toward the sky, is like not throwing a stone into still water. The elephants were noble, the giraffes both detached and vulnerable-looking, the lions bored, the panthers pent, and the apes as smelly as ever.

Lillian said, "When you look at their eyes, they look like ours. Don't they make you feel guilty?" This was in October of 1979, a year before we separated; even innocence, even then, was making me feel guilty. "They look so *resigned*," she said.

Sam at that time was barely seven years old, growing fast but still a baby sometimes, as was his need and right. We were near what Lillian called the low-intensity areas, where you could find unglamorous creatures who tended to ignore humans. A tapir, with his long and nearly prehensile snout, his boar's body and small stupid eyes, was chewing and moving his bowels at the same time. Sam turned his back. He wore a dungaree jacket and corduroys and high-backed work shoes. The wind had made his dark skin take on the colorations of a peach, he was ripe and shiny and enormous tears in single crystals slid down his face.

Lillian, behind him, put her hands on his shoulders. I was in front of him, and I got onto my knees and hugged him. Lillian withdrew her hands, but stayed there, and we exchanged expressions of bafflement, then asked Sam what was wrong. He fought free of me to point. There was nothing there but fence, feed, and a defecating pig with an elephant's face.

"It's the tapir," Lillian said, at home, after a walk, a lot of jokes, and then a smile from Sam.

"A tapir's just another animal," I said low, because Sam was in our bedroom watching a Charlie Chan film on TV.

"No," Lillian said, "it's an animal that makes him cry. It frightens him."

"You think it's because he was pooping?"

"That shows more about you than him, is what I think." She looked so young, I remember, in jeans over loafers and in a thin old camel-colored sweater through which I saw her nipples, or wanted to. "It was *shitting*. Poop you can say to Sam. Though of course at school he probably says *fuckin'* shit. But Sam doesn't have an anal problem."

"You *know* that?" I was terribly impressed by anyone's knowing what such terms truly meant. To me, being anal meant keeping the paper clips organized in a top desk drawer.

"He's my son," Lil said.

"Well, he's my son too."

"So you know it also, yes?"

"Sure. Yes."

"So we didn't need to *do* that whole doody-poopy number. I don't mean to be mean. I'm really worried about that little hysteria he threw."

"Maybe he thought of something very sad. Maybe he'll tell us when he's older. Maybe it isn't too bad, Lil."

"If he doesn't know, then we have to help him find out. That's our job. If he knows, and he can't tell us, or he's afraid to, or reluctant to, then it's very, very important. Because it means he's getting like you, sweetheart."

"And I'm that bad."

Her face was older now. She crossed her legs like a man, left ankle over right thigh. I loved her long legs. I thought, often, of kissing them because they were so smooth. But she slept poorly, and often on the sofa. I wanted to say: Lillian, if I could say it, and if we could have less consciousness of *self*. I wanted to say: I am growing frightened of you; you feel more and more at home in the world, and I feel comfortable less and less.

"No," she said. "And yes I love you. But this isn't *about* you. Except it's difficult to do, always be nice to you very well. Because you're hiding."

I said, "Hey! Maybe it was the tapir's *nose*. It looks like a penis a little, doesn't it?"

"It's hard to remember—no, a *joke*, I promise. Maybe so, though, about the tapir. You know, he's in love with me. It happens at this age. Maybe he's jealous of you, and desirous of me, and the penis-thing became a—"

"—Terrific metaphor!" I said, triumphantly.

We hugged Sam a lot that afternoon and took him to the movies that evening. We made love and we nearly had fun. It happened like that, and I often thought of the order in which it had happened, so simply and so almost pleasantly. And then we had our separation.

And all those years before all that, with Rhona, on a mattress, in a loft, and unafraid, I had spoken of Freud and the putting up of dukes. Forty-ninth and Fifth, a voice behind me on the street—or a voice remembered, or just made-up—and I was shuttling between them, a psychological ferry, riding in my mind from the afternoon at Central Park, and then that night, to the midnight at Varick Street, loving Rhona and telling stories about who I'd used to be. With Lil and me, on that autumn day, it had started slowly. I had hugged her from behind because I'd had those nipples in mind, through afternoon tea with Coke for Sam, and through a neighborhood rerun of *The Great Race* (Sam loved it, Lillian dozed), and through a night of reading the papers, and weaning Sam from TV, a long bath for him, and my pushing into the bathroom to towel him off and sprinkle talcum on his sloping shoulders and on his back, where the shoulder blades protruded and where he could so easily be struck or bruised by a world full of snags. I had had those nipples in mind, and after a while I had them under my palms. We took off Lillian's clothes in the dark living room, and then we took off mine, and we tangled and whispered and kicked on the broad old sofa and, at last, on its cushions on the floor, I came and came, I pumped, I groaned and hosed myself into her, and she squeezed her vagina around me like a hand and shuddered, and we were lost, it was Eden because we were so lost, and Lillian bit me—ear and cheek and chin—and whispered loudly, "I *love* it. I—*oh!*"

And I said, "No, Lil. All right, it's, God, *fine*, Lil."

But she whispered, "Damn it. And damn me too. And you, you son of a bitch."

And all I thought to say was, "No, Lil. Everything's fine."

And on Varick Street, Rhona had danced a fast strip in a cold loft to, I think, a Buddy Holly song on the radio. She had closed her eyes—she was flushed, or blushing, from her forehead to her upper chest—and she had inexpertly, and therefore deliciously combining innocence and wickedness, pulled her crewneck and button-down shirt off while wiggling her hips and behind to a song too fast for such temptings. I had stopped her by pulling her to me, and then onto the mattress. We had together hiked her skirt above her hips. I'd kept my clothing on. I pushed the crotch of her underpants aside, and had swung away to the rhythm of a DJ pushing a rug sale at Gimbel's. And there, afterward, still in her, I had said, "What would Freud say?"

"He should be so lucky," she said, her hair stuck in sweat on her forehead.

"But it iss zo *complex*, no?" And, withdrawing, but not far, and pulling the blankets onto us, I told her after a while about Freud, and the friends in Brooklyn on a Friday night. I could hear the hiss of nylons and petticoats and black chiffon from one end of the living room to the middle landing of the steps, where I sat, waiting to be cute. Some men were in dark sportcoats, scuffed shoes, dark woollen shirts, squat wide woollen ties; some were in business suits, but they were ashamed, I have come to think, because they were the ones who drank the most, while the artists in their proletarian uniforms sat on the sofa or stood, slightly apart from the business friends, and smiled with certainty. The newer friends belonged to my mother, found by her at the school at which she taught. They were eccentric teachers who espoused either blends of socialism or a comprehension of the new technology, which I think she thought would change the world for the better. The old friends, artists, belonged to my mother and my father from the days when they were poor. All the women were dressed similarly, in variations of the long-necked New Look, even if none of them except my mother possessed a long neck. My father chose to compromise. He had begun the evening in his Friday business suit, but had by 8 P.M. taken off his suit jacket and had loosened his tie. He thereby modulated the male signals of those who had sold out to business, those who still loved poverty and the arts, and those who sat back on the sofa and silently laughed at everyone else.

A biology professor, Uncle Bob from Hunter College, has called to me, on the stairs, asking if I would like to play chess.

At eight, and in front of a room filled with grownups, I would like to play anything. "Sure!" I call, and I run upstairs to my room to fetch the wooden pieces in their pine box—received for Christmas, under the awful tree.

As I bounce downstairs, pert in my gabardine pants and sharp as can be, the professor asks, "Did you forget the board?"

I say, "I've only got a checkerboard, Uncle Bob."

The laughter in the room has driven me back up the stairs, and I am lingering too late, but am pampered because my mother thrives on the friends, is flattered and invigorated by them. I regard the problem. The problem lies in this: my father, also invigorated, has drunk a lot of dark stuff with cherries in it, and he is beaming and loud. He announces that Joe Louis has emerged from retirement tonight in order to fight Ezzard Charles. There is a small Emerson TV set in what my parents call the Study (a small room lined with books in the center of which is a dining table with 57 leaves we store in the cellar in case a nation comes to dinner), and my father would like some of the gentlemen to join him for a championship fight. My mother is discussing *Death of a Salesman* with our friend Manny, who supports himself entirely on the commissions he receives from religious institutions for his huge sculptures of large-muscled people wrestling with either famine or death.

The problem has voices which—never mind whose—sound like this:

"You'll pardon me if I sound a little hard-line about this, but any play in which there is an actor who is such a big-nosed Jew and he changes his name to Lee J. Cobb, like a baseball player in a movie, and somebody utters of him that priceless bourgeois sentimentality that he was wonderful with his hands, look, he made a new stoop for the family steps—I'm sorry, Tessie, but this is, at the least, excess."

"You're talking about the end of a very touching scene and you're forgetting how Mildred Dunnock leaves the stage? Something-something, 'We're free,' she says, and she's crying?"

"In a world like this, how can you praise the sentimentality of the mortgage payment? *That's* what she's talking when she leaves the stage with all those fake tears. She paid off the mortgage, he upped and died. What about a few million people, they don't have houses? What about the ones with houses, paid or not, the brown-shirts came to the door and took them away?"

"I'm only saying it's a very moving play."

"*I'm* only saying, if anyone can come out of retirement and take the man who decisioned Jersey Joe Walcott, it's the Brown Bomber himself. Now, I don't want to see him hurt, you understand. It's always risky. But I think he's in good enough shape to take this bozo."

"This is what being an intellectual comes to?"

"Tessie!"

"With a choice in the world of anything to think about and talk about, where else but in a house of college-educated immigrant Jews do you find a professional man drunk and watching a prizefight? Disgusting! No wonder—"

"No wonder what? This is a new tack? A little anti-Semitic self-hatred in case the goyim don't do it efficiently enough?"

"In this living room, Manny, you have all of it: you have the intellectuals, you have the artists, you have businessmen of a certain sensitivity. And you have smelly immigrants who cannot understand that this is the twentieth century, and there is such a thing as penicillin and tranquilizers. But we have to watch a prizefight."

"Nobody has to watch a prizefight, dammit! All I asked—"

"Sure. We're standing here, talking Lee J. Cobb, and you—"

"Jacob, his last name was. You knew that?"

"Tranquilizers, anyway, that's what Orwell warned about in *Brave New World*."

"Orwell didn't write *Brave New World*. Huxley wrote it, and he's a drug addict."

"Yes, but you'll notice he didn't turn his friends in. Like the blackface in the movie? What's his name?"

"For faggotry? Did anyone hear if he turned his friends in for being public queers?"

"Larry Parks. Of course, a Jew also."

"I think homosexuals invented prizefighting, with the Greeks. I think the only people who really follow it are them*selves* homosexuals. I'm sorry. But this is what I believe."

"Because you read some Freud once?"

"He didn't watch prizefights."

"He wasn't a communist, either."

"I happen to think it's very possible Freud was a homo."

"Yes, and look at all the tranquilizers the Freudian analysts give out. Doesn't that tell us something?"

"Huxley is Freud in disguise?"

"And Freud is a prizefighter."

I see my father slide into the Study. I go through the kitchen, around what used to be a pantry and is now a corridor with a desk where my father sits to pay bills, and I am in the Study. My father sits on a chair pressed up close to the little blue-gray screen of the Emerson. The sound is down low, I hear only a high excited murmur. My father sets his glass on the floor and, still staring at the set, reaches his left arm out. I lean against it, he circles my waist and pulls me up to him. We stay like that, and he whispers, "Watch this carefully. The one with the darker skin is named Marx, and the other is named Freud. They are both Jews of Greek descent. If some people have their way, we'll feel awful about watching them. The point of the game is, we stay here like this no matter what happens, and we feel *good*. It's about culture and religion, which I'll try to explain later. Watch."

Or watch this. You could always tell, in the junior high school playground during recess, who was going to do it. If you were planning to do it yourself, you could count on looking the same—an otherwise healthy normal boy suddenly puts his hands conspicuously in his pockets, as if to prove that he's harmless. That starts it. Then he hovers, handless, around a girl with heavy hips and big breasts, who wears, say, a yellow sweater that's tight. He makes a joke and she might even laugh. When she's near him, but is turned slightly away, so that by reaching he can cup her breasts from almost any position but head-on, he cries "Yargh!" and closes his eyes and reaches and runs off, all at once. She blushes. She might cry. If she's a slut ("hoo-ir," we used to say) she smiles a brave grin and might even look mildly amused. He is by now at the other end of the schoolyard, trying to remember what it felt like. He is very much aroused, and throughout the day can only look at her breasts and think of his fingers and wonder whether she might love him. "That's you," Rhona said. "That's you. You couldn't violate anything without falling in love with it."

In high school where I was guilty of intellectual failure —mostly poor grades, no Honor Society, no Ivy League college ahead—there was a tall, square-shouldered girl named Annette who looked years older than the rest of us. She dated a boy who went to college, and she was sad when she spoke of him. I always assumed, because her chest was beautiful and always provocatively draped, that she was unhappy because he used her cruelly. I didn't know what "used her" really meant, but I enjoyed the phrase because it suggested people being tied down and other people having their way—whatever *that* meant—with them. We always checked our trigonometry answers before class because I was smarter than she, though I was pretty dumb, and she was patently failing. Brains and boobs again! And whenever we would examine our notebooks, she would be certain to rest her bosom on my forearm, as if parking her chewing gum or leaning on a wall. Through sweater and shirt, through sweatshirt, my arm and the dancing skin beneath it learned to distinguish nipple from taut brassiere, mound of breast from fat leading to armpit, left one from right.

I sometimes looked at her homework with my eyes closed, the better to taste the flavor of the feel. She knew, of course, what was going on. Perhaps it was nice for her because it was so nice, visibly, for me. Perhaps because there were no consequences for her, she enjoyed it. Perhaps the very furtiveness I gave to what possibly should, in her eyes, have led to open dating and an all-out screw, was what pleased her. I never did ask her out. I was certain that she'd laugh. Our love, that of the legitimated and mutually copped feel, was for the darkness I made by shutting my eyes. She failed the final exams, by the way. I passed. Brains, more or less, and boobs.

The first dreadful soul-twisting wonderful frightening spasms of masturbation were achieved by imagining women cooking in bikinis in a middle-class kitchen in my neighborhood while no one else was home. I used the clippings from *Esquire*, after first being tortured by the dentist from whose magazines I tore them. Sex and death, Freud would doubtless remind us. I was always afraid to buy dirty magazines in the candy stores on Avenue J, so my imagination sufficed, along with a few scraps of pictures, until I could graduate to a firm and habituated vertical stroke, as opposed to a choppy and chopping harsh rub. When I did move on, I relied upon memory—this hip brushed in the hallway, that French kiss, last week's exchange of saliva with so-and-so, the breast explored beneath a brassiere in the Kingsway movie theater.

I eventually branched out. I found that certain historical novels named the parts of the bodies and almost described certain acts. I found that certain books in my parents' library (the Study) offered exemplary opportunities: woodcut-illustrated editions of the *Droll Tales* of

Balzac, certain pages in *Ulysses,* my father's book on Goya, my mother's books on home nursing and biology, a novel by Alberto Moravia—it was all about a whore, and it told how she did it and how she felt. She *felt,* I was astonished to learn, and I was appalled to further learn that I wanted to know more about her feelings. So I splashed their classics with what would become yellow spots on heavy paper: the usual story.

Yes, until I came home to find, on my bed, an un-wrapped catalogue from Frederick's of Hollywood, which had been advertised in some place as innocent as *Popular Mechanics.* There were illustrations of sexy lace and cutaway bras, with promises of fully revealed plea-sures which weren't permissible to print in public jour-nals, they were so incendiary. Of course, I had sent. A plain brown wrapper had been promised. And here it was, opened by the only person now home, my mother, and it was in the middle of my bed.

I played it cool. I didn't look inside—you don't even *care* about this sort of thing, I instructed myself—and, taking it down to the kitchen, where my mother was grading exams and drinking coffee, I said, "Did you leave this upstairs, Mom?"

She didn't look up. She checked off something about protein, and said, to the paper, "Yes, I did. It came in the mail. Didn't you send for it?"

"*Me?*" I screamed with calm innocence. "*Me?* You think I wear this kind of *junk?*" Good word. Go ahead. "You think I'm gonna put on this kinda *crap?*" Very nicely done.

With a smile on her face—patience, victory, cruelty, comprehension, all the good stuff and all the bad stuff at once—she looked up to seize my eyes with hers. She said, "Well, you don't think it's for me, do you?"

Trapped in the logic of the lie by now, and remembering to remind myself to be angry because she'd sprung the trap so well, I said, "Sure. I mean, you *could*. If you wanted to. I mean, I thought *you* sent for it. Who else *would*?"

"You think I should dress like that?"

So, trapped tight, dear Doctor Freud, I said no.

And she knew that I had lied twice. "I guess it's a mistake," she could afford to say, taking the catalogue and tearing it in half. I wonder how long she thought it would take me to recall that the plain brown wrapper had *my* name and address on it. From her smile, as she addressed the papers once more, not long. That night, I spurted onto my sheets by trying to imagine what the models in the catalogue had looked like. Each time a face I focused on became my mother's, I whispered "No!" and tried to picture a girl in my class. When I finally came, my body caught me before I could prepare a woman's face and body with which to welcome the little wrack-and-spurt: I jerked off to a vision of my empty homeroom—vacant desks, the polished dark linoleum floor.

Sex, I therefore learned, is what makes everyone miserable, and sex is that behavior which coexists with death, flight, fugitive lusts and the tempered reproach of a loving mother who has to destroy your mind in order to convince you that being dirty is bad for you. And then there is always Rhona's approach.

She said, "It isn't unimaginable that you love me, and I know that you're . . . devoted to me. You know I feel that way about you. We're both alone, we seem to nourish each other. Do these sound like good reasons for me to move in with you?"

"Are we getting married, Rhona?"

"I didn't say that. Let's not be hurried by conventions."

"But we're living in the same apartment now?"

"Your loft."

"Oh."

So, on a Sunday of brittle leaves, blown newspapers and bright autumn sun which followed shortly after the day of clammy wind and poisonous radiation in Queens, we gave a neighborhood child five dollars for the rental of his red wagon, and we formed a lovers' parade that went from 12th to Varick, no short haul. While Rhona held her horrible bureau, for which she had paid $10 on Ninth Avenue some years back, balanced on the wagon, I pulled. On another trip, we held a long dowel between us as if we carried a howdah, and from it swung her skirts and blouses and coats. One more trip for her schooldays' desk, teetering on the wagon-top, and then we got bored and took cabs for two trips with cartons of more clothing and books. I lived only one flight up, and she was strong, and soon her clutter helped to fill my loft, which consisted essentially of interstices—one huge one, really, between my tin-walled shower stall and rust-colored toilet bowl, and the rest of the large room with its glaring white paint, bookcases painted black, and my mattress on the floor. Now that Rhona was here, we had a desk, we had a bureau, we had a lot of women's clothes, we had a librarian; we were living together, we knew, precisely as the Dharma Bums really did, and other people in books. Except in the morning, she put on stockings, I put on a tie, and we went to work. Except that we didn't sleep well that Sunday night because we weren't used to whom, together, we'd become.

That Monday morning, I took her downstairs for coffee with Lefty. He was late again, so we walked farther back into the kitchen to introduce Rhona to Loretta and Piggy. They were sitting opposite one another, dressed in spiked high heels and fancy dark dresses, patent leather pocketbooks on the floor beside each shabby chair, white waitress uniforms and aprons hanging on the back of a door for when they'd change, and there was the smell of evil midget shrimps in the air.

Piggy, seeming not to look at us, stood and took down two mugs, filled them, and said, over her shoulder, "All right?" And when I said "Okay," she set the mugs down, nodded acknowledgment of our thanks, and went back to talking to Loretta. They didn't seem interested in meeting Rhona. Piggy was saying, "And I tell him, don't you cry! Don't you call your mother from college and be crying in her face because you got yourself blackballed from a fraternity. First of all, what color did you *think* your balls should be? And second, don't you be fooling yourself about white folks and their affections. And third, get educated, not drunk in a fraternity house. Get *good.* Then get rich. Buy the house and jack their rent up and later on, you *fore-close.*"

Loretta calmly lit a cigarette, nodded, blew smoke up at an acute angle, and nodded again. "He thought something changed because they let him into the school," she said. "You can understand that."

"Oh, I can understand it," Piggy said. "I'm just not planning to tolerate it. Understand, but not *stand.* That's where I draw the line. I told him. I told him that. Now he knows."

This time they both nodded, and when Loretta looked up to find both Rhona and me standing nearby, watching them, she raised an eyebrow, like a mother waiting to get tough, and we took off. As we walked out, Lefty pulled up to park illegally and start his day. We were too late to talk, so I called, "Lefty! This is who I was talking about!"

He stood at his Cadillac in the early-morning truck traffic of Varick Street, his one hand on the door, and he looked Rhona over, from her hairdo to her shoes. He said, "Very nice, kid. Hello, miss. You look very nice."

Rhona turned crimson, and I pulled her with me toward the subway. She kept looking over her shoulder, like a man in a bar who wants to be seen by his friends as spoiling for a fight, but is relieved to be taken away. " 'Very nice,' " she growled, in a fair imitation of Lefty's grave-shovel voice.

"He can't help it," I said. "He's really all right. He's an all right guy."

"So were many of the plantation owners. And several sonderkommandos, no doubt."

"He's Jewish," I said, trying to jest.

"So was Goebbels."

"Really?"

"*Zimmer.*"

I have to confess that I loved it: bickering like married people and not alone at night. Maybe it wasn't Eden or pitching for the Yankees, but it beat the former direct route from Strange News About Shoe Polish to what was, without her, a toilet attached to an empty room.

Of course, there was a price to pay. I paid it in the evenings when I met her outside the library and we followed the fascist home. Many nights, he paused and sniffed or shook his head, then hurried, having probably detected us. Sometimes, he just waved his stick and made his way and disappeared into his brownstone basement. Once his sister met him and they walked, in a windy night, around the block, talking loudly, before they went inside.

And Rhona did her homework. Being a librarian, she told me, especially in a public library branch, meant doing a good deal of reference work. The rules for it are simple: you make certain that patrons feel welcome to ask for precisely what they think they need to know or consult; you conduct an interview intended to help them tell you what they need; you don't stop until you've found it, or found someone who can help them further. You do not give up. Rhona didn't. She sent to other branches—Rhona was her own reference patron now—for books on the Iron Guard of Rumania, and on the Balkan fascists in general. She looked at pictures, had photostats made, read memoirs, and spilled so much data onto my lap and into my ears and over the roaches and city grit and dirt of my loft, our loft, that I became confused. I no longer knew how we knew that he was really a fascist, or why we were sure about Rumania, or how it was that his sister had become a part of the story. I was also upset about how he could wear the same brown suit every day, about whether or not he had a choice, and why with a white hat, and about how it was that he sensed us at some times and didn't at others. I was also vaguely, and then not so vaguely, and then quite surely, convinced that I was trading fascist-hunting for Rhona's affection for me—and that given Rhona's equation (not so different from her mother's, really, I thought), I was becoming a Jew. To hunt the persecutors, to be always aware of the awful past, to suspect all, to forgive few, and to be certain that a few wary Jews, perhaps the state of Israel, and one or two pro-Semitic goyim, were all that prevented eradication of all Jews everywhere by a world which wanted to devour them—this was being a Jew. Trust *nothing*. Were there Jews playing forward in the NBA? Where were the Negroes when we needed them—though they expected us to kick in money and lay down life for civil rights? What about the Six Million's civil rights? With Italians and Irish running New York, a Jew should feel safe? A Jew is a vote and donations, is all. We'll still lock the loft at night. All right. It wasn't only lust, it might have been love, it surely had something to do with her being female and me not, and it might have gone back to the days of my Christmas trees and long evenings with my parents' friends—I can't tell, though Rhona thought so. "I am summoning you," she said one night in bed. At first I thought it was the name of a wonderful position, new to me, which she had decided we should try together for the first time. Then I understood that I was *summoned*. I didn't feel that way, only sad for the dead, horny for Rhona, happy in her company much of the time, and tired of hounding a blind man.

HOW TO UNWIND
Feeling like a wound-up clock spring lately? Then it's time to unwind . . . get rid of the tensions caused by business and the everyday, minute-to-minute routine of work, work, work. *Children's games*, say leading educators, are one excellent relaxation—for adults!

And so on. I had discovered the ellipsis, dot dot dot, and a new depth of making little sense: "the everyday, minute-to-minute routine of work, work, work." It was worthy of the entire stenographic pool of the House Un-American Activities Committee as edited by General Eisenhower. But I really didn't care; fortunately, neither did the client, a producer of a kids' board game too tough for kids—for I left work to chase a blind man in a white hat and brown suit from the library, in which he uselessly sat some of every day, to the cellar flat of a brownstone on Irving Place, into which he dived like a guilty soul pursued. And from there, I went home with Rhona, the spirit of an armed Israel and of atonement for the children of Terezin, the daughter of the Holocaust, a sexual athlete, and the person who in my loft and in my life kept me from what I seemed to fear, in all the world, the most: Zimmer alone.

Dot dot dot and it was Columbus Day already, mid-October, a full moon having leered the night before over Manhattan, corpses doubtless awash in the Harlem River and down at the pilings of the Staten Island Ferry piers, a full quota of crimes against the person and portable property having already taken place, and both Rhona and I had the day off to celebrate the possibility that an Italian, working for the Spaniards, had discovered America. *I*, in fact, had discovered America, and as we mounted our watch I was telling Rhona what I thought I had learned: that America's newspapers, for the sake of whose unimpeded function there was an entire article in the Bill of Rights, were willing to print what Zimmer, in the service of Max, construed—rat killers, baby's games, capitalist jingoism, etc. That America ate poison shrimp in egg rolls manufactured by five familiar hands. That America had blackballed Piggy's son. Rhona was telling me that I was juvenile and jejune, and I was trying to get her to admit that she had no more idea of the definition of jejune than I, when the brownstone's cellar door—we could see its corner move, under the arch at right angles to us, beneath the first-floor staircase —that door opened out. We paused over our hot tea in the slop shop which had become our command post for the persecution of old immigrants. Rhona took my hand. "Something is happening," she whispered.

It was the sister. In a man's cardigan, in lace-up oxfords, in a dark tweed skirt, with a ritzy-looking yellow silk scarf at her neck, she stood in the traffic flow of Irving Place, opposite our luncheonette, and she waited for us. Her face made that clear: *Come on*, it said.

"She wants us," I told Rhona, as I rose.

"No."

"Rhona, it is time. Either we fish or cut bait. Hey! Now I understand what that means! You've heard that expression?"

"Zimmer—this is no time to become chipper."

"I devour you with my eyes. I kiss your fingertips." I did both. "I grow mountains in my molehills on your behalf." I gallantly gestured to the south. "But either we go out now and cut them down, or torture them, or whatever we ought to do—call the FBI?—or I'm quitting the private-eye part of it, Rhona."

She clicked and made sticking, sucking, spitting sounds with her mouth—a Jewish songbird's scorn. But she stood, she counted the tip I had left, and we went outside to where the sister now stood, on the sidewalk in front of her house, touching an illegally parked panel truck, her arms folded across her flat chest, her chin raised, her large dark eyes, with folds of brow beginning to descend upon them, sending long scornful looks at us. Rhona was pale, her mouth was partly open, she was panting as we walked. With her right hand, she held my arm; I thought that she might fall if she didn't. And I? I grinned. I almost shoved my arm out for a hearty handshake. I grinned and showed my Nazi-tended teeth. It seemed a friendly moment. I kept telling myself *Fascist!* but all I could respond with—to her presence, to my reminder—was the great American smile.

"You follow us," she said, in a very low voice. On the telephone, it might sound like a man's.

Rhona, in a shaky voice, sounding young, with her hand squeezing my arm, said, "We know who you are."

The woman's mien collapsed; her strength washed away before us, and her eyes lost their hooded glint and became just an old lady's eyes. Oddly enough, they reminded me of Mrs. Glinsky's. "You know us?" she said.

Rhona nodded. I shrugged. I flashed a little of the grin again, but it didn't help. Rhona must have felt the smile, because she pinched the inside of my arm.

"How do you know us?" the old woman asked.

I couldn't speak, and Rhona didn't. The sounds of traffic at that moment would have obscured our words anyway. But I had none to risk.

"And you never forget?" she said.

Rhona found her voice: "Never!"

"But—there is nothing you can do now. Nothing."

"Don't count on it," Rhona said, like a kid insulting another kid. Her iciness was somehow innocent, and I felt sorry for all of us.

"Do you understand how this terrifies my husband?"

"Your brother," I corrected. The eyes swiveled to me, I saw the rage in them, covered my mouth as if I'd belched, said, "Sorry! Sorry. We thought he was your brother."

"I am a woman with a blind husband. I am required to perform therapeutic exercises at Saint Vincent's. And you follow us because you know what we are. And you are not ashamed?"

"Aren't you?" Rhona whispered. Her lips were so dry, I could hear them tear apart as she spoke.

The old woman stared at her, at me incidentally, but mostly at Rhona, and then she turned, limped slowly away, and with great dignity, and slowly she shut her door—as if to remind us that she could do that when she wished—and slowly, distinctly, she latched, shot a bolt, then turned a lock, three punctuations of her clear statement: There is nothing you can do.

Rhona was sniffing, her shoulders were shaking, she was gripped by a rage that seemed to leave her barely breathing, and I was as frightened by her pain as I was strangely comforted by the old fascist lady: she was just someone on whose toe you might step in an elevator, and who would give you a hard time for being clumsy.

I said, "Rhona."

And she said, barely forming the words, "Shut *up*."

But she let me lead her away, as if there had been a wreck, as if she were wounded. I took her home in a cab. I put her into bed, clothed, and she lay under the covers. She shook sometimes as if with cold, and she fell asleep, a person whom the world had helped sicken. To be a Jew, I thought, is to be willing to accept that sickness. I sat with my health and listened to the gentiles on the radio name music by Italian composers in honor of the holiday for which we had been given a day's rest. I thought of how Rhona wouldn't talk to me in the cab. And while Rossini made tempestuous foreshadowings on the airways, I composed The Strange History of Immigration:

> Ever wonder why, in emigré circles, the halt *do* lead the blind? Why the European art of persecution has come full circle on New York's Irving Place? Sociologists tell us

but I stopped because I didn't find myself charming anymore.

Sally and I weren't good in bed, or at sly loving, or in any kind of secret, really. She had always been the one to give away clues to office intrigues among the staff, or to let slip to one author how much another had received as an advance against royalties. Once, when a young writer of ours was cruelly reviewed in the *Times*, and she had found out on the Tuesday before the Sunday on which the review would appear, she waited until Friday at 5 P.M. to call him; when the call went through and the author answered, she started to sniff, and there were tears in her eyes when she told him the news. I had watched her do that, and I'd admired her. So at sub-rosa lust in the Hotel Royalton (we told our authors, when we installed them there, that it was nearly identical to the Algonquin across the street, but much quieter) Sally was pretty much of a flop. And of course I was too.

It probably had to do with her youth. I could wink at her and could make her blush, could be called "mister" (very nearly in bed, I should add). She was pretty, still fresh in the world, something of an innocent person, I suspected, and trying to claim her—isn't that what our chilly-skinned coupling was, at least on my part?—constituted my effort to appropriate what I knew the world would soon enough possess and make sour. In other words, I wanted possibility, I think. And of course, I wanted her tongue in my mouth, her gentle small fingers on my balls, her hand kneading my buttocks, and all the sounds she made, I suspected, because she felt that she should.

My heart, I was telling Sally on that afternoon in New York, was broken. And, quite possibly, I was making a gesture that I hoped would provide, one day, a demonstration for Lillian, a statement she might somehow grasp: I am screwing someone else because you're hurting me; I am trying hard to hurt you in return. This was before Lil decided that we ought to live apart.

Except: I knew that Lil would know that I was hurt far more than she was. My little sexual disobedience was admission, should she learn of it, should I blab it as I thought I one day might, that she was more important to me than pleasure in bed, or the feelings of Sally whom I somewhat adored, or the self-respect I had just about vanquished by signing into the Royalton after two tasteless drinks at a little table off the lobby of the Algonquin, where authors reeled in search of permanent importance or another reason not to write. And because Sally was awful at secrets, I did suspect that Lillian soon would know. I was, I thought, being majestically utilitarian and practical. In fact, I was just being sneaky.

"Wouldn't that make me something of a parent-figure?" Lil would say to such connivings. "Something of a mother?"

Lillian! Why do men nuzzle a woman's breasts in love, rub their penis between them, kiss them, suck at them

—for friction or milk? Or is it because the mother is available after all these years? Or is it—Freud, put up your dukes—because we need some comfort as well as the screaming loss of self in love? Maybe good love leaves some of the self in place.

Okay. But meanwhile I was using Sally, and she was using me. "What do *you* need?" I asked her as she turned her back to me and dressed. I turned her around and kissed her throat. It wasn't right for us to be so parted in so small a room. My own throat burned, and so did my eyes. I wanted to weep for her small mouth and straight nose and little blue eyes, and her hair which was so fine that it refused to retain any of the artful shapes she insisted it into. I hugged her and told her, "You're my good, decent, damned fine friend, Sally."

She was crying too, very gently, carelessly, and there wasn't love for me in that, I saw. She was crying for herself. From the Radcliffe Publishing Program to a year at Little, Brown to a year at Harper and Row, to us, to this, to me: the usual story, except that I wasn't as handsome and daring as were most of the older men on whom such younger women broke a part of themselves and so became clichés.

"Your wife wouldn't mind this," she said. "Do you know that?"

"Well, sweet Jesus, old friend Sally, I don't think you should tell her anyway. Do you?"

"Oh, I wouldn't. I want to keep something for myself, first of all," she said, tying a silk tie that matched her blouse. "I don't intend for this to happen again, and I want it. I liked making love with you, even if the two of us showed about as much ardor and skill as a couple of flatfish drowning on land." In something deeper, perhaps intended to be my voice, she brayed, "Make a hell of a fine metaphor for something, eh?" And then, in her own tones, she went on: "You're a gentle man and I felt good being with you. And please don't go getting the guilts all over. I wasn't crying because I've been seduced in the big city. I have to confess this—I was crying for you. You need company. And I don't want to spend a bad year giving it to you. I'm sorry. Because that *would* lead us noplace. But you're a lonely son of a bitch. And I think, if you could get your wife back—well, not *back.* I mean, if—"

"Back is just right," I said. "So are you. I wish you were my sister or something."

"Incest," she said, putting a camel-colored woollen blazer on, "is where I draw the line."

"Well," I said.

"Thank you," she said, kissing my cheek.

"Thank you," I said, kissing hers.

"Thank you," Lillian said that night, when I came home from ostensibly entertaining the author whose trip to New York had really been cancelled by bad weather in Minneapolis. I gave Lillian the basket of giant apples from Seattle which I'd bought on Sixth Avenue, and she tore one apart with her fine white teeth. She loved good food—food not made of cholesterol or sugar—and she took on health, visibly, each time she ate what she liked.

"God, I love your metabolism," I said.

"My metabolism is a piece of ass," she said, wiggling her own in black wool shorts she wore over cream-colored tights.

"I am *so* tired," I said.

She startled me by reaching forward and seizing my scrotum. She nodded. "Nothing," she said.

"Give it a minute, can you?"

"After Sam goes to sleep, you've got fifteen minutes," she said. "Then I crash."

I sat on Sam's bed in his little room. He had been washing the lead knights I'd brought home from a business trip to London. They lay in a puddle on his floor. His bed was covered with stuffed animals, which he retained there to keep him younger than eight. I couldn't blame him. So, with a hand on a furry dog and a leg crushing a lime-green koala bear, I ran my hands over his head and smelled the boy of his scalp and neck. His breath was like apple juice and toothpaste together. His skin was shiny and taut. His long lashes lay over his closed eyes and his breathing was regular. I leaned down to sniff again, and to kiss him goodnight. His eyes opened and startled me. His mouth opened too. He bared his teeth, made his eyes wider, and snarled, "The Hulk is pissed off."

I pulled back at the hands he'd put around the back of my neck. "What kind of talk is that?"

He showed his teeth and laughed. "School talk."

"Well, it isn't *home* talk."

"Not even if you and Mommy sometimes say—"

"No! I don't want you talking back, Sam! *No!*"

So he hid. What else was he to do? He took his arms back, and his expression; he closed his mouth and let his eyes go dead.

I said, "Sam?"

In a monotone he said, "Night, Daddy."

"Night, Sam. Maybe we can try a little better in the morning." I didn't say at what, or who would make the effort. I didn't know. "I love you, Sam."

"Okay."

In the kitchen, I made a drink and poured it out. I found some ginger ale and drank it from the bottle. Lillian, wearing my pajama tops and the tights without the shorts, came in. She looked at my face. She said, "Never mind."

"What?"

"I thought you might want some sleep."

"You mean, some sex."

It didn't faze her. She was used to saying what she meant. "I thought you would sleep. I hoped for some sex. I think that you're going to get neither, and I think I won't get much of either myself." Her voice, in its expressionlessness, had been like Sam's. Or Sam's had been like hers. I was impressed by my ability to slaughter animation regardless of generational differences.

"Do you know that I love you, Lil?"

"Yes."

"Do you love me?"

"Yes."

"Does it help us any?"

"No, sweetheart." Her handsome long face went soft, then. She was moving large, fruit-shaped magnets on the white refrigerator which hummed at us. Glass bowls and pitchers on top of it were subtly vibrating against one another, and in the half-light of the kitchen, with its one window looking over Manhattan at night, with the stars invisible in the lightbulb-glow the city threw up at the sky, I felt as if we were in the cabin of a ship, humming and burring and banging our way somewhere. I was panicky, then, because I didn't have any sense of any control of the vessel.

"That would be one hell of a metaphor," I said, and then realized that Sally would understand me more than Lil. "Never mind. I'm thinking of something else, and I shouldn't be."

"No," she said.

"Because I really love you. I really want to take care of Sam and make him feel good, and I really want you to be happy. I want you to *love* me."

"But I do. I told you I do."

"But I want you to *like* it. I want you to enjoy it, loving me."

In my pajamas, her breasts swung and her shoulders moved and her strong arms gestured. "It's difficult, right now."

"But can you tell me *why?*"

"You know that the sex thing is a problem."

"But I *love* your body. I love making love to you."

"You know, you're so repressed. You're so fucking *private*. So am I. It could be a curse on us, you know?"

"And also," I begged. "Also? Isn't there something else? Is it just my cock and balls? A tale of *tits?* Isn't there *more?*"

"Well, you *know* it, sweetheart. I mean, you may not know what it is, but you do know there's something. You're so desperate. You are so desperate. Do *you* know why?"

"Could it be that turning-forty business? You know, a case of time? And that would be all? Look back and see what you did with your life and you didn't do much?"

"You did me. You did Sam. I would like to know what else is more important. That is *precisely* what I'd like to know."

"*Me!*"

She came closer and hugged me. I felt her flesh as soft, not hard, and I loved it for that. I grabbed handsful of her strong but malleable ass. I squeezed it, worked it, and she let go enough for me to hold a lot of it at once and make it move. My hands moved lower on her, deeper, and she leaned in, kissing my jawbone and saying, "Yes. Isn't that it? You're so locked into you? With nothing more important at stake than yourself . . . I'm being facetious. See, I don't *blame* you. I understand a little bit. Really just a little. You're trying to find out if you're alive outside of me and Sam. And you love us. And we're also getting between you and yourself. I didn't mean it to be funny. I don't know if it makes sense. I mean, I think it really does. But I don't know if I'm—oh God, you better—mean this." Because I had reached down and behind and had seized her groin with one big hand, and then had moved the other hand to the front, and where my fingers met, they met in her, and through the moist tights. Which then came down, and so did my trousers, while we kissed and licked and breathed all over each other, and there on the kitchen floor, or in the so-called cabin of the so-called ship on its so-called voyage through what you might as well call life, I remembered making love to Sally—in infidelity to both these women whose secretions were smeared on my loins—and I went limp. To her credit, because she is a generous person, Lillian kissed me, once, on the mouth. She held on to me as she lay on the floor beneath me. And she whispered: "You won't forget this. But also don't forget this part of it. It was your mind that went bad on you. Your dumb prick is as obedient as ever. Could you let me up? I'm going to bed." But she stayed there, and she cried so terribly hard in the cabin as it shook and jingled and swayed while we traveled on.

Rhona and I had troubles too. We did live together, and were a strong redoubt against the outer storms. But no matter how well *it*—what magazines and friends in analysis called The Relationship—was going, *it* was also a nexus of anxiety. Rhona was frightened by her meeting with the fascist's sisterly-appearing wife. She was frightened away from our routine of peeping and following, Laurel and Hardy. Her lessened zeal made her less zealous for me. When she doubted herself, I think, she lost her fire to hunt and punish; when she lost her easier angers, she lost her faith in whatever she had reposed it in to begin with; and, losing that certainty, she lost what she could—or would want—to give to me. She didn't need me just then, because she no longer knew what she knew. Those hooded eyes, that almost-withered leg, the actual voice of a woman on a street and in the world— these had frightened Rhona from a haunted life she'd thought routine.

And I? I read about agony, about feces, about bread stolen from friends, about husbands and wives torn from each other in a nightmare. I read of survivors who stopped sleeping and those whose children stopped eating. I read, with astonishment, about the shallowness of those who did the killings. Not those who killed to survive: they were trapped in humanness, they would either no longer eat or sleep, or would eat satisfactorily, sleep pretty well, and either forget or remember. No: the ones who gave the orders. They were all involved in a giant game, complete with uniforms and thundering boots and the blood of old people on cobbles. It was called Jew. You hated Jews because they were Jews. You hated them because you did. You could, to help the historians and never-silent Jewish analysts of their own destruction, come up with socio-historical-economic-political-psychological reasons if you liked; you could even talk about the murder of that bad Jew Jesus, if such was what you wished. But what you had, at last, was that the game was Jew, you were the winner and you polished them off, and usually you did it efficiently. To be the loser in the game called Jew, you let the winner call you Jew. You were not given a choice, but more often than not you volunteered; no one could tell you why. And then when I was reading about the medical experiments, I simply stopped altogether. It was no more than two or three days after Rhona had collapsed in the sights of the sisterly wife—the purest case of evil eye I'd ever seen. It was during the middle of the week, I remember, and I just decided that I wouldn't read anymore. I remember deciding that I didn't owe this to anyone, and I didn't want to know now. Not even for Rhona. For no one. I didn't want to have this anymore.

Of course, I had made a similar decision when I graduated from college and left home. My mother had wept on the phone when she called twice during the first week, three times during the next. And when at last I had told her that I had friends there, and when she wondered why I mightn't bring my new friends home, and when I had lied that these friends were really *this* friend, and that *this* friend, well, actually, she didn't have any *clothes* on, and when my mother had said, "Oh!" and then had hung up—I remember telling myself that I didn't want to have that anymore, and that I wouldn't feel guilty.

After one night, I'd called home to ask if I might return alone for dinner.

My mother, no doubt thinking that we were all being very adult about it, had said, as if surprised, "Of *course*, dear."

It is possible that Rhona, too, might have said "Of *course*," and in that very way. But I didn't mention it to her, and I wasn't sure that it was worth too much mentioning. I had simply been glutted. I was dying of everyone's death, I was in the middle of loving, perhaps, a witch, my entire life seemed to me to be in progress, not yet shaped, and I was curious about where it was headed and who this woman was, and who I was too, and enough dead Jews. Rhona made no protest as I reduced the stack of books by the bed, and started in reading that famous homo drug addict Huxley, just for fun. Rhona was having a difficult period, she was enduring herpes simplex cold sores, terribly painful, on the inside of her upper lip—she slurped and seethed aloud, she couldn't eat or drink unless I brought her milkshakes, and then she wetly whispered that I'd make her fat. She was also suffering from herpes zoster, a name I loved but which merely meant shingles, and she had what looked like a quarter-inch-deep bullet wound in the back of her neck. We put salve on it and I looked away; she kept her hair in a bun so that it wouldn't collect the salve. At home, she left off eyeliner and sometimes skipped washing. She never flushed her tampons down the john and I held my nose when I took them down with the trash. They didn't smell, it's just that Jewish kids are taught, no matter how informally, that menstruating women smell. Unclean! It was not a bad test for the earlier stages of devotion. She went to work, we didn't meet for dinner, and afterwards, at home, I cooked. I cooked Spam and fried eggs, rejoicing in her digestion of the fatty pork—perverse Semitic man. I made stuffed breast of veal without the stuffing and without defrosting the breast: cold tit, no substance, that's life, Rhona, and it was going badly for us, I felt. At night, we listened to music while she poured honey-glycerin fluids over her simplex and spread cortisone cream over her zoster. From across the room came the *pfft* of another tampon wrapper being torn open. I read Huxley on eternal life, and Rhona read Saul Bellow, and I was pained by guilt for the Jews who were dead, for my mother who was distant, for my father who was tranquilly far away, for Saul Bellow whom I should have been reading instead of Huxley, for Rhona whom I should have been loving better—not like a sick smelly sister—and for her mother, whom I thought about as I thought of all those tiny gray broken stick-people, Jews they called them in the great game of Jew, whose lives and dreadful dyings I had put behind me for a long time while I played Careers.

BAD FEELINGS ABOUT GUILT

Have you ever wondered why, when your parents have moved to Florida, and your life is going with mild satisfaction, at no expense to them, you feel that you've done something wrong? And you know if you call to say so, your mother will agree that you *have?* What you need, in that case, is this study, by a team of psychologists, about the ease with which you can *transfer* that guilt, or guilts about the murder of infants, or the deaths of old men, into an enormous boil that grows on your forehead! *Bring Things to a Head*, or BTH, is the name of this therapy. Find out why it's sweeping the nation. Why *presidents* employ it! Why clergymen adore it! All the facts, in a story that will leave you sick with pleasure.

Well, it wasn't a herpes of any sort, and it wasn't on my head, but the truth of the matter is that I did develop an ugly whitehead in the left-hand corner of my mouth, and it was not because, as we'd been taught in high school, of shellfish; for otherwise, living where I did, I'd have been a mass of whiteheads. No, it was because of feeling bad; Rhona and I were sharing it, as well as the rent, and it was time to take measures.

"Rhona," I said, over the sound of WQXR one night,

while she was listening to Berlioz, "Rhona, we have to take measures."

"I wear a diaphragm, stupid. Or did you think I was dusting my thighs with cornstarch. And anyway, you haven't touched me for a week."

"I did too *touch* you, Rhona."

"Zimmer, you know what I'm saying. It's all right."

"Grr." I didn't actually say it the way it sounds in cartoons, when little tigers do it. I actually snarled, I roared, I kicked a garbage pail and scattered soiled tampons wrapped in toilet paper and Kotex pads which were not wrapped. It was a bloody mess. I held my breath. I forced myself onto my knees and with my bare hands picked it up.

Standing again, and not washing, I watched her watch my fingers. She was doubtless waiting to see if I'd run to the sink screaming like Lady Macbeth, I could tell by the way her lips were twitching and her eyes, for the first time in days, were shiny and alive. I said, "We are taking measures, as I said." I was as calm as if I had not just growled, kicked over a garbage pail, and sunk myself to the elbows in womb-lining. "We are going to Irving Place. As soon as you feel okay. We are going to, you'll pardon me, breast the old man. Confront him, maybe kick him in the knee and run. But I want this over. I want it ended. Then you and I can fight our Jew-wars for my soul, and let's see what we see. With apologies to the blind and the halt and the rest of us."

Rhona opened her arms—they had started to move with the word breast—and we actually made love on a damp bathroom towel, with Rhona pulling (as she liked to say) the plug, and with me pretending that her vagina did not feel lined with alum, hard as coral, dry as an old man's heart. It was not wonderful for her, either, but we loved each other then, and a little sacrifice was called for. We both groaned so loudly that we each, on hearing the other, started to giggle for the truth, and then I relaxed, and she did too, and we had a mildly satisfactory fuck, and some good laughs, and we went to bed happy for the first time in days.

As I told Lefty when I returned from work before Rhona, one mid-October day, "Love is a difficult job, Lefty."

He was pretty drunk by then, and he'd stayed late at work presumably to sober up. It was the same tic of slumbering nerves which made him stay on the road as he drove his Caddy home through traffic. So, staying alive, Lefty sat in the steams of Mexican shrimp and formaldehyde, sweating, drinking applejack and waiting to be sober. He leaned back on the aluminum chair and said, his face shiny and broken, "Love is not a job, old pal. Love is a sentence."

I was still living in the fog of words I breathed each day at work. I said, "What? You mean like in jail?"

Lefty was patient because so drunk and because shrimp, I think, promote torpor if inhaled in large quantities. He nodded his battered head and said, "Sentence. Like in jail. Workhouse. Prison farm. And your own personal favorite, concentration camps."

"A sentence?"

"Well, listen, kid. This love—are you having a wonderful time?"

I stared. I took the cup from his hand and slugged some down. It was icy cold, it was powerful in the back of the throat—a variety of kerosene made from fruit. It was what I needed. I slugged once more, then placed the mug in Lefty's hand. His fingers received it gently, happily, like a baby's around your thumb when you poke it into the carriage to say hello.

He said, "Is it fun, kid?"

"Well. Relationships take—"

"You're *serving* time, kid. Don't tell me nothing about relationships. You're serving *time*. You're a nice guy. I hope it works out nice for you. I hope nobody busts your hump. They bust your hump, come on down and have some Jersey Lightning with me, and I'll tell you some terrific lies."

Nobody busted my hump after I said goodnight to Lefty, wished him survival on a major municipal roadway, and clumped upstairs to do what I had done since I was sentient—change from "school clothes" (later "work clothes") to "play clothes." Each day of my life in school I had returned to take off my Thom McAns and either dark-blue or dark-brown corduroys, then put on sneakers and jeans. I did the same now, and Rhona came home with a little book to make the "play" my clothes were named after seem more like the "work" I was presumed, by dint of my costume, to be done with.

We kissed. She hung up her coat. I took a beer from the little icebox and she poured herself a slimy-looking vermouth. We made small talk. We paused, giving each other a chance to interrupt our monologues about the boring day we each had spent. Each did interrupt, and we took turns, leapfrogging dull stories about mediocre hours, trying to pump enough interest into the telling to encourage the other to be absorbed by what only could hold the teller's attention. We called it "debriefing," after the questioning which spies were said to go through upon returning from missions into enemy territory. Uh-huh and then he said so I said then we both said uh-huh oh really? well I never heard of it done that way you'd think uh-huh so would I well what the hell she's a jerk he's a fool they're a bunch of crooks uh-huh so how do you why do you when do you, and we were rolling right along through the daily winding-down, feigned interest based on real affection, and then Rhona reached for the little book at her feet and set it on the kidney-shaped table, and there it was.

The author's name was Andreoscu, and the paper was splitting—it shattered as I looked at a few pages, which were thick and brittle, yellowed, brown at the edges, filled with a tiny print that never lay across the page in a wholly straight line. "What's that?" I said, "the kind of book you make with your Dick Tracy stamp kit?"

Rhona pulled a torn library card from the place it had been preserving, and, holding the book open, she offered it to me once more. Bordered in black, with mostly darkness within the border, there was a tallish man in a hat. He looked at the camera; no, he looked as if he didn't know the camera was there. He wore thick glasses. The hat might have been part of a uniform, and so might the collar.

"So?" Rhona said. "You recognize?"

"Rhona, this could be anybody. It could be me."

I didn't want to speak like that. I wanted to wail—for love or confusion or both. She knew that love was a sentence, didn't she? Or something of a chore, at least. She wanted to rekindle me to the cause, and therefore —assuming I caught the spark again—make me more attractive to her. I, in turn, knew that I had no choice but to be rekindled. Either that, or turn to celibacy and dark reflections on fate. And stay away from Irving Place.

So: one protest for the sake of honesty, or something like it. And then: "Well, maybe."

"Maybe?"

"Maybe."

"A maybe is better than a no," Rhona said.

"A maybe's a maybe, Rhona. I won't give it a yes, but I won't say no. It's a solid maybe. Find someone who can read it, will you? What language is this? Is this Rumanian?"

"What else? A book about the Iron Guard killing Jews in Rumania. What else should it be? Sure. Rumanian."

"How do you know that?"

"Zimmer. You're talking to a librarian."

What I was talking to was a woman who wanted something. Either she wanted me, or what I offered to her life, or she wanted to hunt Nazis because of how she felt about her mother. Which was that she either loved her, or hated her, or felt bad about not doing either as well as she might. But the book was to excite me in the hunt. And the hunt was to make me a better lover or a better Jew. I was to define my life, on her behalf, in terms of a history littered with murders. And I cannot say that I believed a word about the book. Nor can I say that I saw it wholly as a lie—goad for the dancing bear. But I don't think that I believed very much about it. So there must have been a good deal of affection—we knew each other too well, by then, for me to be only excited by lust—because I didn't toss the book away, and Rhona too, and insist that we live with each other instead of the six million dead. It was not quite a *folie à deux*. But it surely was a *folie à une et trois-quarts*. I went along with my Rhona, and no one made me do it. That was what I wanted to do.

She said, "A solid maybe, Zimmer?"

"Maybe, but a solid maybe. Yes."

"Zimmer, do you know what I would do for a solid maybe from you?"

"You must show me sometime."

"I don't know if you're old enough for this."

"I don't know if I'm old enough for any of this, Rhona. I'm telling you, the old guy with the cane could *maybe* be the guy in this book. So could my managing editor. Where did you dig up the book?"

But by then she was showing me how much a maybe meant, and she was not dirty in the inspired, lascivious way I'd expected. She was sweet. She kissed me in the corner of the mouth, she kissed my nose, she kissed my ear as if we were teenagers, and I became excited by her innocence. The two of us, plotting to annex one another, plotting together to haunt a man who walked, sightless, with a white cane, and there we were, in a dirty loft above a shrimp-stinking public endangerment, being innocent. It was one of the moments for which I afterwards most loved us.

It was for similar moments that I remembered Madeleine. I told Rhona a good deal about her, and she was tolerant, as one should be of teenagers. I told her we necked in cars, in public parks after dark, in dormitory rooms during visitors' hours, and even in empty classrooms. We made what college kids in those days thought of as love. There were clothes off, condoms on, flesh on flesh, and an absence of sex manuals. So you did what you were advised to, or what you'd heard of, or what you dreamed about. And with Madeleine, it was fast, and fun, and furtive. But she *smiled* when we did it, usually, and she laughed as we shuddered at cold floors or muddy fields, and she was innocent. And so was I. I regard us both, now, the way a grandparent must regard his children's children—what they do, their fumblings and errors and triumphs, must be very rewarding and very distant: precious in the mind's eye, and nearly not seen, more nearly remembered, but as if on behalf of someone else. And I am coming, more and more, to remember that innocence of Rhona's in the same way that I remember Madeleine's—fondly, and down through distance. Lillian, very much present-tense, urgently seeking me on the kitchen floor, and Sally in the Hotel Royalton—innocents all, each in her way. Am I the corrupter? Or, worse, am I merely corrupt? I want to be as they are! That is my plea: innocent.

What an irony it is, what a folly, what a joke, what a farce, foolery, outrage and idiocy it is: whores on Eighth Avenue fuck pox-ridden key-mold merchants from New Jersey, and amateurs in bedrooms fuck governors and little dukes; in cars, there are girls who gobble cocks because their lives haven't come yet; and in the backs of subway trains to Salsa rhythms and in Liberty, New York, inside ranch houses built of chipboard, and in Portland, Oregon, in the rain under the enormous orange moon they hurl their loins and grunt and do not think of it before or after. Yet there is Zimmer, who cannot screw with his wife. Zimmer, the joke about sex. Zimmer, who can make *anything* that is normal and pleasant into the most unquotidian of nauseas. Zimmer, whose wife must leave him though she loves him—*because* she loves him—and whose son must be towed like a serving-cart on wheels away from Zimmer's life: you've had enough. Zimmer, who, no matter what he says or tries to say, won't *say*. Say: sex would be a dandy metaphor for that, wouldn't it? Zimmer, as his separated wife

152

is wont to tell him, can make a secular mystery out of the holiest simplicity. And Zimmer can only agree. And I did, on a Tuesday, shortly before the countdown to Christmas had begun on Fifth Avenue and shortly, therefore, ahead of that voice—"Will you *wait?*"—and shortly, then, before I had to choose: past, present or future, Zimmer. Which will it be?

When I told Rhona about the erection of the dead when I was in college, she snorted at the synagogue parts and snarled at those about my girlfriend's parents' comments on my wardrobe. And yet she was not wholly un-sympathetic, since so many survivors, she said, named their children after victims of the Holocaust, hoping to in some manner resurrect them, keep them in mind.

"That's naming," I said. "That's what Jews keep doing. Adam."

"Bullshit," she said. "A Jew is *not* sentimental. Didn't I teach you that? Adam wasn't a Jew. He was a story about Chaldeans and Phoenicians and people who wor-shipped a goddess with four breasts. So Adam names the creatures of the world. You remember that poetry per-son at NYU? *He* would appreciate your little story about Adam. As far as I'm concerned, I worry most about that little girl getting her hands on your ass. Is that likely to happen again in the near future?"

"Not if you keep your hands there now," I said.

But she didn't. She was a very good listener: she paid attention. And she wanted to hear it all. I think, in fact, that she was somehow excited—I never was: I hated hearing about her hours in bed with men I deemed un-worthy of her (yet somehow, maybe, worthier than I)—by stories of what I had done, and how, with whom. I told her that my childhood, as she had already heard enough to guess, was blessedly usual. We were not distinguished by pain, though my parents remembered childhoods of poverty, and (on my mother's side) of awful orthodoxy, and (on my father's side) fierce anticlericalism. There was more than enough to eat, when I was a child. And as their income increased, I was told that I might wish to know we were now of the middle class. I thought of rungs on ladders, but the idea of vertical mobility made no other impression on my life.

It did, by the time I was in college. I was always broke, and therefore always borrowing money from my parents and from my friends. The money was for girls, and I telephoned home to beg for checks. My father sent, my mother scolded. I practiced vertical mobility, climbing toward heaven up the bodies of girls, whining my way and bowing my way, as old men daven up and down at prayer, bobbing my head and my ass while worshipping the body of a girl, or the bright dream of my own body's promise, and, like all pilgrims, dying on the way, and that was fine with me. I came in cars and various beds and on creekside gravel, I worshipped and whimpered and blessed all the stars she lay looking at because at this moment she is actually letting me touch her *here*, and oh my *God* she is going to—indeed, it was vertical mobility. It was Madeleine.

When Madeleine's uncle died, things grew difficult. He was a gentle man whom I had met twice, and who had been able to say nothing to me because probably, I thought, I was a coarse person. Madeleine's father had agreed. The uncle was tubercular-looking and in fact had died of lung complications which Madeleine's father traced to the TB the uncle had suffered while fleeing the Nazis. I wondered whether they were exacerbated by the cigarettes he chain-smoked, but Madeleine's father would not discuss the matter with me. The uncle's younger brother, Madeleine's father, a widower, was tall and strong and always angry at the depredations wrought by college boys—by *me*—upon his only daughter. He was a German Jew who spoke only German with her, no matter how she blushed, or complained, or answered in English. With his long, flaring nose, he resembled a horse standing tall. With his large muscles bulging custom-made suits, he was a stallion to my burro—my *goat* (as I, in other ways, was his). He phoned each night that she did not call home. He never asked after me unless she was late to the phone, and then he asked plenty. And though he was pleased that Madeleine was friendly with the son of an accountant (how friendly, I suspect, not even his nightmares could tell him sufficiently), he made a point of informing her how miserable my clothing was. He was accurate. I did a wash toward the end of each semester. In my closet I hung a huge laundry bag. When I ran out of clothing—say socks or underwear—I reached to the bottom of the bag, on the theory that the oldest clothes had been there long enough to be purified by trapped bacteria, and I wore those.

But Madeleine's Uncle Herman died. Two events intersected. Her father—this was after weeks of telephone calls, visits home without me, much wailing and gnashing—mailed her a package he'd instructed her to forward to me. It was one of Uncle Herman's larger suits. It was for me. If she had to hang around with me, let me at least be well-dressed. That was the first event.

The second was Passover, which happened to occur that spring near the death of Uncle Herman—near enough for Madeleine to be overwhelmed with drama, sanctimony, and obedience to her father's flared nostrils. She sought out a temple, and in that area of Pennsylvania, her search was not a simple one. Imagine going into a gas station in Macungie, Pa., and asking the man at the gas pump, "Excuse me. Do you know if there's a synagogue in town, and whether it's reform?"

"Ooh. I dunno. You talking about a *Jew* church, now?"

But she found one. The suit had sat for a week in a wad on the floor of my closet. I had vowed never to wear it, to refuse to be buried alive in it, not to put it on if I were commanded to live or die in it wholly for the sake of love.

We had fallen asleep on the rancid daybed in my dormitory room. We were naked. *I* was sleeping, I should say. She was bending to me, licking and kissing and nuzzling and telling me, between mouthfuls, how sweet and small it was, and then she nipped its head, sucked it in with an expertise that horrified me—where had she *learned?* Sure, I wanted a veteran lovemaker, but a virgin one—and then, opening wide, breathing above it, watching it rock and roll in the perfume of her breath, Madeleine wondered if I would reconsider wearing the suit when I accompanied her to services.

I said no. She nipped, I cried a thousand times no. I watched her shiny brown hair dip and swing. I touched her thin strong shoulders, unblemished because, probably, for years her father had fed her the milk of pregnant tigers. I felt the warm air expelled from her long curved nose. Her breasts crushed against my thighs as she curled, moved, pressed, opened, received. I was amazed to find that years of omission, with some latent Semitic anti-Semitism, and the long rise up—not to heaven, but the ranks of the middle class—along with the usual theoretical objections to worshipping any god at all (taught by my father casually; gratefully learned by me) all came together at that moment, and I felt that I must say no.

On the other hand, it was crucial that *she* not say no. And I did love her as boys love girls. I was pleased not only by the painful pleasure she inflicted on me, and by her generosity; I was also startled by, and then happy about, her efforts to bribe me. Even though she did it, most likely, for her father's sake, and even though I never had been to shul before, and even though my principles and those of my grandfather and father were sorely outraged, I said yes. "It was almost what you think, but not completely what you think," I told Rhona.

She said, "It was a blowjob."

I said, "It was young love."

She wouldn't even answer me.

Uncle Herman's legs were slightly shorter than mine, and so were his arms, I told Rhona. My flesh therefore protruded, though my wrinkled shirt and soiled socks were stretching because I constantly, in a boil of anxiety, writhed to pull the socks up, whirled my arms to shoot the stiff cuffs down. Nothing worked for long, and my flesh leered from around the dead man's suit. I wore my own tie, of narrow woven wool in a dark brown, which I thought might contrast nicely with the corpse-gray of the silk suit, the label of which was in characters I thought to be Chinese. While narrow lapels and small notches in them were then fashionable, I had notches with an underbite, the bottoms protruding an inch farther out than the tops—as if someone had cut someone's father's double-breasted suit into a single-breasted model. While my friends had flaps over their suit pockets, I now wore a jacket with little open bags sewn onto the sides. My friends wore pants with belts in the back and no pleats in the front: guess what I did not wear on the back and did wear on the front. And guess whose trousers were bell-bottomed several years before *that* particular style returned to fashion. The jacket was tight on my waist, but I wore it buttoned: I was going to temple, after all. As they'd have said in the old neighborhood, after calling me, once more, an impostor, I looked very much like a schmuck. With, as they used to say, earlaps.

It was like a ski chalet or a small fancy train station—maybe a private airport serving executive jets. Fancy blond wood all over, high ceilings, tile floor, echoing voices, and the clopping footsteps of men feeling important and showing it—rushing here and there, performing chores while calling attention to their performance: I could see them doing that when they were little boys. Madeleine wore a dark-green dress that made her look about thirty. In constant motion to pull my socks up, pull my shirt down, keep my suitcoat buttoned, make my tie stop choking me, keep from starting to neck with her there—I had a reward to claim—I felt fifteen, and covered with boils. I was the abridged version of *Every Boy's Book of Job*.

I looked around for things to kneel before, or bow to, or for mats on which perhaps I should hurl myself full length and wail in the voice of desert warriors. I saw scrolls on display, and I didn't know what they were, and I realized that any Jew-baiting bigot from the college, accustomed to weekly church *plus* enforced chapel during the week, would better know how to behave in this noisy room than I ever would. Church is church, I realized; a Jew is either something different from a worshipper, or all the anti-Semitic prejudice I'd heard of and experienced was wasted. Give history a break, I graciously told myself. I solemnly agreed. A Jew was different from these people around me in their dresses and suits, or at least a Jew was more.

The rabbi looked like a track-and-field-day organizer, but in a suit so stiff with richness, the jacket never moved when his arms did. He announced a reminder that on Passover the Yizkor memorial service is said for the dead. Madeleine began to softly weep for Uncle Herman. A woman, wrapped at the shoulders in a chain of six dead weasels, each biting the tail of the one in front, each staring at Zimmer, the infidel, began to weep as well. "And I remind the youngsters," the rabbi said, in his lanolined voice, "we mourn in the Yizkor not only our own, but each and every one of the Six Million." A man beside me, who smelled of cloves—Sidney the dentist! a Nazi in the synagogue!—stood and walked out. Others did too. The rabbi frowned, but paused. Madeleine whispered in my ear that some people with living parents will leave a memorial service so as not to curse them. I hoped we would leave as well, but we didn't. And I sat beside the girl who fasted (I did not), and who had attended a seder, with other Jewish students (I had not) at the home of a family who lived near the school.

I had been jealous of the hungers she experienced without me, and of the seder she had been to, and now, in the synagogue, I was jealous again. After all, she knew this world and I did not; she belonged to it, and I never would. The jealousy was edged with sorrow because I learned in shul, wearing a dead man's suit for the sake of love (as a ship might fly false flags for safer passage), that differentness is the final and fearful truth, even in love. The second emotion was lust: our flanks touched, and while I sat beneath the roof of the Lord, or His tenants, anyway, I thought only of collecting my reward for wearing a tubercular suit stripped, for all I knew, directly from a corpse, in order to be presentable among some well-dressed strangers who did nothing but call in an alien tongue, and stand and sit like any other people in any other church. The language I didn't speak was *worship*—which particular dialect, I did not care about. But I was to be paid for my services, I was trafficking in love, and I was tumescent much of the time. When I tried to place her hand on my erection when we sat, she flinched as if I'd burned her. She turned red. She bit her lip, looked from the side of her eye at me. Her dead uncle hardly intervened, I thought—unless it was grabbing a cock beneath *his* pants which made her excited. It made me excited, I decided, but she removed her hand, shook her head and looked around as if to find the Torah. I couldn't find it. Was the Torah the same as the Scroll? What was the Ark of the Covenant, then?—and I understood, or pretended to. Love of the Lord, thousands of years of tribulation, the death of the beloved, the stallion-father having his way, the boyfriend in the clothes of the avuncular dead, the worship—of what?—in a building belonging to others, and never to me: all these facts, and the two hard emotions, jealousy and lust, along with all my doubts and fears, were crowded into the blood that brought my penis up as hard and unquellable as it ever had been. She knew and was pleased. I knew and was pleased—her pleasure then meant pleasure later—but I was also sad: we were bound to be separate. And the cock that told me how we'd come together soon was also throbbing its little jungle rhythms about how, and soon enough, we'd be apart. So I sat with it between my legs, and stood with my hands above it as best I could. I was in an alien place, and my wilful penis rose for hunger and sorrow while the fellow-worshippers rose in the secret name of the Lord. "If you had been there to look for me, Rhona, I'd have been the one in the bulging clothes of the dead," I told her.

"Very dramatic. Bulging clothes of the dead."
"You should have seen it."
"You should be less dramatic. Look—you've got a hard-on. Zimmer, you're arousing yourself!"
"And you?"
"What was that about how she breathed on it? What —wait, if we just open this and *confront* things. Yes. Now, she must have been—like this? Um. Um?"

But what else I came to later was, indecently enough, more important than such delicious listening by Rhona Glinsky. I came, again, to Queens. I did not want to, nor would anyone. We were on the IND again, in a filthy car ankle-deep in newspapers and old shopping lists and candy wrappers. We were with six or seven people, all of them short and wearing thick glasses and staring warily at us because we were speaking, very loudly, about a subject they didn't wish to study anymore.

"Your Andreoscu," I was telling Rhona, "if he was in the Iron Guard of the Order of St. Michael, he wasn't a Nazi, probably. You should know this."

"Fine," she said. "I do know it. So what?"

"So a Nazi isn't an Iron Guard. I don't understand this, Rhona. If you know so much about the guy, and you consulted this reference librarian at the Grand Army Plaza branch who speaks the language, then you should know that."

"I'm lying to you, Zimmer?"

And still, I hadn't the courage to say it. "Listen. There was this time, I forget when it was—'Forty-one? 'Forty-three? The Iron Guard went crazy. Planned crazy, of course. They killed the Jews, you understand. They didn't put them in camps. They killed them. They raped them. They bludgeoned them to death, and shot them, and fucked them with knives and ran over them and

burned them in the ghetto houses and what was left of
the shops. For three days, I think it was. They had a hell
of a fine time. Then the Nazis had the Rumanian government *arrest* them. You understand? I'm talking about
politics. The Iron Guard types fled. Because the Nazis
didn't trust fanatics. They wanted *method* in their allies'
madness."

"So that's what I'm saying. They were crazy fanatics
who killed Jews. How can you be asking me for *more?*"

A little man with a fur collar on his shabby cloth coat,
whose cordovan shoes were highly polished but whose
small feet made him appear like a schoolboy and not an
old man, sat up straight. He nudged his little wife, whose
collar was also fur. They turned toward us. They listened.

"But I'm saying, you don't have the facts. Outside the
obvious: half the world tried to kill the Jews. But this
Andreoscu book? The picture? The translation I never
get to read because you can't get hold of it? The notes
you lost from when your friend told you what the book
said? A killer sitting in your *library?* Rhona!"

"Why now, Zimmer?"

"Why now what?"

"Why is it now you have objections?"

"Rhona, I've always had them. Had—difficulties with
the whole cloth."

"Very mercantile, Zimmer. Whole cloth. So why do
you tear it to little pieces *now?* And why have you never
told me?"

"You never thought I had suspicions?"

"No! Suspicions? No. Troubles, yes. Hesitations.
Sure, why not. Me too. But *suspicions?* You're telling
me it's my *motives* that worry you?"

We swayed over Queens. The answer, of course, was

that her motives didn't worry me. I knew them. They were to lure me to her with guilt about the Jews. They were to lure me to Jewishness with her love. They were to find what had driven her mother half-mad and punish it. They were to punish her mother for being removed from her daughter by madness and war. And why not? At least, that's what I thought for a fraction of an instant: why should she not have what she needs? A grateful nation had let Richard Nixon and Senator McCarthy invent communist conspiracies and intricate designs of doom. The world had let the Third Reich be born, and the Stalin Trials proceed: why should Rhona Glinsky not be permitted to pursue a possible—a barely possible—renegade blind man?

The husband and wife watched me from within the comfort of their collars. I raised my brows and shrugged my shoulders at them. Like typical New Yorkers, when acknowledged in public, they made their eyes go dead and forgot they'd seen me. I leaned over and kissed Rhona on her brow, and said nothing more. Let her carry the whole cloth to her mother, I thought. As for me, I still carried with me the tatters of what I had done that day—How to Cut Your Risks in Advertising, and then Try These Winning Ways with Carpets ("What are the newest trends in carpet colors? Which carpet fiber offers the greatest protection against *pets*?")—and I sat on the shivering train next to Rhona, leaning against her as our car chattered and scraped, smelling the old breaths which rode with us in Queens.

And there, in that apartment, its expensive decor in that awful building making it something of a jewel in a dungheap, we ate baked chicken in a blanket of herbs that made my mouth pucker. We drank sweet wine. Our dessert was junket, which I hadn't eaten since I was small. Our after-dinner conversation took place at the crumb-littered tablecloth over which we called to one another across the wide wood. Mrs. Glinsky looked smaller than last time, and even more lacking in sleep, and even balder, and more in pain. Again, she wore long sleeves—a brown velvety fabric, this time—and more clanking jewelry all over. Mr. Glinsky wore his day's business suit and a matching tie and shirt: three shades of green. He smiled, he twinkled, he showed his teeth and gums, the insides of his lips, his very uvula hanging from the back of his throat like a symbol of his generosity to the world. He worked, that little man, unrolling long, rich carpets of conversation up which Rhona and I had to walk; we thus were prevented from saying anything— Christmas trees, the nature of salvation, the sundry ways of worship—which might distress the woman Mr. Glinsky loved so well.

What are the newest trends in carpet colors, I wanted to say and didn't, as we strolled up a discussion he'd construed for us. But Rhona, who enjoyed pulling rugs out from under folks (Your sentimental treatment of the death of a rodent, etc.) merely reached beneath her chair, took up the dark-blue book, and plunked it on the table. "Andreoscu," she announced.

"Rhona," Mrs. Glinsky said, "this is good for my digestion or bad?"

"Andreoscu," Mr. Glinsky said, rubbing his little chin with his clean little fingers, showing a little linen under his cuff. "Andreoscu. Rumanian name, am I right? The book is from twenty years ago, so Rhona is going to tell us about wartime Rumania, which is during the time of the fascists there, am I right? The Iron Guard, yes? Wonderful, very nice. Daddy's little girl is going to tell us about killers in middle Europe, hmh? Rhona . . ."

Mrs. Glinsky was nodding, smiling, tuned into her husband's monologue, really appreciating him, and I think—in that herb-smelling apartment, with a clear plastic cover on a wing chair with new fabric, and with death in the air like a mist—I really envied Mr. and Mrs. Glinsky, that moment, of all the lovers I had known. "Let her tell us," she instructed her husband. "Maybe it will be good for us to know something about the less fortunate peoples of the world. It's not all perfume and light, after all, life, you know."

Rhona did not stand—I waited for this—to rage at her mother about having to be reminded every day in her childhood about the camps and the permanent nightmare in which her mother lived. I admired her for that much silence, though not, to be honest, for what she did next: she opened the Andreoscu book to the picture of our old blind fascist and she pointed, pounding on the feathering page with fingers I had recently kissed. "Here. You see this one? A colonel in the Guard, it says here. Zimmer and I have seen him in the street. We follow him to his house. He lives here, in New York City, and nobody knows it except us!"

Mrs. Glinsky cried. As simply as that: looking at her daughter, listening, watching her fingers dance on the book, her eyes filled and ran over onto her cheekbones and her sunken pale skin, running swiftly down to her mouth. She licked her tears and stared at her daughter.

"We don't want to know," Mr. Glinsky said. "They are all over the world, darling. They are in the government of Germany, west and east. They are in Austria. They own Brazil, Paraguay, Nicaragua, Uruguay. They work for America putting rockets into the air and they sit in the government in Washington and tell the spies how to catch the other spies. The only place we *think* they don't live is Israel, and this is probably self-deception. The Nazis are not new, you understand. There is nothing new about a Nazi. Once, they worked together in the same uniforms with the same boss. Now, different. But still essentially the same. It's all the same. The Jews have always been the same and the Nazis have always been the same. I don't read books about the Nazis or the camps. I don't read articles in the newspapers either because what else bad news do I need? Your mother, in her heart, carved on her soul forever—what is it you think she needs from you in the way of news about"— he began ticking off in choppy motions on small fingers —"the barbarian savages, the cannibals, who killed your grandmother, your grandfather, an uncle from Lithuania, an uncle from Galicia, an uncle who was an architect *in Berlin*, and therefore, I say it because those monsters have always enjoyed ipso facto and other logic, an aunt from Galicia, an aunt from Lithuania, an aunt who resided in a swanky neighborhood in Berlin near a bridge with wrought-iron rails carved in a very elegant design. They killed a total of seven small children in your mother's family"—the little fingers danced now, playing the cruel tune, and it was a Disney night of death, I expected to see his hands holding sticks which banged on Mrs. Glinsky's bones to make this music—"and one of them, as I think you know, was four when they took him. A little boy of four who looked at the men who broke his mother's wrist because she didn't move quick enough to suit their requirements. This I know, and it lives all the time in my heart. Your mother is some nights not alive because of it. And look at what it's doing to you, maybe. Why, sweetheart, would we need to know more of them?" He stood. He ran around the table. He took his daughter's big shoulders in his short arms and hugged, with his eyes closed. Mrs. Glinsky had stopped weeping, Her eyes were open. She looked at her daughter. Over the father's arm, the daughter looked back. I looked away.

As if they were used to long wailings and short grudges, they became calm. Rhona sat. Mr. Glinsky returned to his seat. Mrs. Glinsky wiped her face and looked at me—I could feel her—and waited for me to speak. I didn't. I watched Mr. Glinsky pour alcohol with which to pacify us. I watched a dessert spoon spin in my hands, again and again. So because I wouldn't venture out, Mrs. Glinsky came in after me.

A finger pushed my arm. It was a skeleton's bone, and I was in the dark of Hallowe'en, too young to be alone with skeletons. She said, with the tone of humorous patience in which Yiddish-speakers specialize, "So, you too are pursuing this Jew-killer?"

"Alleged Jew-killer," Mr. Glinsky said.

"He is," Rhona said.

"Excuse me," her mother said. "I asked the boyfriend. I can call you that?"

I said, "Yes."

"To both?" she said.

"Yes."

"The boyfriend I can understand. My daughter is crazy, but appealing. She comes from a crazy but appealing family. But why—what would you call yourself? An agnostic? A reformed Semite Agnostic? Or just Protestant? Hmh? Why would you be hunting this—outlaw? Rhona, she does it because of me and the dead ones. And she tells me so I should feel nauseous that she is maybe becoming a monster of revenge. This pays me back too, you see. It's a problem of Jews. But you?"

"Loyalty," Mr. Glinsky ventured. "Devotion is so hard to understand?"

She swept his suggestion away. Her bones rattled.

Happy Halloween. I was sweating and starting to itch. As she stood, in her bony thinness and high bright mounding skull, I clasped my hands, as if I were at Sidney the dentist's.

Mrs. Glinsky said, "Devotion is not hard to understand. Sex is not hard to understand. Sightseeing in somebody else's life is not hard to understand. Betrayal is not hard to understand. Rumanian is not hard to understand. But *you*, Mr. Zimmer, I do not understand."

"No, no," Mr. Glinsky said. "No, no."

And Rhona said, "Goodbye. That's all. Goodbye."

And Mrs. Glinsky's face, its haunted, eaten features, and her high harsh voice, her hairless scalp, and her exhausted eyes which looked so long at things—these are what I saw when Mr. Glinsky danced with coats and chairs and doorknobs. "You'll come again. We'll try again. We're getting there, yes?" he said. I walked down the stairs as if still in her vision, and on the wide deserted street I looked up to see if Mrs. Glinsky was looking down.

Rhona insisted that we ride a taxi home. We rode over the 59th Street Bridge and were downtown in a hurry. Rhona pulled me upstairs. I knew what she was going to want: sex, dirty sex, wonderful nasty sex, with tongues here, and fingers to follow and this over there and that under here—

I went into the bathroom. I locked the door. Ah, days of yore! How many minutes—hours?—had I sat as a boy on the closed toilet, furtive in my silence?

"Zimmer," she called.

"I'm sick."

"With what?"

"Giblet gravy."

"Zimmer, we didn't have giblet gravy."

"Herbed chicken."

"Thyme, basil and tarragon don't make you sick."

"They make *me* sick."

"I don't hear any gas coming out, Zimmer."

"*Rhon*-a."

"When you're sick, you have gas."

"Do we really know each other this well, Rhona?"

"So either hiss for me, or come out."

"Rhona?"

"What now?"

"I have a headache."

"With your poisoning from giblet gravy that we didn't eat? With your terminal tarragon poisoning? Also now a headache? Zimmer!"

"And I think I'm getting a sore throat."

"It's the giblets again. No doubt. Goodnight, Zimmer."

"Rhona?"

"What."

"I love you."

A long silence. Across the loft, the sound of bedclothes. Then: "Zimmer. It's all right. You're a true Jew. Don't worry."

TOOTHSOME AND ROMANTIC: THE HISTORY OF PRETZELS

It seems unbelievable that the pretzel came into being almost by accident, but it did. Legend has it that in the year 610, after baking bread, an Italian monk had dough left over. He twisted it into forms resembling hands folded in prayer, baked them, then presented them to dutiful youngsters as a treat. These "pretiolas" grew popular, crossed the Alps, and were translated as "pretzels." They crossed the Alps on elephants. I quit. I quit. I quit.

But I didn't. I went on to Free Things to Write For— how many puns about America as "the land of the free" did I write that day?—and I even started The Amazing New Highway Story on behalf of some insurance company in a midwestern state I knew I'd never visit. That morning, when Piggy had said, "All right?" I had answered her with, "No." She didn't care, I thought, but Lefty did. He was standing in sleet that evening after work, wearing an elegant brown leather coat, with one arm pinned, that creaked. He looked like a hood about to shake me down, and I didn't want to talk to him, so I stood still at 5:45 P.M. of a dismal Thursday in October, and he came after me.

We faced one another on emptying Varick Street. He looked into my face and said, "Come in here, kid. In my office."

I followed him to the Cadillac, he unlocked the door for me and even held it. He locked me in, as if we were going for a long ride. Then, having locked himself in behind the wheel, he looked pointedly at a plastic tray which rode on the driveshaft hump which swelled the center of the floor. There was a cup of applejack which he had placed there before I'd come home: he'd been waiting, and seriously, and he wanted me to know.

That close to him, in such a small space, I smelled not only shrimp in formaldehyde, and rancid celery, rotten gluey sauce, but the harsh high smell of the applejack itself—it wasn't clean that night, like apples: it was dirty, like a stranger's sour lips. I leaned back.

"We know each other a long time, kid."

I nodded, rather than say *We know nothing, Lefty.*

"We go back a ways. I like having you here. It feels safer, somebody living over the shop, you know? And you're a nice boy. You're bright. I like it that you do PR work—a little class, where I come from. So what I'm saying"—he sipped, sneered at the pleasure in his throat, swallowed, sipped again—"is I feel like we can talk. What I'm trying to say is: buck up. Love is tough when it's *good*." He sipped. "And it's never that good, that I know of."

The sleet collected, melted, ran and pooled, so that the windshield of the Cadillac was glazed, impenetrable. We might as well have been driving down Avenue W in Brooklyn or a side street of Evanston, Illinois. I felt as though we were traveling, and I felt as though I were traveling with a drunk who was getting us lost; I had to stay awake, lest we get so lost we couldn't retrace our errant path, and yet I didn't think I'd be able to, I was so groggy, and there was Lefty—would he get us killed, I wondered.

I looked up to check the oncoming traffic, promising myself that I would sleep after one quick look. There was no one beside me, and no traffic, of course. And I had slept, and not long enough. I was cold, felt hung over, and was embarrassed to have died on Lefty like that, when he was offering his generous and not very useful advice. I shook my head as if I were a dog, then stepped from dryness into the wet of the autumn storm. There was Rhona, crossing beside Lefty's car. She stopped, stared, stepped closer. "Where have you been?" she said.

I said nothing. We walked past Lefty behind plate glass; he raised his white mug in a parody of toast—*And it's never good*—and what I said was, "Waiting for you. It's time to see the old man. I want to know what he thinks we've been doing to him."

"He came in again today," she said outside our door, formerly my door. "He sat, he listened. He *looked* as if he listened. That's all. He left. He wore the same brown suit, and it was clean. As usual. You'd think a blind man would spill some soup on his tie. My father is neat, and *he* spills soup on his tie. You spill soup on everything."

"Racial trait," I said. "Onan. He spilled his soup upon the ground. I want to go *now*, Rhona. I want this over with."

"What?"

"You know."

She looked at me so sternly that I felt wrong. Then I grew angry and my anger made me loom. She shrank before me at the door. I therefore felt guilty, and I urged her to go upstairs, as she wanted me to, so she could change before we left.

In Abromowitz's office, 18 years later, Sally told Abromowitz, "But we advanced her ten thousand dollars."

"Call it back," Abromowitz said.

"I never heard of that," Sally said. "Anyway, let the other houses do that. We're not like that, are we?"

"We sure as hell are," Abromowitz said. "The girl wrote a halfway decent book that did okay." He was rustling the printouts he didn't understand, but which Sally always broke down for him as the meetings got underway. "We sold some copies, Book of the Month came through with a QPB adoption, we came pretty close. It was all right. So an advance for a good book, ten thousand bucks, I can see it." Sally was blushing. She was the editor of the book which was exploding beneath her. "But she hands in—"

"Trash," Sally said, shaking her head. "It's horrible. There isn't a sentence here that's *written*. It's as if she took it out of her college files—it's so *bigoted*."

"Against whom?" I asked.

"Other women who aren't as angry as she is," Sally said. "It's kind of lesbian-feminist. This woman works in this huge office—sounds like IBM. There's a lot about computers, and she doesn't make it very clear. She's fighting her way up the old corporate ladder."

"Vertical mobility," I said.

"But there's this other woman. Very pretty and sophisticated. Old family, not much old money left, lots of pretensions about class and breeding. She sucks up to the men, tries to be one of the old boys, you know? And this fierce fighter, she nearly loves the male-chauvinist woman. But she's also disgusted by how she's using what all the *tough* women have done so she can get ahead. It's a love story, I guess. And a politics story. It could be *good*."

"But it isn't," I said.

"Listen," Sally said. " 'She thought of Arliene's white thighs, round and spread, leading to her love-gash like converging parallel lines, but of flesh, seeming to meet but not meeting.' Do you see?" Sally said. "Her thighs never meet. Don't you *hate* it?"

"Love-gash," Abromowitz said. "It's like something in a skin magazine."

"It *is* something in a skin magazine," Sally said. "She sold serial rights on two chapters."

"So reject it," I intoned, waiting to move on.

"But—"

"Get the money back," Abromowitz said. "Sally'll spend the rest of the year putting this shit into shape, we'll publish it, we'll maybe even make some money, and we'll lose our reputation. We're too good for this book. When we do trash, we'll do it like a classy house—memoirs of fag ballet dancers. None of this love-gash trash.

You tell her agent, Sally. Say it's not in acceptable condition. Say any advance is refundable unless the contract says nonrefundable. Does it?"

"No."

"Get the money back."

Stottner said, "I think we have a commitment to the author."

Abromowitz said to Sally, "Have Wally here help you on this. He can talk to the agent too. She can see how it's hard for us to take the dough back. But that we're gonna *do* it. After, maybe, lunchtime? We'll have lunch, and I'll tell you how to figure out with them the ways they can pay us back. Don't forget—we got about fifteen hundred bucks held back, yes, for returns on her first one? We can work the rest out. Anyway, we'll get what we can, lose what we have to, and forget this book. Done, okay?"

"She did write a good book last time," Sally murmured. Sally was a loyal person. I winked at her, she blushed back, and we were friends the length of the table, and not in bed anymore, and colleagues at work, and what more could I ask for?

Paul Celan. I was reading out loud to them, for goodness' sake, shouting over the dusty harvest table at Abromowitz, who let me and Sally publish poetry because he thought it was our necessary and nonprofit contribution to the western races, not because he cared much for it. I was reading:

> *we are digging a grave in the air there's*
> *   room for us all*
> *a man lives in the house he plays with the*
> *   serpents he writes*
> *he writes when it darkens to Germany your golden*

> *hair Margarete*
> *he writes it and steps outside and the stars*
>   *all aglisten he whistles for his hounds*
> *he whistles for his Jews he has them dig a*
>   *grave in the earth*
> *he commands us to play for the dance*

and Sally had tears in her eyes, Stottner had his face covered with his hands. Abromowitz was furious, redder than Sally, a dangerous red that made his muscular jowly face look explosive.

"You're using dead Jews on me to make a point?" He said it very low, and he sounded as though he might walk the length of the table and attack me. "You're using Jews killed by Nazis to help me understand something?"

"I'm trying to demonstrate something. I've been telling you about this guy for months. Now I'm showing you."

"But we said no. No means no. We voted. We decided. Then you use dead people on us like a fucking *lever?* You think that's friendly of you? You think it's reasonable?"

"I don't want to apologize for using the man's work to help get it in front of readers."

Abromowitz said, "Then how about apologizing for reading it at us like we're a fucking bunch of fat Germans in a restaurant who don't mind the light from Jew-tallow, instead of people who know what's what and what was and the answer is no and stop *bullying* us."

"Bullying?"

Sally nodded, her mouth twisted in apology. She shrugged her shoulders.

"It's apt," Stottner said.

"I thought you liked Celan's work."

"We're not talking poetry," Abromowitz said. "We're talking people. You and me. You and us. Here."

"I'm breaking up the family, huh? Over a bunch of poems and a bunch of Jews?"

Sally was pale now, and she was sad for me. I thanked her by winking slowly, to show I wasn't angry at her, but the wink was just a tic, and she knew I was angry at everyone. Abromowitz passed the printouts over to Sally, ruffled Wally Stottner's handsome hairdo, stood up, sucked in his belly and adjusted his belt, then nodded at me, said, "Go home and rest and tomorrow remember how important you are to this publishing house and to the rest of us. Personally." Sally flushed this time. Stottner looked away. Abromowitz tried to smile. "We'll be all right," he said. "Maybe I shouldn't yell, huh? But I'm pissed off at you, buster. I want you to think about why. You're my senior editor. Please think about that, all right? You're the guy I have to trust the most."

"So I should leave myself out of it."

"No. You know better than that. Leave the dead Jews out of it. I got enough problems in my life already. And how did you think my cousins who aren't around managed to die thirty-five years ago. Will you fuckin' *think?*"

I couldn't. I left the office, my raincoat flapping, my chest flapping too. I was almost dizzy, my vision was on the edge of drifting to pieces, and my heart felt soggy in my chest, there was a weak wet mushy rhythm to its work. I walked uptown, stopped at a riding apparel store, looked at leather boots and whips and jodhpurs, and I thought of arrogant lean officers with high boots herding prisoners. I thought of Paul Celan, who could write in French and who lived, after the war and the Holocaust in which his parents died in the camps, in France. He insisted on writing his poetry in German, though. What a way to assault the masters of the camps—writing in their language. What a way to assault himself for having lived when others died. But what did I know about poetry, or concentration camps, or poor Celan's nightmares? And why had I attacked Abromowitz and Sally and Wally Stottner with Paul Celan's words? I had done it on my own behalf. I would therefore be enriched if we promoted his poems about death and the awfulness inside the mind. But why? Would I be a better husband? Father? Citizen? Jew?

None of the above. But I might see myself, more fully, and maybe more deludedly, as suffering. Why was I trying to suffer? For Lillian? For *Rhona*? Remember Rhona? For Sam? For all the dead strangers? Or just for myself—world-class self-pity.

And Abromowitz was right. I was using the dead as a club. I was swinging away at the world, myself included, using the dead in their graves and chimneys and ashes and memories—in the poems and leftover voices—as a tool. I was an artisan of corpses. I was home. I was at my door, and in, and Lillian was shouting at me.

"He just rang the bell and he was inside."

"No, Lil, you keep the door locked. He was inside because you let him in. Why did you do that? Why're you home in the afternoon?"

"Because Sam got sick in school and they called me. They always call the mother."

"Is he all right? Where is he? What's he got?"

"He's got what makes them throw up in the hallways at school. He's in bed and he's asleep and I had a mass murderer in the apartment!"

"Lil."

"He just rang the bell, and when I asked who it was he said 'Me.' "

"So, naturally, you felt obligated to let him in. Not wanting to deny anyone their right to selfhood."

"I thought it was you."

"You thought it was *me*? I never come home this time of the afternoon—whoops."

"That's right, you son of a bitch. Whoops. It sounded just like you. And here you are, this time of the afternoon."

"You think I've got a doppelgänger running around New York, drooling over people's doorknobs?"

"It sounded like you and don't make *jokes* about it."

"I'm sorry."

In her dark-blue suit with its white pinstripes, with her fine yellow hair blown up by static electricity, catching light from the bright wide window behind her, without shoes on, her long strong feet rasping on the wooden floor through stockings, she looked so competent and pretty, so much a part of the world in which women wear suits and at the same time come home to be barefoot in another world—I moved toward her, thinking of Celan, and Jews, Abromowitz, and little Sam, stuck at school, cared for by this woman, his mother. I was nearly incoherent with impulses that had no name, with blind feelings of celebration, need, and fright of course: a fearful man had been here, and she'd mistaken him for me.

"So you let him in—did Sam see him?"

"No. He was asleep by then. I saw him. He's this squat guy in khaki clothes, like a janitor. He *stinks*. It's the worst smell." She gagged. I wasn't too impressed by that, because Lil could gag at will, as I could belch whenever I wanted to—grade-school tricks we'd retained, our souvenirs. "And as soon as I saw him, of course, I slammed the door. But he stuck his foot in it."

"Just like the movies," I said, still standing just inside the door.

"Just like the movies. Except I kicked him as hard as I could in the shin."

"And he fled?"

"No. I'd taken my shoes off. I hurt my toes." Lil began to weep, a slow, quiet crying of real misery, and what I wanted to do was step forward and comfort her, hold and stroke her back and the back of her neck, where the fleeciest soft blonde hair caught the light. But I thought of the man with my voice, and somehow I felt as though I smelled like him. I was afraid to go too close because I would drive her away. "He took off, anyway," she said, pressing her nose first. She sometimes did that to make herself stop crying—as if she had a nosebleed and a pinch of the capillaries cut off the tears. It didn't, but it made her take a deep breath, and that self-consciousness sometimes made her calm down. It worked this time, though I wanted to say something about tears, capillaries, blood and dandy metaphors, and she read my eyes and grew wary. "He ran when I shouted and screamed."

"So he didn't hurt you, and Sam didn't know about it."

"That's right. I want a divorce from you. I want us to be divorced. Are you sick too? Is that why you came home?"

"No," I said. "I'm all right."

"Okay," Lil said. "Then I want a divorce."

"But why? Why *now*?"

"Because the first thing I thought about was telling you. When it was happening, I thought about you right away. Then I thought about making us a cup of tea, or a big bastard of a drink maybe, and telling you."

"Yes," I said. "Yes. You should. I'm glad you wanted to. Shouldn't you? Isn't that right? I mean, why would that make you want to leave me? Lil: don't leave me."

"Because you come home and I tell you something

terrible and Sam feels sick, and all you can say is 'I'm all right.' "

"Oh, Lil. I was trying—"

"Because you're not all right. You're going a little nuts now, I think, and you aren't telling me."

"Don't leave me, Lil."

"And because I know you. I know your eyes. When I was telling you about this maniac here, you were throwing off German words at me, and thinking about something else. Weren't you. You were thinking about *you.* You were thinking in *your* terms. You *weren*'t thinking in mine. Because you are almost, not entirely now, I wouldn't claim that, you are almost someplace else. Or I am. And Sam? What about *Sam,* for godsakes, when there's a monster at the door who smells like a cesspool and I say who is it and he says 'Me' and it sounds like you. What about *us?*"

"Don't leave me, Lil."

Once upon a time, Rhona and I took a sabbatical. Probably, we had grown disgusted with ourselves and our search (for different reasons, of course) and probably—this was during our second week together—it had been a remark I'd made about how well-pressed his brown trousers were, and with what style he wore his shabby clothes. He became an actual person for a time, and Rhona, fleeing such reality, decided to take me away from Nazis and the blind toward Eighth Street, then across to Greenwich Avenue, where we sat to sip coffee and listen to a man in an oily white tee-shirt and jeans read poetry. A woman with the face of a baby, the body of a twenty-year-old dancer, and the defeated shuffle of someone married too long, walked among the small square wooden tables, carrying pots of tea, cups of silty espresso, and little French cakes. People about us leaned back proprietarily—they were in possession, their bodies said, of art and artful ambience—or they crouched in toward one another, saying with their adjunct torsos that they owned one another and the truth of lasting love. I sat up straight and Rhona did too, and we listened to the poetry for a while. I was, of course, very much afraid that the poet, who had no hair anywhere on his visible body, would say something about mourning or praying or hearing or wishing or dreaming or thinking like a Jew. Rhona, shifting her eyes toward me and then away, said in a stage whisper, "Don't worry. I won't persecute the artist."

She had parodied a tough-guy's aside from stiffened lips, and the pure pleasure—this was the tantalizing part —of not being politically, historically, religiously, and morally *aware*, the quiet delight in the ordinary, in the possibilities of joy in our ordinariness, made me open my mouth and show all my molars and waggle my thick red tongue and laugh out loud.

Little espresso spoons stopped softly chiming on cheap espresso cups. The chewing of sweet French cakes declined into slow mushing of crumbs. The poet stopped and looked over the fug of Gaulois smoke and coffee steam, and he shrugged his shoulders at someone nearby and said, in a friendly low voice, to all the room: "Friends. I am pausing for a prick who thinks that Hiroshima was cute."

My eyes bulged and watered. I held my head still on a neck that felt a foot and a half long. Rhona was red. I felt red. We looked at one another. The silence thickened like a starchy pudding. "Schmuck," someone said, a woman, with no scorn, just the necessary emphasis for description. You'd say it of a bird observed: "Thrush," you'd say. She said "Schmuck."

Rhona said, with equal objectivity, "Bitch," loudly enough to be heard, but with no special punch in her voice.

"How about death-lover?" a man near the vocal woman asked.

I cleared my throat and said, "Let's listen to the author, friends." But it came out as a whisper, and when I tried again, what emerged was: "Why don't you put your nose back in her lap and let the guy read his poems, huh?"

"She doesn't have a lap," Rhona said. "It's all stainless steel."

The woman, who now stood to reveal more hair on her face and bare arms than the poet, pointed at our table and said, "Bomb-dropper. Baby-killer. What's ya hobby, honey—lampshades in concentration camps?"

Rhona went as stiff as I had been.

I said, "Don't."

And she said, "Don't be ridiculous," her face relaxing into a smile. She stood, looked over the room at the woman, and said, "You deserve congratulations, you very short person. You have more hair in your moustache than my boyfriend. And you have shit for brains." She swept out, leaving her coat and her pocketbook, but receiving the applause of two men wearing matched Eisenhower jackets dyed black. I retrieved her things and waddled after her, too embarrassed to do more than study the floor as I told myself, *Don't trip!* I didn't, we met outside, I handed her the coat and bag, we both laughed and then stopped, then laughed more, and held hands like lovers in Greenwich Village, not hunting anything. *It could be like this*, I thought. And the evening made me sad.

And that night, while Rhona sat on the mattress and read, blankets swaddled around her legs which she had gathered beneath her, wearing a nightgown of figured blue flannel which made her look young and innocent and all the more desirable to me, I sat a few yards away on a wooden milk-bottle crate and watched her look uncomplicated. It was a happy time, not sniffing motives and sensing needs, but just watching someone be at ease and therefore being easy too. The light was dim, the loft was chilly but not uncomfortable, the smell of shrimp had more or less subsided, and outside there was little noise of traffic. I felt as though we might be somewhere else.

"Did you ever read *Robinson Crusoe*, Rhona?"

She looked up, she blinked in confusion, her dark hair shook as she nodded. "Sure. I guess so."

"I read it three times. Made my father cry, I think. I know he really thought about it. I was young, I think I was nine or ten, I read all the time, I guess. You'd have been proud of me, the way I used libraries. I was reading *Robinson Crusoe*," I told her on that gentle evening in our fourth week. "And there was all this wonderful *detail*. You know, he had so many casks for water, and enough gunpowder for so many weeks of hunting and so on. And at one point, before he met Friday, he said he threw his knife down and ran to do something. I don't remember what. I read for a while, and it didn't mention the knife. So I went downstairs and I asked my parents —I remember, my father was reading *Life*. He loves his newspapers and magazines. And I asked them. My mother was doing lesson plans. She was terrifically con-scientious about teaching: vitamins, minerals, muscle tone, all that stuff. And I asked them, and they thought about it, and of course they didn't remember. So I went back upstairs and I looked ahead through the book, then shut the book and listened to the radio instead. There was a Dodgers game, and I was one of those kids who died later on, about six pounds' worth of death, when they left Brooklyn. I never cared about baseball in the same way after they went to L.A. Anyway, the next day I come home from fourth grade, grab the usual snack of thirty or forty Oreos and a quart of milk, then walk over to 12th and J, up to the old library. I take out three other books of *Robinson Crusoe.*"

"And you *quit* graduate school? You stopped doing research?" Rhona said.

"You guessed, huh?"

"You were comparing the editions, yes?"

"To see if there was anything about the knife."

"And there wasn't."

I said, "Nope. So I didn't finish the book. See, I didn't want him running around out there, all over that desert island, with his knife lost."

"Is that anal compulsion, Zimmer?"

"It's being afraid of losing things, Rhona," and my voice was that larded with jest, I think. "You know, of getting lost and losing things and being unprotected. It's probably not about books at all, and it's probably all about being endangered. Vulnerable."

And just as I had hoped—I didn't realize it as a hope until I watched her eyes while I spoke—she loved me for my fearfulness. Like Othello wooing with his stories of danger in savage places, I was a contemporary neurotic, seducing my girl, again, with stories of ineptitude and bookishness and fear. Her eyes were huge with affection, and I felt as though I'd won something and, enjoying such triumph, I realized that we had a good deal, Rhona and I, to lose.

And weeks later, having lived together and ferreted one another's needs and secrets, and having given a great deal up for, and over to, the other person in the sprung mattress on the floor of the Varick Street loft, we made ready to hunt the blind man from the Iron Guard.

We dressed for the event as though for a social evening. I wore my most emphatically Ivy League clothes:

khaki chino trousers, polished penny loafers (no tassels), thick blue wool socks, a blue buttondown broadcloth shirt, a maroon crew neck; over them all I wore my father's graduate-school-admission gift, a Burberry trench coat. And Rhona: she shamed me, as so often she succeeded in doing, and she made me feel, once more, separate from the group-of-two, the alliance I always felt we nearly were capable of forming. She dressed in dark-brown tights, first of all. When I saw the tights slide up her thighs, I felt as though I saw an old woman in her intimacies. She wished to be older than I, that night, and she was succeeding. I felt no desire, only embarrassment for each of us. She put on oxford shoes with laces and flattish heels; they were scuffed, and instead of polishing them, she had covered their wounds with the brown liquid dye which mothers put on children's shoes in grade school. The Nazis were going to bring us together, I wanted to tell her, but they made us separate people—they *proved* us separate people. Over it all, then, a horrible brown corduroy dress that went almost to her ankles in a swollen A-shape from the waist, and which fit her torso like a shirt with bunched shoulders, and sleeves to the wrist. It looked as if made for doing penance, or changing bandages in slum hospitals. The color, right for her rich skin, still seemed somehow wrong. The cloth was scuffed, like her shoes, and with her dark eyes, and with the refusal of the dress to fit her body, she looked—yes, I saw it clearly under the buzzing lights of the former shop in my Varick Street loft: she looked like an immigrant Jew-child in the New World. Worse still: she looked like an overgrown, exaggerated photographic Jew-child, the one seen wearing a yellow armband in a Prague street, say, or in front of the stables at Lidice, just before they fire the guns. She wore her old melton cape over that costume. And we were ridiculous: the Ivy League wonder and the victimized Jew. We didn't speak. Not touching, the Old World and the New walked over to Irving Place through first-of-November winds. Though our teeth chattered, we acted unmindful of the cold.

It was seven o'clock, by then, and Fourteenth was uncrowded. Car lights gleamed on the street, still wet from early rain which had stopped by then. Stores were closed, many of them barred for the night with expansible brass gratings, and despite the flow of cabs from the FDR Drive I felt as though that section of the city were deserted. It wasn't. A very short Hispanic man wearing a large child's costume—fluorescent skeleton painted on a plastic one-piece suit of black—staggered eastward toward us.

"Hey, baby," he said, pausing to lean against a plate glass window behind us as we turned to look. The window said Invisible Mending. His face was smooth and pale, his clipped mustache waxed or dyed so that it gleamed even in the darkness of the orange light which dripped from the old iron street lamp at the curb. "Hey," he said, "trick oh fuckin' *treat.*"

"Hey," I said.

He said, "Hey."

I said, "We'll take the treat."

He slid around the corner of Invisible Mending so that he stood in the shop's alcove, sunk between its two protruding display windows. From the darkness there, he called, "Hey, *wha?*"

I said, "You told us trick or treat. I said we'd rather have the treat."

Rhona said, "Zimmer, we don't have time for this. He'll either vomit on us or hold us up. Come on."

The skeleton loomed, began to glow in the oily light from the curb, and then it writhed. It shuddered and flexed, bending, reaching, mewing with discomfort and then crowing triumph: "Hah!" the Hispanic skeleton cried. "You wanna treat, you gonna receive you *treat!* Dig on it, Anglo!"

And there he stood, at the edge of Invisible Mending, a baby-faced mustachioed Halloween skeleton, 24 hours late and drunk as anyone could be while still walking— or just plain crazy and therefore, in all probability, the happiest man just then on Fourteenth Street. He stood, between darkness and light, offering us our treat: a fairly standard example of the human penis, shaking up and down in his bright hand, the organ and the organ which held it both white in the night, but not so luminescent as the painted bones on dark cloth above them. *"Treat!"* he called again. He was wasting Rhona's time, though.

She stepped forward from behind me, made as though to study what he offered, then looked the skeleton in its hidden eyes and said, loudly, "Interesting. It looks just like a penis, only smaller." The skeleton gripped itself and stared, and we walked away.

At the killer's house, we did some lurking. Irving Place was deserted-feeling too, except for the night-lights in the closed luncheonette, which made me feel less alone than I would have with only Rhona nearby. For she was silent, she was clicking her teeth, she was walking in tight little patterns on the sidewalk in her refugee's cloak and jumper. She was a figure by now, a dark shape in dark-ness, a bright face in the brightness of a passing car's lights. But she wasn't Rhona, I thought. I thought that I would remember her when I was miles and months away. *Then,* I would sense the moment of her wakening, and I would waken too. *Then,* I would feel her body as it worked in her sleep. And *then*, I would know what long tracks she rode upon, old trolley tracks down a crazy street designed by someone too large and thoughtless for the arrivals and departures of little people like us: it went from her mother who wore the skin of someone who had died, to her father who preached and chattered at the darkness until it held away a while, to her, that night, in love with death and hating death and seeking vengeance and a God one of whose names, if there had to be one, ought (I thought) to have something to do with comfort, or love.

I was thinking of a blind old man who pissed at a wall in Macy's while I studied his prick. I was thinking of Lefty, in a steam of bad shrimp, while he told sad jokes about Jews. I was thinking of Rhona, at her library or in our shared bed, or in the lobby of the Eighth Street Theater, snorting when the tall pale girl offered espresso as a favor to the groundlings. She had replied, demurely, "Just a glass of saliva, please."

I took two giant steps to catch up with her as she walked to the basement entrance and brought her hand up in a sideways fist—the famous knock in the night—to hammer at the wooden door.

There was no reply. To the right of the door, outside the arch supporting the first-floor entrance steps under which we stood, were two narrow windows with metal bars, painted brown like the brownstone, to keep the neighborhood Visigoths away. Between the vertical bars, and then between the horizontal slats of the venetian blinds, I saw two lights, or lighted rooms, go out. And then, a knock of the door later, a tiny argument or change-of-mind later, the two lights went on, and then a light behind the small barred window of the door at which we stood, and then, in a sweep of violent resignation, the heavy door opened in and the panting wife stood before us.

She did her best to loom protectively, but though she was tall, she was frail, and her bony body, swaddled as it was in a hooded dark-blue sweatshirt and dark-gray skirt, woollen stockings and fur-lined slippers, looked meager. She could not protect herself, much less her house and husband. Her arm fell from the door, and she said, "We thought that it was you. Because you never will forget us, you decide. So. Now?"

"The Nazi," Rhona said, looking at the floor as if embarrassed. Then she looked up and raised her voice: "The Nazi."

And the old woman raised her arm from her side and jabbed a crooked forefinger at us, holding the finger in the air at the end of the gesture. "There you are," she said in a thin voice, angry as much as frightened. "There. You should one day see yourselfs."

"Actually, my friend meant Iron *Guard*, I think," I simpered.

Her face changed. The hooded flesh above the eyes stretched upward, the bony sockets themselves seemed to withdraw. Her eyes, huge now, lightened and glowed. Her mouth was an O. She hung her head to the right, like a dog watching the movements of a leaf in gusts of wind. "Wait," she said, motioning us forward as she limped into the darkness at the back of her foyer. She paused to look, this time in a bird's manner, neck so stiff she seemed to have been frozen while we watched; she turned her torso around so that her eyes might hook us: "*Wait*, I say!" she called, gesturing us to follow.

So I pushed Rhona forward—she was planted, I remember, and might have stayed there for hours, caught in her life—and I closed the door behind us and we followed as the tall old woman limped, offering glimpses of a brace beneath the long skirt, while we turned too many corners for a small apartment, walking short corridors in each of which she turned on single lights. We went past dark paintings or prints hung at face-level, past lace constructions framed under glass, silhouettes cut out in black paper and pasted on paper turning ivory with age. There was a jetton, I think, nailed onto the wall, and next to it what looked like a New York subway token, and many colors of ticket stub, and photographs of cities I knew I'd never been to, and a small triangular metal vase holding dried grasses on the wall, and a small shelf bearing a tiny white statue of a seated woman. Rhona shuffled, and I kept my hand on her back.

And then the living room: it was small, and though she had lighted it—two globular glass lamps on wooden stands, one lamp an inverted brass vase with a great white shade above it, all glowing, and all nevertheless somehow accentuating the darkness of the room, the textures of the dark. The sofa was framed in a grotesque turning of wood in which every fruit I knew, from pineapples to guavas, seemed to be carved. It was covered with a dark, and possibly blue, velvet-looking material which in turn was littered with six or seven pillows, some of the material of which crawled with amoebae and seemed to be from India or Burma, and some with the grave dark prints of France. In front of the sofa was a basic American coffee table, shaped like a tombstone, glowing with synthetic grains. Straight-backed chairs with carved legs stood against the wall, a long table at one short wall was covered with books and with what seemed to be photograph albums, and a curiously high typewriter. There was a sculpted model of the Globe theater, a map of Russia, a picture of what was clearly a city hall in someplace distant and Balkan-looking, and there were reproductions of paintings—a Rembrandt self-portrait with his mildly alarmed and disappointed heavy face, a Turner of Venice, and a photograph of coal lighters on the Thames. A record player in several aluminum parts stood, hooked by wires, under the table, connected to high speakers. There were stacks of record albums—mostly operas, it appeared. There was a wall of books, the shelves seemed to explode with books, and most of the title I could read seemed not to be in English. There was barely room for the sofa and the scattered chairs, I saw, and the one or two ornate end tables on which the lamps sat as they disturbed but didn't solve the darkness.

"He will come," the old woman said. "I will fetch him, and then he will come. Please pause." She left the room. Rhona didn't speak. We had come to the point of whole separatedness, I knew. I thought we might not see each other after this—whatever *this* might be—unless something wonderful happened. What, for us, in such a puzzle as this, might something wonderful be?

"Rhona?"

"What?"

"Is the sofa as uncomfortable as it looks?"

"Now how would I know that, stupid?"

"Rhona, you're sitting on it."

I heard her clothing rustle as she studied herself and where she was.

"I don't know. I don't feel anything, Zimmer."

"Well, you're confused, probably. Probably you're having a lot of emotions all at the same time."

"My *body* is numb. It isn't working. I can't feel my legs."

"Suggestion. She's lame, he's blind, you're just getting in on the act."

"Zimmer."

"What?"

"Don't be glib."

"I'm not being glib. I'm being nervous. I've never helped anyone hunt anyone down. And because of us, also."

"I don't want to talk about us now. Don't trivialize this. There's time for soap opera later."

"Certainly," I said with cold dignity.

"Sir," the old lady's voice said from the doorway around one of its corners, "lady and sir, may I present my husband for who you have been thinking you are hunted—hunting, I mean. I present my husband. They are a young man and a young woman. He is like anyone you see in the street but broad and with spectacles and peculiar eyes. She is—she is a type I cannot name yet. Handsome, surely. Both dedicated, the girl more than the boy. I do not know to what." She led him to a straight-backed chair and he sat with poise. He was giving us an audience. In his brown suit and brown shoes and bright orange tie on a tan shirt, he was receiving supplicants. I saw that his socks matched his outrageous tie, and I thought of her selecting them for him. Then I guessed that the typewriter cut Braille into those large stacked books, and I saw her typing for him every day so that he could read with his fingers as once—I looked at the leaking shelves—he had read with his eyes. I was very uncomfortable. For, while it was wholly possible that Nazis and their spouses helped each other with Braille rather than eat one another's entrails, there was simply too much musty devotion here, and to decent things, for them to be bad. Though *that* particular perception was responsible for a lot of dead Jews being stacked like firewood, I reminded myself. I got tough. I sat on the edge of my chair. I waited for the criminal to speak as I looked at his face, which had always only been a nose and closed eyes beneath an unseasonable hat. Up close, the skin of his face was a baby's. There were lines, and deep ones, to be sure, at the corners of the mouth and eyes. There were deep tracks connecting lips to nose —peculiarly vertical, so that the center of his face was in parentheses. His lips looked soft and full. His flesh looked somehow oiled; it glowed with good health. I felt that I was looking at a happy man. I envied his health, I resented his happiness. And I knew that he had never called the police out on us, his pursuers, because he had come to feel proud of his courage. She believed in danger, I thought, while he believed in the virtues that danger might bring.

With his right hand, he reached confidently to the drawer of a side-table. He withdrew a candy bar—Suchard's Milk Chocolate. He stared to where blind people look. His thin fingers with their long nails slit the wrappings and offered them on a palm. She took the papers. He ate. We waited. I thought of my father's pre-college advice. I thought of people starving in the camps. I wouldn't know her anymore, I thought, when we were outside of this apartment.

His beaky nose and hooded brow came up, as if he sniffed the air. Behind him was a *menorah!* I gestured, smiling for the wife, but moving my nose for Rhona. I pointed again with my characterless nose toward the candelabrum on a shelf behind the blind fascist. But his wife's eyes fairly drew blood from across the room: she thought I was mimicking the blind man's questing motion. And Rhona didn't notice me at all. She studied the old man as if hypnotized. I wondered if she were beginning to suspect that the apartment was littered with the valuables of Jews he'd sent to death.

His high reedy voice said, "You pursue me. I feel you in the street. I hear you, the woman, in the library, when I sit."

"*My* library," she cried. "Mine, where I work. What right does a blind man to have to sit in a library filled with books that you read with your *eyes?*"

"In the United States," the old man called back impatiently, but with little strength of lung, "it is permitted that the blind may read books they cannot see if that is their wish. This is called the Bill of Rights. Blindness is not a crime."

"Criminals can hide behind blindness," she said. She had rehearsed, I realized. "The blindness is a redoubt and no longer privileged."

The old man said, "Pardon?"

She stumbled, he had broken her rhythm of accusation and reply, parry and riposte. "You—huh? Wait!"

But his patience had cracked, and why should it not have? "I am an author. I have been privileged to write elegantly in Rumanian and speak what was called an almost flawless French. It is proper that I sit in libraries, because I am a man of language. And I add this thought: I should sit on a bench in the wind and let dogs and teenage hoodlums urinate on my shined shoes? *You* try being sightless."

She was frightened into haste, I realized. She had evidently rehearsed the building-up of the case against our fascist, though why she bothered to reason with the unreasonable I didn't, I still don't, understand. If you try doing that, you might as well pray: same impulse, same result. The night still falls.

But her mouth was working, her eyes were blinking, her knees jerked, her shoulders quaked, and she said, in her loudest voice, "Of all the fascist states, of all the countries in mittel-Europe, Rumania was the most viciously repulsive in its anti-Semitism."

He nodded impatiently, sucking at chocolate on his teeth. He moved his cane. He raised his nose. She hadn't paused. She wasn't seeing him.

"The Iron Guard broke their windows, closed their shops, they couldn't work, you didn't *let* them work. The beatings! In the street, humiliations, crawling in spit! And book-burnings, oh yes. And you ran them over, you shot them, you burst in their doors, you were in *heat!* And you *killed* them!

"So we followed you. *Certainly* we followed you! Some evidence turned in to the Immigration people, and you're out of the country. Maybe in jail. For life. I smell the smoke from their burned bodies. Don't you? I smell their vomit from cholera in the camps—the ones you let live. Don't you? I hear them *cry!* Don't you? You are a monster. You are a monster. You are never to be forgiven. You are evil in the world, snakes in the city, everyone must *crush* you now that Andreoscu has proven who you are!"

I looked away. As it was, I mourned to hear her. Only secular, only civilian, I mourned, for myself, for having lost her to history.

The old man made a squealing sound. His mouth opened and remained open. He squealed again, as if Rhona had suddenly struck him. He placed his arms across his chest in a parody of pharaoh, in a need for self-defense. His wife's mouth opened too, replicating the little hole which opened in her husband's face. And then I saw that it was laughter, not pain, which came from his mouth, and from the wife's as well. He clutched himself in delight.

I watched. I saw Rhona's poor earnest face working,

the eyes dark now with unhappiness and fright, embarrassment, bewilderment. She was a picture of someone trying to hurt herself. Her mouth moved, her teeth shone white, her tongue danced on the dark air of the Balkan room, and in her dowdy brown jumper and shabby fat shoes she was ugly enough to need me once more. I would have married her that night, moved her to someplace strange—say, Omaha or Albany—and started us up in a luncheonette, playing Muzak all day in the greasy restaurant so that her brain was too bothered by noise to boil itself among the dying and the dead.

The old man stopped laughing. His wife's profoundly relieved guffaw slid across Rhona's last word—of course, it was "Jews"—and then there was silence. I clasped my hands hard, as if I were at the dentist, under torture, or in a synagogue, bursting with sex. "I am Andreoscu," the old man said gently, almost comfortingly, and with perhaps a tone of possible apology for what he did to her. "I am the one who asked of your colleague at the library that she obtain my book. How else would such a neglected volume appear? Months, it took her. You did not know? I hoped someone would wish to peruse it, I confess."

She said, "What was—who?"

"I am Andreoscu. I am the man. I am an author, my dear, before I am a Rumanian or a refugee Jew. So: what do I do? I sit in the nearest library, and I wait for someone to ask for my book. I am not *much* of a Jew anymore, I must confess. His Highness's delightful amusement at the persecution of His people has somewhat taken away my pleasure in bending an old knee, His Highness might like to hear a bone creak now and then. But I am, I believe, what you might consider *drôle conte*—a joke. I am the story about the blind Jew who sits in the library, hating His Highness when I bother to think of Him at all, waiting for somebody to ask for my book in which I give a detailed exposition of how the fascists tortured me and mine for being Jews. This His Highness would appreciate. He is a big-deal comedian, yes? It was printed in London, as you perhaps have noticed, by devoted fools who fled like me and Gretchen here." She raised her head and nodded. We were being introduced.

"Rhona Glinsky," I said, pointing to her.

"Zimmer, shut *up!*" Rhona whispered, she was as pale as I had seen her, and more stricken. She was being devastated.

"So," Andreoscu said, "this is why I have been followed into the large apartment store. *D*epartment store. And through the underground, down the streets, out of passageways and into the backs of little shops?" He nodded. He nodded again. "So," he said. And I couldn't tell whether he was speaking with rage or humor, or if they had to be separate.

"We thought it was because we were Jews," Mrs. Andreoscu said. "You see? We thought, again it happens. It *could* happen in America. Who knows? Your Ku Kuggel—the fascists who hate Negroes? It could happen anyplace, I think. And so, two old Jews with three good legs and two eyes that are working: we were frightened, you will understand. I at least was."

In a dead voice, in a voice filtered through a mouth filled with pebbles and mud from the grave, Rhona said, "This is a joke."

I'm afraid I nodded. Gretchen Andreoscu nodded too. And the author smiled. He said, "Exactly. Now." He folded his hands and settled his head on his neck, composed his blind face. His face was like a bird on a perch

—restless, then still. "Now," he said. "Now that we know what is what, we should asking—"

"Ask," Gretchen said.

He said, "Yes. We might say: what we have learned from you? From this." He plucked his cane up and swung it urgently before him. His face knotted, then smoothed.

"Gently," Gretchen said.

"So?" he asked.

Gretchen said, "Wait."

He knew, as I did, that she meant for him to go on, so he did. He stood, and he leaned the backs of his legs at the chair. Again, he prodded the dark air of the dark room with his extended cane. Rhona stood too, in her immigrant's costume, with her fine broad shoulders high and gathered, as if she cowered, or as if she would make herself small. He thundered, a theatrical professor in a European classroom: "What you have *learned!*"

Her face was like a bone. It gleamed, all its life stripped off. Her eyes were huge. I waited for her to speak of her mother. She swallowed the dead air stuck in her throat. In the museum of the blind author, whose days were spent in listening to a library's patrons talk of books, and maybe one day his, she swallowed again and clamped her teeth. I saw her jaws grind. She kept, as some might call it, her peace.

"Would cocoa be useful?" Gretchen gently inquired.

"I am sorry," Rhona said.

Andreoscu said, "That is happy."

"I *am.*"

"So. Very happy."

"Sorry."

"Happy. Thank you."

"Sorry."

"Yes."

I did the most I could—put her cloak on her shoulders, walked her through the dark little corridors and, eventually, out. Behind us, the cane scraped, a foot dragged. Rhona didn't sob or heave. She walked like someone wounded. "Thank you!" I called as we left.

That did it. On Irving Place, in shock, in disappointment, humiliation—in the throes of an undeniable joke, and undeniably its chief fool, and nearly its inventor— she said, low and lethal, "Thank you for what?"

"Form," I said. "You just say that."

"Oh. And loyalty?"

"What?"

"You have no loyalty?"

"Rhona—we've been persecuting Jews here!"

"You dare—"

"I spied on his cock in *Macy's*, Rhona."

"You *dare*."

"We should've put a little sweater on his dick, you know? A dark little—black little sweater, maybe. Then we could pin a little yellow star on it, right? A cockband."

"You *bastard*," she said, walking from me.

I caught up with her around the corner and tried to hold her arm. The cloak disguised her body, though, and I couldn't find limbs. I pushed, I pulled, we both stumbled, and in front of Invisible Mending I fell to one knee. I stayed that way. She stayed erect. When she spoke, I was laughing too hard to hear.

She moved backward, her face changing, and the Hispanic skeleton, slightly late for Halloween, but timely nevertheless, came forward to shine his chemical bones.

I felt the laughter dribble out, then stop. I pointed at him, but turned to look up at Rhona. I remember that I screamed. I screamed, "That's what you love! That's what you love! That's what you love!"

And because it was an opera, she extended both hands through the cloak, and her fingers writhed at me. I saw her mother's hands. Her face was broken.

The ghost of Invisible Mending said, "Trick oh fuckin treat, man."

"Young lady," Andreoscu called, walking around the corner into sallow light, following his cane. "Young lady: from shame and guilt comes a little wisdom, sometimes. Come. You are a librarian. Come. Talk a little bit with an author."

He marched toward Invisible Mending, his cane and free hand extended, his brown suit black in the night. Clanking her iron brace, at least I thought I heard its noise, Gretchen turned the corner, tugging her crippled leg toward us.

"This ain't *nooo* treat," the skeleton announced, retreating into the darkness of Invisible Mending's alcove.

So there I was: Halloween (a day late) became, eighteen years later, late October but nothing so awesome or dramatic as Halloween—just a day in autumn, with Sam very pale, eight years old, tall and sturdy and with Lillian's Norwegian bones rounding out the flesh beneath his eyes, and with what must have been my dark stare sitting above those cheekbones, and with the sort of question you wish they wouldn't ask as your wife moves you out of the apartment and down to a waiting cab: "Do we still get to have Christmas, Daddy?"

He cried, then, and hugged Lillian and stuck his head into her belly. She cried too, and pulled him into her. May I say that I was also broken by his voice, a little hoarse as it was, yet still the voice of my baby? I knew the wisdoms about man as a creature who was always alone. And in the books we'd discussed at our Tuesday editorial meetings—eagles in the sky, homosexuals on the ground, all the available literary solitudes in between

—I had surely found some dandy metaphors. But there was nothing like that question, in that voice, emerging from that face. He was my baby.

I said, "Honey, I'll see you very soon. I love you." I'm certain I said it. To me, it sounded as though someone had thrown gravel onto a rooftop, or a coffin, or simply at the window of a passing car. To me, it sounded like something to do with dying. But Sam, ever polite, aware always that fathers need attention too, made sure to nod his head while burrowing at Lillian. We stood in the harsh winds of a Saturday morning in October in New York. We stood beside an old-fashioned, high-roofed Checker cab, bright orange-yellow in a day of orange and yellow and green leaves that were driven through the air. Above us, there was a high sky of murky blue. The wind smelled of gasoline and diesel fuel and all the stone of which the city had been built—it was pretty clean, and so were we, in our Saturday sweaters and casual slacks and desert boots. And there was the luggage. And here, around us, the city was having its Saturday, and over us the sky was satisfactory for walking beneath, if you could hold one another's hand, or be in love, or not be forced away, or have, that moment, at least something in your life that you required. "See you soon, darling," I said to Sam or Lillian or both of them. The cab held two suitcases and one camp trunk we'd carried with us since we were married. We had bought it in Macy's to use as a coffee table and a place to put our winter clothes, in moths balls, when summer came to New York. We had often dined on scrambled eggs and the fumes of camphor, and I still smelled the camphor in the cab. The driver, as we bucked downtown and were passing City Center, smelled something too. He asked me if I smelled gas.

"What, in New York? On Broadway? Gas?"

"Oh, sorry," he said, with no malice.

"Are you writing a book?" I said.

"No. I'm driving a cab."

"No," I said, "it's just that a lot of people who drive cabs nowadays are also trying to be writers. I thought maybe I could be of some help to you." I noticed that the back of his neck had those diamond-shaped wrinkles I used to think, when I was a boy, only occurred on the necks of old Italian construction workers.

"Hey," he said, "you sound like a nice guy. But"—his thumb pointed over his shoulder, over his seat, through the bulletproof glass which separated us, and over my shoulder, and my seat, and the glass behind me—"who's gonna help *you?* If you'll pardon me for asking."

"Oh," I said, "that. Listen. It's temporary. It's just a marital dispute. Family strife is all it is."

"Okay, mister. You're the fare," he said. "But couldn't you say, if you don't mind me saying it, that World Wars I and II and Korea and Vietnam and the Reds dropping into Afghanistan was your basic strife?"

I said, "You know, I really don't need this shit right now. You know that?"

"You're the fare."

"Stop the cab."

"You mean it?"

"Stop the cab."

He did. He said nothing more. We sat at the curb on Broadway and about 59th. I pushed the locking button down. The driver, activating it with a lever in the front, raised the button. The woman opened the door and held it for me.

"I'm not sure I'm leaving," I told the woman. She wore dark glasses, the red frames of which matched the color of her raincoat and her lipstick and, I saw, her fingernails and leather-and-canvas bag. She had fat ankles in red shoes, and her cheeks were puffy, downed with dark hair, well-rouged.

"He's having a domestic crisis," the cabby said.

"I'm having a luncheon party, and I have to get to Mamaroneck," the woman said. "In or out?"

I said, "I'll give you a lift downtown."

"I don't want to go to downtown," she said. "I want to get to Grand Central Station."

"Too far east for me," I lied.

"*I* don't mind," the cabbie said. The meter ground and clicked, the little numbers rolled up, and the cab shook in place at the curb.

"I don't know if I want anyone in here with me," I told the woman, as frankly and unaffectedly as I knew how. "I was going to get out of the cab because this man, at least as far as I can tell, feeling the way I did a few minutes ago, was overstepping the bounds of—well, just bounds, really. And he was telling me—"

"His old lady kicked him out," the cabby said. His face was lean and pointy, the nose descending to a rising upper lip, the skin a bumpy red—he matched the woman's raincoat, I thought—and his eyes were intelligent, superior, amused. His voice was kind, though. He was relieving the boredom of what was just another day. "It's a marital dispute," he said. "But he don't think it's hopeless. He don't want it to be. He's very upset. I'm pretty sure we'll be proceeding, ma'am."

"I think you're both crazy," she said.

"Yes," I said. "Possibly. This is difficult."

"Bye, ma'am," the cabbie said, and she dutifully slammed the door. "You ready?" he called over his shoulder as he looked in his side mirror and pulled out. With his lever he relocked the doors.

I nodded. He wasn't looking at me. He was taking me

away from Lillian and Sam to the Tudor Hotel. He seemed to know what to do. So I just rode. And there I was, eight years before, the very excited Lillian Zimmer phoning the office to ask me if I had read my morning's *Times*. I told her no. She told me that in a little AP piece there was a story about a Klan rally outside Cooperstown. Since we each had certain proprietary interests in Cooperstown, and not only because Lillian was already planning to go there for the July induction of Reggie Jackson, in no matter which year that event might transpire, we discussed with dismay that such a pretty place could be the scene of such ugliness.

"It was almost funny, I think," she said. "They announced this thing in all the upstate papers, apparently, and nearly nobody came. They had thirty beer-brains there, with sheets and crosses and heaven knows what else. It seems, from the article, that there were more state policemen than demonstrators for *or* against it. Isn't that *awful*? That nobody *cares*?"

"There's this dreadful Sinclair Lewis novel," I told her. "It's called, *It Won't*—no: *It Can't Happen Here*. About fascists taking over America. It scared the hell out of me when I was a kid, I remember."

Her voice broke. I mean, it absolutely started out on one plane, then cracked like a piece of pinewood, and then continued at a lower level. "I know," she said. She kept saying it. "I know. I know. That's why I'm so frightened, all of a sudden."

"Oh, Lil," I said. "Don't be scared." Like a man who knows nothing recent about fear basically because he hasn't been frightened during the last few days, I became pompous, I'm afraid, and patronized the woman to whom I spoke. "There isn't anything to be—Lil, for heaven's sakes. The KKK has about as much chance in New York. Lil? Are you listening? There isn't *any*—"

"There is," she said. "There always is. You know that. Take a little subway ride late at night and tell me about the world. Look at Richard *Nixon*. It can always happen. It always *wants* to happen. The only place where you can run to, in the entire *world*, I'm saying, is Israel."

"Israel?"

"Come on," she said. She nearly was shouting at me. "You've heard of it. Home for the Jews? Remember? That's why there has to *be* an Israel, so if somebody decides to really do the KKK right, you can run there. And take me along. But I don't know if they would let you do that. But you can go there guaranteed. It's called the Law of Return. Right? I went to the library before I came in. It's called the Law of Return."

Naturally, I said—my mouth said it, my pancreas, my sub-brain; I insist that I, myself, did not—I said, "Rhona!"

Lillian said, "What?"

"Whoa, now," I said. "I said, 'Whoa, now.' Slow down, Lil."

"And we're going to have a baby," she continued. "And what kind of a place, with the KKK upstate, are we bringing a kid into? And what if there *is* some kind of trouble? You know what the Law of Return says?"

"Lil? A baby?"

"It says the mother has to be Jewish. Did you know that, stupid?" She was shouting. And I'm afraid that all I was able to do was say her name again.

"Lil?"

"You really have to think about this," she said.

So I did the other thing I do well: I shouted. "Lil!"

"What?"

"Congratulations to us."

"Thank you. I mean—"

"I love you," I said.

"Ditto."

"And the fascists won't get us."

"Big talk from the Jews. Ask the KKK if the fascists will get us, then you can tell me."

"You know," I said, "you're beginning to sound more Jewish than anyone I know."

There was a bit of silence, and then Lillian's usual voice—low, firm, and from the throat and quite provocative: "I'm a Jewess by injection," she said.

"Would you care to meet for a little midday injection back at the apartment? Hey! You can *do* that when you're pregnant, can't you? Without hurting anything? And when the hell is it *due*? And is it normal? Are you? Will you *tell* me?"

And she said—and I could have predicted that she would: our domestic politics were of the most exciting sort, one always depending on the weakness of the other for a surge of strength—"Calm down," she said, "calm down."

That afternoon, at one o'clock, we asked for the room I had reserved by telephone at the Waldorf. We made love during the afternoon at the hotel which hosted Richard Nixon during his New York affairs of state. Afterward, she laughed herself into hysterics over my insistence on bringing a large attache case, which I had filled with old proofs, make-believe baggage of respectability. In later years, I grew more sophisticated about the midday use of hotels, and I came to travel light.

*I*f only life had chapters in it! Then, between the madness off Irving Place, with Hispanic Halloween skeletons swearing and slinking, and Rhona crying out to me and to her mother's life and her own, and with me laughing like a frightened fool, and with the Andreoscus coming toward us out of the darkness, dragging braces and swinging a white cane, the Jewish joke personified (or was that me?), then I'd have only to jump to the next chapter and tell myself that Rhona had left me, it was over, I was alone.

But what really happened was that I stopped laughing, because it wasn't funny anymore. It really hadn't been more than sad, ridiculously sad, and while sadness deserves some laughter too, it called for less than I had offered. The Andreoscus stood a few feet away from us, listening—I saw that the author's wife had closed her eyes, as if to perceive this night as her husband would, no less, no more. Rhona stopped making noises. The drunken skeleton walked away from us, and from Invisible Mending, and he disappeared, as minor characters must. We were left with the scrape of passersby avoiding us, and the drift of lights up 14th Street, and the TV sets above us in apartments, the windows of which had opened when we all began to scream. We were left with embarrassment, the sting of our recent interview—my face still hurt because I'd been clamping my jaws so hard —and with each other. I held my hand out, she accepted it. Her hand was moist. Her face was moist. It was blurry; the interior tensions of mind controlling nerves, tightening muscles, all had let go—with the loss of her ideas, she had lost her face. It was the same general face, of course, on the same general Rhona. But its slackness made her look unfocused, as if her skin tone and tautness were the product of how I saw her, not who she was.

But she took my hand, she walked with me to the curb, she stood with her side touching mine while our backs were to our former quarry and his wife—the end of another New York literary evening. Rhona did not speak. She sagged against me when we sat in the taxi. "Goodnight, young lady. Do not be too unhappy. At least you paid attention! Good night," the author called to us. "Good night!"

The driver didn't know where Varick Street was. That was when Rhona began to cry again. The cab smelled of cigars and rum and wet cloth. The driver was unapologetic, very tired, and unsympathetic. I told him to turn onto Seventh Avenue, and to follow it past the Village as it became Seventh Avenue South.

"There is no Seventh Avenue South, thank you," he said.

His accent was Balkan. I was afraid to ask if he were Rumanian, because I feared that Rhona would attack him. "Take my word for it," I told him.

"Very well," he said, turning up Brahms on the radio. "I will take your word for it."

"Thank you."

"You are welcome."

He showed no surprise when I proved to him by virtue of our arrival that there actually was a Varick Street in Manhattan. By then the night was very cold, very dark, very wet, and Varick Street was deserted. He was anxious to be away from our block, and he accepted too much money with no demurral. Rhona had made something of an attempt to get into her handbag to pay, but she hadn't gone hysterical on the subject of independence. The independence—not hysteria, though—emerged again as a vital subject, once we were upstairs and had changed into jeans and sweaters and were drinking the sweet tea I had brewed.

Rhona sat on the wooden milk crate, her legs protruding unbent, crossed at the ankle. Her feet were in old, soft half boots, and she looked very . . . equipped. From the way she wore her fresh jeans and thick woollen white turtleneck, I knew that she was going to make something happen. But first she had to speak. With Rhona and me, while it was hardly all talk between us, there was much that depended on words.

"Zimmer," she said.

I was leaning on a wall—the usual New York illegal loft wall, half chalky plaster with cracks, half stamped tin. I stood straight and away from the wall, and made ready. I knew that I was going to receive.

"Zimmer, I've been a pretty big jerk. All that fascist shit. You were seeing through me half of the time. Was I doing it more than half of the time? I don't want to know. Never mind. Look: I really made myself believe he was a fascist. You knew I didn't get the book translated. I did believe it was him—I really did. I halfway did. Sometimes. You knew that, and I counted on your generosity. You've been a generous man."

If I'd been Rhona, my face would have been flaming. I think, as it was, that I stood with a red face beating before her. She looked into my face with her big dark eyes opened wide, as if she were forcing herself to stare and not flinch. And her face was pale, almost blue-white. Her hair looked darker and richer, then, and I thought that I could smell her skin, the warm and perfumed smell I was used to, during the best of our pleasure, at the end of a day. That made me as sad as her pain did, and our mutual humiliation.

"I went after you," she said, "because I wanted you. I kept after you because you were worth keeping after. And—this is true: it wasn't just your silly stumpy body I wanted, though I did. I was thinking about—all right," she sighed, as if she had to confess something awful— "your soul. You could be a Jew, Zimmer. You really could."

I tried to smile for her—smile of thanks, of eagerness to be a Jew who was saved for the service of the Lord. But it was a terrible smile. It was merely the bones of my mouth showing. Her face in response told me that.

"So I did a great deal of play-acting, for myself and for you." There were tears in her eyes, but they didn't come out. I had never seen her hold them there. By accident of surface tension or by force of will, they collected, and they stayed in place. Her eyes glowed and the light in them shimmered; she didn't blink, and no tears ran from her face. "I did a lot of pretending. I also didn't pretend. You understand? I did a lot of just being—true." That last word came out small, and her voice, from this point on, was hard for her to control; she worked on it, though. "I made love to you because I wanted to do that. Also, and it's true, because I was hoping to use my terrific crotch to lure you over to the Jews' God. It's our training—some of us are temple whores." We both smiled bones at each other. "For the lies, or the pretending, the whatever—thank you, and I apologize. For the rest of it, just thank you."

I lifted my forgotten mug of tea, and I was about to respond, though with what words I cannot imagine. But she stopped me. For what she'd said had not been the point, apparently—not without what had to come next.

"But for what you did tonight," she said, "I cannot thank you. Almost, but not quite, you were wonderful, superior, a man among men. Nearly. At the end, in the living room of those people—those refugees, those *zeroes*. There, at the end you abandoned me. And on the street, in that somebody's-nightmare with that silly man who was so drunk and—listen! with your poor girlfriend who was crazy and deluded and hysterical. There you failed, friend Zimmer. You left me alone. You chose between life for Zimmer without trouble, and life with Rhona that was so much pretending and whackies and woes. So: You chose. Life for Zimmer. No more problems. *That* I don't forgive. At the gate to the camp, Zimmer, *the* camp, Auschwitz, with the cute little motto about labor setting them free and *how* free they already suspected, you'd be surprised how many of them suspected. At the *gate*, my beloved, they clung to their children unless they thought that giving them up would save them. At the actual *gate*, in the smell of the dead, the husbands and wives wanted to hold on to one another. This I have read, and heard, and I believe it. And you, in a little panic and craziness and social dilemma and Rhona being strange—you gave me up. Didn't you? You were teaching me a lesson, yes?"

My voice came out with difficulty, and it was low. "I was a bad Jew, Rhona, for one thing. I don't know what a good Jew is now. Not for me. Sometimes I wish I did. I was trying to tell you that you were loving death. You *are*. That's what you think about, you know. Death. People killed in the camps, in the pogroms, in the ghetto fires, in the ovens and furnaces and Zyklon-B showers and in the cattle cars. You love the God of the Jews in the deaths of the Jews. I was saying that. Yes."

"And the laughing? Never mind the infantile notion that to be a Jew is to conveniently forget the history of persecution we were marked and set aside for. Matzoh balls don't make Jews, Zimmer."

"The laughing was sadness," I said, smiling, and thinking of shrimp egg rolls and matzoh balls and how alone I was going to be.

"You laughed because you were sad?"

"I laughed, Rhona, because I knew that we were leaving each other. And because I felt—peculiar. Sometimes, when I'm crazy, I smile a little. You know? You remember?"

"Abandonment, Zimmer." But she nodded, because she did remember.

"If that's what you want to call it."

"I call it what it is. And never mind about dead Jews—I do not require any lectures on dead Jews, thank you."

"Rhona, isn't this *sad*?"

She nodded. The tears worked loose, and then they ran. I turned from her—she had been right, I guess, about our separateness—and I leaned my face against the wall, and I cried too.

Later, I washed my face at the sink while she put some clothes into an overnight bag of mine. "I need your little suitcase for a while, all right?"

"Sure. You have money?"

"Yes," she said, "thank you. Would you walk me to a cab? Or the subway?"

"Maybe a cab, this time of night? Where are you going, by the way?"

"I am not going to Queens, I assure you. I think the Albert Hotel, you know that one?"

"No," I said, "please. Bad choice. It's all whores and bedbugs. I've heard nothing but bad things about it."

"Well, uptown, then? Barbizon for Women? Sixty—what: Sixty-seventh, I think, maybe above that. A cab driver would know."

"It's supposed to be cheap and clean, sure. You have money?"

"I'm fine. Yes." By then we were walking downstairs and I was carrying her bag. She was calm, and so was I, and though I felt the truth of what she'd said about me, I didn't feel more than that justice had been spoken. There wasn't, at least then, the awful weight, along the shoulders, of ruinous self-love. The night was inky and a fine cold mist fell upon us. I suggested that we walk west, to catch the cabs coming uptown, and we strolled, like lovers, the only people there in a city closed down. But of course there wasn't romance between us. There was the phlegm-taste in the mouth, and the relief to be done without harsh talking, and the clear knowledge that in hours, maybe minutes, there would be an intolerable certainty of loss, palpable absence. We encountered no Hispanics in costume, no roving street gangs, nothing like a cab. We said little as we walked. Rhona told me that she would feel better sleeping on her own. I agreed that she was wise to obey such feelings. She told me that she would return, if I had no objections, for her clothing and books, when she was settled. I told her that there was no rush.

And then I saw the cab and whistled. I saw its turn indicator blink as the lighted roof began to drift toward us. I said, "I'll miss—I'll—I am so sorry, Rhona."

"I am too." She smiled. I kissed her eyes. The tears were in there, flooding her mascara, and they were black on my lips, I suppose. We hugged. She patted my back, as if I were a boy, or a sick brother, a friend about to travel. I squeezed her hard, and she squeezed back, our dry mouths cupped with a little suction and then were pulled apart and she went on while I walked back.

I went to work the next morning. I wasn't very good, and typed up and tore the projected titles I'd have expected of me: Treachery Facts and Fancies, I typed, and The Long History of Short Love. I even did some labor —three synopses for a not-yet-existent article on ballroom dancing. My title was You—Dancing in the Dark? Promising greater social achievement and deeper self-confidence, and nearly everything else except untold wealth and curlier hair, I wrote the last sentence: "All told in a story that will have you gliding in the spotlight, instead of stumbling in the dark." I liked that, it was awfully clever, and it would have made, I told myself— or did I tell it years later?—a dandy metaphor for something.

Lefty came upstairs that evening, when I, having come home early from the office because I was exhausted and mired in dismay, was sitting on my milk crate and looking over the wide mattress at Rhona's books and the essential singleness of the bed. Redolent of poisoned crustaceans, carrying with him a bottle of Laird's, Lefty came in. He said, "Your girlfriend came by, did you know that?"

"She was getting some clothes, probably. She still has to come back for the rest."

Lefty stood, so I stood. He looked at the empty coffee cup in my hand. "You want some applejack in there, kid?"

I shrugged, so he poured, and we stood, the resident one-armed bandit and his tenant. "From what she said, it's all over between you guys, huh?"

I nodded.

"It don't do you no good, understand," he said, "but you're a young boy. You'll grow older, and before you get to be too old, you'll meet a woman who will stick by you."

"It's the other way around, Lefty."

He was wearing a brown suede sport coat with the left sleeve pinned up with a giant blanket pin. It matched his brown suede shoes, which were tasseled suede loafers. I thought of my own boyhood browns, and of telling their story to Rhona.

Lefty said, "Listen, I can give you some more cheap advice."

"Thank you," I said. "Thanks. "So—uhm, how's business, Lefty?"

"In New York, you want to make a living, you can do a lot worse than egg rolls. Next to hot dogs, knishes, and soft pretzels, it's a great market. Who don't eat egg rolls?"

"Geez, that's great. Great."

"You want another drink, kid?"

"Lefty, I really don't. You mind? I mean, thank you. You're a friend."

"No, kid, I'm just an acquaintance. All it is, I like you. That's all. You can do better for friends. You'll see. You'll find somebody'll *stick* with you. That's what you want, right? Somebody'll stick."

"Well," I said.

"How bad a shape are you in, kid?"

"Well, I'm not going to die, Lefty. I feel horrible. I feel

bad. I think I'm a bad person. But I'll live. How about that?"

"You want me to hang around a while?"

"I'd really rather be on my own, Lefty. Which seems to be the trouble."

"I can understand that," he said, his bulbous nose moving as, not understanding, he wrinkled his face. "So I'll take off for home, and I'll see you, right? You'll live."

"I will."

"Listen—as long as you live, 'as long as you got your healt, tank got.' You remember, kid? Take it easy."

"I'll take it easy, Lefty. Thank you."

"Because you *will*."

"That's right."

And, all those years later, I was struggling to say to my son, "Sam, Mommy and I have been having some tough times."

He would be wearing jeans and probably those miniature running shoes that go for thirty-five bucks a pop. And I would be all over him, I thought, though striving to seem tranquil and so much less greedy than I really was: rubbing his hair, holding his head, kissing his cheek, and looking into his nearly black but really dark-brown eyes, and rubbing his belly and back, idly swatting his bottom to keep from just holding it. And he would be itchy and bored, I thought, because he would want to be off. Though when he is tired or, especially, ill, he seeks me out. To me, disease is emergency; to Lillian, it's what slows you down until it makes you go to bed until you're better, at which time you get up and get on with your life. He goes to me, in illness, with darkness under his eyes and the fine skin drawn too tight on his face. He asks, almost embarrassed, "Daddy, can I sit on your lap?" And I put my knees together and sit up straight and he climbs on me, knees in my thighs, elbows in my sternum, and turns until he is soft, and breathing at my rhythm. When sick, he grows suddenly warmer, as if permitted, now, on my lap, to be feverish, and he sleeps as I hold him, and as I, sometimes, remember to be grateful—used to, I thought.

I wanted to say, "Sam, Mommy and I have had a kind of—*sickness*, really. We're trying to get better now."

I wanted to go to her office on Pine Street; beg the curious receptionist for admission; stand before the secretary she shares with several other consultants, and say that I *must* see Mrs. Zimmer, and that my name is Gossage—the pitcher on the New York Yankees; watch her office door explode toward me, watch her falter as the baseball fan feels true disappointment, then anger, and wait as the wife, estranged but still wife, grows curious, and then invites me on to further talk.

Would we sit at a restaurant table? Fraunces Tavern or a bar on Whitehall Street? Or would we sit, hands folded, across from one another, at her bright birch conference table, in the glare of downtown Manhattan, in the thump and whistle of ferries and tugboats in New York Harbor?

And could I calmly stand, I wondered, and take my raincoat off, and then my tan suit and blue-striped shirt and maroon-figured necktie? Drop my trousers and hurl them onto her desk? Tear my shorts off? And stand before her, maybe shrunken but also possibly swelling with self-sacrifice and love and lust and need, nobility—God-*damn* and curse forever consciousness!—and say to her, "Lil. I'm still wearing my shoes to make doubly sure I look ridiculous. So you can laugh at me if you want to. Please have me. Please take me back, this is what I am, Lillian. Are you hearing this? Do you see me? Can I offer it? *Lil?*"

Or perhaps, I thought, I could just telephone: Lil, I've been thinking. About us. About life, actually. Let me try and be better for you.

Or, face to face: Lil, I want to be better. I love you.

Or: Lillian, please?

Or: Lil.

I kept on hearing her not answer. I knew her voice and didn't hear it. What if I had truly been hearing Rhona's voice but didn't know it anymore? If a whale could be sent after Jonah, then mightn't Rhona appear, after eighteen years, on a corner of Manhattan where my life and my memories seemed to be having a reunion?

The old mosaic threatened, my vision started to break into the little fragments that insects are said to see. I didn't want to be blinded in midtown, a panicking frantic middle-aged man, hyperventilating his way beneath the wheels of fast cabs. My hearing was threatened too. I imagined my own voice, parroting Celan to my colleagues, *he shouts play the violins darker you'll rise as smoke in the air.* The shoes of walkers became hard to hear, and then the wheels on wet blacktop, the engines of cars and their horns, and the voices of everyone separate from me in New York, all receded. I heard myself breathing. This was what Lil so detested, I thought: the only hearing myself.

I wanted to whine. I wanted to say, if she were *kinder* to me, then I wouldn't hear only my breath, see only pieces of the world that swam in a blood-red brightness and jumped before my eyes.

"What we have learned," she said. I remembered Andreoscu posing as question what she said, from behind me. I turned, there was no reason not to turn, there seemed so many reasons to turn, my arms partly extended for balance, to squint and peer. I saw her, taller than I remembered, far less hefty than she'd been, though broad-shouldered still, and statuesque. There were lines around her proud nose, her mouth, and on her brow. Her skin was red with cold and walking and possibly excitement. In a sailor's long coat, her hands in white mittens and clasped before her, graceful in high-heeled boots, Rhona smiled with joy—it looked like joy at seeing *me*—and she said, "Zimmer! Get over here! Come hug me, Zimmer, dammit! Come here!"

So there I was, and she was true. I betrayed her at once by humming with happiness at not being wholly crazy. Then I stepped toward her and embraced her, smelled the city in her hair, and cigarette smoke, dark perfume. She leaned back and then leaned in to kiss me on the jaw. "I thought it was you, Rhona," I said.

"Is that why you ran? I was chasing you."

"Leviathan."

"Who?"

"No, no, no. Could I have another kiss, please?"

Because it was romance. It was a chance meeting on the sidewalk in New York at Christmastime, and we had loved each other and been strange together, and I had been alone, and now I felt a good deal younger. I felt—possible. I kissed her on the lips. Her mouth began to open, and mine did too. She stepped back, and the large brown eyes, less angry than I remembered, looked happy and puzzled. And I saw, too, that the eye makeup was gone; her eyes looked softer, I thought, thinking too that someone had made her feel lovely for a change.

"Zimmer," she said, "you want to come and spend a little time with me?"

"Please," I said.

We didn't hold hands as we walked to the subway entrance: she held my hand in both of hers and tugged me, though mostly she just prized me (so it felt), and I'd have sworn the heat of her palms beat through her thick white mittens to reach my skin. She paid my fare, and she led me to the train. We took the IRT to 42nd, and there we waited for the Whitehall train on the downtown BMT platform. Among the usual graffiti and litter, we sat in the most difficult position for speaking—side by side. I would have asked her why intimacy and proximity seemed so difficult to reconcile sometimes, but the train was roaring under lower Manhattan and, besides, it sounded like the sort of question you ask on a nervous date. Our legs touched, and in spite of the thickness of her long coat and my heavy raincoat, I felt the pressure of her thigh and knee, and I was bloated with language-less, imageless lust: I was all tumescent vessel. I felt that if I opened my mouth, the same tunnel-roar of the dark train would come bellowing over my tongue, a vomit of grope and clutch and shove.

The lights went on and off as we began the long slowing turn to South Ferry. The train inched, the metal wheels screamed so high against the rails that my mastoid glands clenched up, and I tasted sourness. I turned in the flickering brown light to look at her hair—still glossy, thick and dark, cut short—and her large nose, her soft upper lip, the dimpling at the corner of the mouth, her clean and unemphatic eyes: she used to look like a predator only I knew to be innocent, and I wanted to take her clothes off and roll between her legs, and hike myself up and down her skin and slide home into her while a distant audience cheered.

She was looking at me. "Me too," she said, before she looked away.

At the platform's edge, while recorded, amplified voices warned everyone to stand back, a metal grillwork slid from the rounded station at the end of the line—the train would continue uptown from here—and when the grilles touched the train, our doors slid open and Rhona, taking my hand again, led me to the ferry.

"You're married, Zimmer?"

"Are you?"

"No more. It was not very long after you and I stopped, actually. I married on the rebound, according to some people, my ex-husband included. A Turkish-Armenian Jew. Very cute stuff, and an okay poet. He was a rememberer."

"A match made in heaven," I said.

She bent my fingers back to punish me. "Except Turkish-Armenian Jews," she said, "they can't forgive the Russians, the Germans, God, and especially *themselves.* Mostly, once he did his rape, loot and pillage routine on my—you perhaps noticed?—substantially thinner and good-deal-firmer body, he whined about how the Arme-

nians endured rape, pillage, loot, and of course exter-
mination at the hands of the Turks and nearly everyone
else. Most boring, most crazy, and most second-rate
man I ever knew."

"You've always been very tough on poets," I reminded
her.

"I'm a more tolerant person," she said. "And while I
would suggest the probability that the entire world *does*
want the Jews to die, still, I am also a follower of opera,
books about criminals, and don't ask me why, please, the
Pittsburgh Steelers football team. I think it's their *gorgeous* quarterback. You know his work?"

On the Staten Island Ferry, I smelled gullshit and car
exhaust and rotting wood and the clean thrilling saltiness
of dirty water on which oil made rainbow patterns in the
lights from the slip. The ferry's engines throbbed, the
hawsers were cast off, and in the darkness of winter sunset we chugged toward Staten Island, where Rhona now
lived. I wanted to see the Statue of Liberty, which I
hadn't seen since I was a boy, and I wanted to see simply
the water itself, which Melville, I remembered, had
come to stare at, pulled away from home toward the
blankness he finally knew as God because he couldn't
ever locate what he was supposed to love.

But the water was black, and the rails were crowded
with homebound commuters and with kids who thought
that standing over dark dirty water on the Staten Island
Ferry was romantic, in spite of the ride's now costing two
dollars. I had ridden the ferry, in the name of romance,
for a nickel each way. They were right, though: it was
romantic. The city shrank back, the harbor was like a
mirror of sky, with blue and red and yellow lights instead
of the hard silver stars; I felt as small before the harbor
as I did beneath the sky, and I didn't want to be alone

against immensities, and suddenly, again, I was very happy that Rhona was with me to keep me from that loneliness, and suddenly, again, I remembered asking myself if that's why I clung to Lillian and Sam, and suddenly, and again after eighteen years, I wondered if that was why I needed Rhona too.

She was leaning against me, her hands tucked around my arm and buried under the armpit of my coat. She was saying something: ". . . *all* craziness, though. Remember? R. D. Laing and those characters—the only madness is sanity, the only way to get healthy is to get crazy."

"What?"

"Crazy."

"Yes! That's right. Like Laing—we were all like that, a little."

"That's what I was saying, Zimmer."

"That's what I said."

"Are you jumpy about running away with me? Because of your—Lillian? Because of your wife and your Sam."

"No. No. I told you. We don't live in the same place anymore."

"Much as you'd like to."

Lillian's note, those years before, had borne no heading. It lay on top of the glass coffee pot. Smoke issued from around the paper she had written on, and the coffee was nearly boiling, the paper almost steamed through. I turned the coffee down and felt sick when I leaned above the pot: it was like smelling awful heavy oils from some grim industrial process. I didn't drink any coffee, but carried her soggy note to the small table at the window of the kitchen. Looking over dark browns and dark reds and the occasional yellow windows of early

Saturday risers or insomniacs, at five in the morning, wakened by her absence—probably, I had rolled to my left and had encountered nothing; in my marriage, I was used to, dependent upon, encountering the resistance of spirit and flesh—I sat in grimy light and read:

> I'm walking around. Nobody's going to rape me. I'm too dangerous tonight to get raped. I dreamed about you. We were in that terrible hotel in Italy where the dwarf carried all our bags up and disappeared under them. You said to me in a whisper that you didn't know how to tip someone you couldn't see. It was Florence. You kept talking about how brown and yellow everything looked. You said "ochre" all the time. I kept trying to get you into the sack. Do you remember this? Because I am sitting here at this crappy little imitation walnut table in our crappy little kitchen and I am furious with you when I could be doing something useful. Like walking around without having to write this. I hate writing notes. I dreamed about you in that hotel. We drank grappa on the balcony and sang. I was in my nightgown and I sat on your lap on the balcony and we made love that way. I thought somebody was going to have to come and throw a pail of water on us to make us stop and go to bed. That's what really happened in case you forgot. But you better not forget that one, fella. That was one of our half a dozen finest hours. But I dreamed about the little man with the suitcases. His head was shiny and his little voice kept coming out from under the suit-

cases. He kept saying Prego, Prego. I dreamed it was you. You were covered with suitcases. I dreamed you were dying and it was an accident and somebody dumped all these suitcases on you and you couldn't breathe. You kept moving around like some kind of little suitcase toy but I knew you couldn't breathe. So I kept on screaming and chasing you and pulling the suitcases off you. I finally got you against the wall and pulled them off. They kept turning into this gelatin stuff. You were tiny when I got to you. You were smaller than Sam. You looked up at me like the little guy who said Prego. You smiled at me. You said Can't you see I need to pack my bags? Can't you let me get my soup into the bags in peace and quiet? The soup's for me, Queenie. That's what you said. So I want to know who the fuck Queenie is if she's anyone. And if it was all just dream stuff, I am still totally pissed off at you. That's why I'm walking around. Just in case it isn't your fault. But just because it was my dream you were in, that doesn't mean it isn't your fault. So watch it. I'll be back later.

L

Sam came in while I was reading. He was three, he was in white pajamas with feet, he smelled like fresh milk and shampoo and sleep while he sat on my lap and leaned against my belly and chest as I read.

"Can't you sleep, Sam?"

"Where's Mommy?"

"Taking a walk."

"Can Mommy sleep?"

I left the note on the table and carried Sam to his bed. I tucked the quilt around him and kissed him on the head. He was already asleep, and I wanted to lie beside him—I needed a body beside me in my life; I couldn't live alone for long, I thought—but I didn't want to be out of our bed in case Lillian came back. So in the kitchen, I put her note back on top of the coffee pot. I turned off the lights and shucked my bathrobe and got back into bed, cold enough in just my shorts to sleep in the morning chill, but fighting to stay awake so that when she came I could seize her and pull her into bed and make such love to her as possibly hadn't been made since the small peach-marble terrace overlooking Florence in our very early days. I was also trying to think of who Queenie could be. And I was wondering how much of her dream I must be responsible for. A new category for marriage counselors: the other party's dreams.

I fell asleep anyway, dreamed of nothing that I remembered, when the lock snicked and I heard the rustle of a raincoat being draped over furniture. I heard her footsteps as she walked around the corner into the kitchen to, I assumed, see if I'd wakened to read about the wandering small husband and his gelatinous suitcases. I heard her shoes thump. On bare feet Lillian came in. She took her clothing off. I heard a nightgown sliding on. I coiled. She sat, sighing, on the big bed's edge. I sprang. She shrieked. I growled into the side of her neck, "You think you're too tough to get raped this time of the morning, huh?" She stiffened, went softer, and then lay back as I pulled her onto me. My hands were under the nightgown, on her buttocks, still cool and very strong, and she was whispering, with a purpose and vigor I found exciting, for it was, then, something like a rape, those tones of resistance, "Bastard, bastard, bastard, bastard."

And of course the lights went on. Of course, Sam stood at our open door. He said, *"There's* Mommy."

Lillian rolled from me and pulled her nightgown down. She said, "We were just getting warm, Sam. Brr. It's *chilly.* Want to come get warm?"

He walked, then skipped, then hopped, and was bouncing on our bed and into Lillian's circle of arms. I threw my own arm around them, but also threw a thrust of hip at Lillian's backside, to remind her of what had been firm between us a moment ago.

"Oh, my," she said.

Sam said, "What?"

And I said, *"Prego, bellissima signorina. Prego."*

"Zimmer, what?"

"What? Oh, I'm remembering, Rhona. Rhona, how crazy were you? I don't mean about primal scream therapy in the *Zeitgeist,* shit-scribbling on the walls, and the old rape-your-puppy-for-effect syndrome. I mean us— you, anyway: I was stone sane."

"Nearly, Zimmer. You nearly were, weren't you?"

"It's a curse."

"I believe it."

"But you *were* a little nuts. You had this crazy Vienna turn-of-the-century-madness look around your eyes with all that mascara you wore. And you wore these costumes sometimes."

"Like the night at the Nazi's?"

"Which he wasn't—"

"Relax, I know that. I do. Remember? I think I told you so right after. When it broke."

"Broke—"

"Us?"

"Oh, *us!* That. Yes. I remember you said that. So you weren't crazy."

"So I *was*, Zimmer. Because I wanted that so much. I did want you, you know? Also."

"I hope so. I hoped so. We were in *love*, Rhona."

"Probably were."

"No. Listen. Not probably. Listen. What would you call it, otherwise? I mean, in retrospect. Say you were writing down the history of us."

"Slender volume, first of all."

"All right. I'll give you that chuckle. But I want to know."

"But we're here on this ferryboat, and we're shivering because it's so cold, and we're talking into the wind, and the wind smells like old peanut butter mixed with gasoline, and you are really asking me, right now, after we just barely met for the first time in eighteen years—what was I saying?"

"How can I ask that?"

"Ask what?"

"How can I ask, you were asking, how you'd describe us in the past tense."

"Zimmer—that's right. That's right. Zimmer, how can you ask me something like that now? You planning on a quick separation after you just barely found me? I'm a dish now, Zimmer. Well, I'm not. But I'm a grownup. And I'm barely nuts anymore. And I'm standing out here in all this fog and wind and peanut butter for you, rubbing up and down on your arm and asking hardly any questions at all because you keep turning—I could have seen it then. You were going that way then. You keep on getting like some retired soldier of fortune. That's what you look like, you know. A beat-up old mercenary soldier who used to shoot people in Africa and then got nearsighted and put these glasses on along with a hairy suit. What was I telling you? Okay: don't turn me down, or into history right away. You're not turning me down, are you? You get me nervous, Zimmer. Come home with me for a drink so I get calmed down. And stop talking about being crazy. And stop telling me and asking me and alluding at me about what we could be calling ourselves. Let's go get something *done*, first."

I wouldn't have known what to say even if she hadn't pulled me into the passenger lounge and insisted on some scalding ersatz coffee for us. She did make me speak, and the more I answered simple questions—the ones she'd said she wasn't asking—the more tranquil Rhona became, with fewer fidgets and a lot less cuteness around the eyes and mouth. I talked a good deal about Sam, especially about how he played baseball and how he sometimes, at good times, forgot he was playing and actually made those deft gliding motions of the professionals. I didn't talk about how Lillian, when things were tough on her or him or me or all of us or the firm or the city or the world, might kick and push and tug at furniture until the long living room was a narrow ballpark on the carpet of which she bounced grounders to Sam, who played at being the Yankees' third baseman, fielding the ball and throwing out runners. At such times, I didn't say, Lillian escaped from us and herself through the motion of glove and foot and ball, and through her imitation of Phil "The Scooter" Rizzuto, venerable former Yankees shortstop and now their play-by-play announcer. "Holy *Cow!*" Lil would cry in the Scooter's voice, "did you see that guy *throw?*" I went into a lot of detail about the office, *we drink it and drink it*, and I talked about books we had done and would do because it was good to talk about the surface of myself to someone who didn't seem to mind.

Kids were smoking, doors were slamming, the ferry rocked in the wind. Rhona was talking about her job at the Berg Collection of the main branch library at 42nd Street. She was going on at some length about a donation of Wilkie Collins papers, asking whether I had read *No Name*, which was about a vengeful young woman unsubtly named Magdalen. She didn't wait for me to answer, though I was shaking my head. "I love the work, you know." she said. "I love the *order*. Sifting through papers, arranging for their storage, exhibitions, checking their provenance—we get a lot of forgeries, I guess by mistake. Not forgeries: people just think what they're giving us is good, and all it is is stuff that looks good because of its context, it's surrounded by other stuff that's more or less all right. I don't care. I like to check it, find it, correspond about it, go after it. I'm still a little bit of a detective, Zimmer. You know?"

"I do know. I'll get you to write a book about it someday. You want to do that? Do you have any good scandals you can make a book out of for me?"

"I hate writing," she said. "I don't even answer letters from friends. Yuck. But aren't you the big-shot publisher, though?"

"I am a hot youngish middle-aged editor," I said. "Novelists hunger for my editing, and sly biographers of minor dead lyricists yearn to be in my stable. Also, I'm impatient and a liar with some of them. And I recently published a novel about a *very* important daily book reviewer on which I managed to screw up so badly, no one in New York got excited or upset. We dropped a bundle, and I think the author is leaving us. I don't blame him. I would, too, if I could."

"I missed you."

"I felt like I betrayed you."

"And you missed me?"

"Yes."

"And now you're so happy to see me, Zimmer."

"I am."

"Except you're worried that this is too—sentimental? Romantic!"

"It is. But you're wrong. I'm not worried. I was thinking about you."

"On the corner? You were trying to justify running away."

"I didn't know it was you for sure."

"In case it was."

I kissed her because I didn't know what to say. I didn't want to think anymore. I wanted to be in love and on my way someplace and feel as good as new. And, as we came to the pier, because it was so dangerous in the middle of a life, I gave orders to the boiler room to Make Smoke, and sent a screen of words up as we disembarked.

I told how, at thirteen or so, I had taken the same ferry to Pouch Camp, where Boy Scouts could find isolated woods and meadows, and set up pup tents, chop on their shins with hatchets, cook bad food, sing smutty songs, not wash, and still be only half a mile from a phone booth. As leader of the Alligator Patrol, I told Rhona as we got into her car, I had taken a new kid on an overnight. The chubby Natty Bumppo of the halvah set was going to teach the wisdom of the woods. "I forget this kid's name," I said. "But he was as boring with ineptitude as I must have been with trail lore."

We had pitched a tent. I slashed some perfectly good saplings down to lash a tripod on which to hang, under a dripping canvas waterbucket, our chopped meat. I told the kid it was a woodsman's refrigerator. He kept telling me how brown the meat looked. I told him it was The

Woodsman's Way. He told me it looked poisoned. We cooked half and saved the rest for the next day. We talked, grew bored, the day grew dark, I taught him how to tie a bowline, we went to bed. In our sleeping bags, we passed wind and speculated on what they did with all the electric trolleys they were taking away from Coney Island Avenue. And we slept some, and then the kid screamed, "Bear! Bear! Bear!"

I reached for my sheath with my left hand and pulled the long knife out with my right. Patrol leader at your service: bears dispatched with knives. But it seems that I had been, myself, apprehensive that night, in spite of my extensive Boy Scout survival-in-the-face-of-nightmare training. "See," I told Rhona, "I *already* had the knife out of the sheath when I went to bed. So what I did, I pulled this big damn blade along my five little fingers when I whipped it out, and simply slit pretty near down to the bone."

"God," Rhona said, turning onto the Staten Island Expressway. There was a lot of traffic, and I was surprised, for I remembered the place I'd been telling her about: green, vacant, a constant memory of summer with few people in it. She said, "We're going to the West-shore Expressway and then Bloomingdale Road. I live in Woodrow. In case you're looking for landmarks. But that was *awful*. Your hand. Are you still telling?"

"Still always telling. I wouldn't know the landmarks."

"You used to tell me stories all the time. Do you remember that? About your parents, and your parents' friends. I didn't ask about them because I was afraid they're dead."

"No, they're alive. They're completely crazy, completely happy, therefore, and *they* keep telling me stories too. My mother sends me little postcards—'I was thinking of you when you were twelve and went to the Planetarium and got lost on the subway.' "

"That's sweet," Rhona said. "That's lovely. Your mommy loves you."

"My mommy loves me. You know the thing I said to my grandparents one night at dinner after I heard my mother bitching about them to my father? They were his parents. I was a little kid. Seven, eight. It was something I heard on the radio, I guess. Maybe Henry Morgan, it sounds like. I peep up in the middle of the soup and I say, 'Outlaws I can deal with. It's the *in*-laws that scare me.' My mother blew soup into her centerpiece. My grandmother smiled. Her English was very bad, and I was adorable."

"Adorable," Rhona said. "This is the Westshore. Meanwhile, of course, your hand is bleeding all over your pup tent. While your grandmother is beaming into her soup and your mother is spraying it. See what I mean, Zimmer? You're always telling. You live in sixteen different times at once, you know that? You're seven years old, you're—what? thirty-nine? thirty-eight? Zimmer! *Forty!*"

"Forty."

"So you're seven, you're forty, you're a thirteen-year-old cupcake of a Boy Scout with his hand cut down to the bone. You're always in more than one place. Time, I mean. Well, place too. You should stand still, Zimmer. Not that I don't love the stories. Really. I do. But you must get tired, running all over the place like that. Now Bloomingdale."

I didn't look at the streets or the houses, or the dark lanes of what must have been Woodrow when we got there. I suppose I was trying to be miffed, or rebuffed, or silenced. I was none. I was riding next to Rhona, and

I was telling her my life. "So I start screaming," I heard myself say, "and the *kid* is still screaming 'Bear! Bear! Bear!' and I'm up and out, going 'Oof' and 'Ah!,' you know, pain-noises, and of course the porcupine or whatever it really is, *he's* long-gone, I'm bleeding to beat the Boy Scout *band*, and the kid, by this time, instead of helping me, is out at the tripod with one of those right-angle khaki-colored belt-clamp flashlights."

"And he's complaining that the meat's all gone, right?"

"Almost. He's complaining that the meat's all *brown*."

"Oh, Zimmer. Does that prove, disprove, or ignore the fact that God works in history?"

"It proves that God is brown meat."

"Probably," she said, slowing, downshifting, then turning up a short steep driveway. "Probably, God is brown meat."

"I left the kid there, and in smoky long johns and unlaced boots I walked on some road we probably drove on tonight until I found a phone booth. And I'm in there, bleeding all over the phone, not dying, and not in danger, but *scared*. You know. The collected wit and wisdom of Lord and Lady Baden-Powell had not, after all, sufficed. So I called up, and when my mother answered, I said, 'Can I come home?' Do you understand? I was crying. I was asking my parents to please excuse me from being a thirteen-year-old manlet. 'Can I come home?' You know how many times you can get tempted into calling somebody for that kind of permission?"

She sighed. She leaned over and kissed my ear. I responded even in my feet. "I understand," she said. "I've been warned."

"Warned?"

"I'll explain it later. Come in. Come in, now."

It was her little house now, she told me, courtesy of

the Turkish-Armenian poet, whose parents had kicked in for the divorce settlement. She took no money, but she had wanted the house—isolation, countryside and appetite: "I wanted *revenge*, Zimmer. The son of a bitch actually *hit* me. I clocked him, I broke his nose, but he kept *hit*ting me." Downstairs, the door off the driveway opened into a wide cluttered room, all sofas and old wing chairs covered in dark blue, a floor of polished wide boards, a bank of curtained windows to the right, with low bookshelves—like a library—beneath them, and a small black stove set into a stone fireplace on the left-hand wall.

"I burn wood," Rhona announced.

"We're publishing a book about burning wood."

"Oh, yeah? I'll have to get it."

"I'll send it to you."

"Do you think we sound nervous a little?"

"Yes," I said. We didn't snicker.

"The kitchen's out there. The bedrooms and bathroom are upstairs, the steps are around that corner. Should I get us a drink or tear off your clothes?"

"One drink, maybe? Or—"

"What the heck," she said. With her coat off, in soft slacks and a dark sweater, she was leaner, and longer-looking, and more alien while still familiar, and surely more exciting. I did feel like a youngster on a date. I wanted her to tear my clothes off, but she was bringing me a drink. Her face was bright with excitement.

And, being Zimmer, sipping Irish whiskey on ice, I had to say, "Aren't you—concerned about this little movie of ours?"

She sat on the coffee table, facing me, while I sat on the sofa, facing the woodstove behind her. "You mean you might not stay here with me in my enchanted cottage in the woods?" She laughed, drank a sizable gulp of Irish, let her knees touch mine, and licked the whiskey on her lips. Then she leaned forward and licked the whiskey on mine. She said, "I intend to take as much of you as I want and can have. If it turns out that you became a bigger fool than you were, okay. I'll show you. I promise. Grace under pressure. Any woman who has spent some time with you, and then a suffering Turkish-Armenian Jew whose biggest problem is which loss to celebrate first, she can handle a little misery in her liberated forties. I'm resilient. I am more graceful under pressure than Hemingway on top of Amelia Earhart. Yuck. But I do like seeing you again. I like it that your Lillian threw you out. Avoid shiksas. Didn't I teach you anything. Zimmer?"

I kept wondering what or who had taught Rhona. She had grown, of course. A precocious kid with a graduate degree is very different from a forty-year-old woman. A divorced woman is different from a woman whose second great fling is with some Zimmer on Varick Street. I thought that, with her reference to shiksas, I might start hearing more in Yiddish, and about Jewishness, and about our folly with Andreoscu, and her chirping father, her sad mother, arrested young by Nazis and forever arrested—not to stay young, but to always be sad. Of course. I said, "When did your mother die?"

Her eyes grew wet, but the tears remained on their dark surfaces and didn't run. I remembered that. She moved her head forward, as if in the chilly room she needed my heat. She didn't, I think; she needed my silence. I was pleased she didn't buy it by kissing me. Because I did, like a kid, like a fool, like a lover, want her to want my kisses because they were mine.

She left the whiskey beside her, withdrew her knees,

and then the rest of her. At the stove, the door of which was small and square and had two little wheels in it, she kneeled, balled some newspaper up, threw it in, then threw some shiny sticks on top of it. "Fatwood," she said. "It has a high resin content, so it's good kindling. Of course, high resin means a high creosote yield on the chimney and that's not desirable." She put some split wood—"This is the hardwood," she said, "less creosote, more efficient heating"—on top of the tinder, lit the paper, shut the door, opened the valves to admit air, and then sat, legs crossed, palms flat down on her knees. "But you are," she said.

"I am what?"

"Desirable."

I blushed.

"You're blushing. I forgot that! Oh, I love it!" She was watching me. "What, Zimmer?"

"Nothing."

"Your wife? Your—Sam? What did you think of?"

"You're desirable too."

The hardwood had caught. Its moisture was hissing, and she turned the wheels, cutting some air off. "You'll feel the heat soon," she said.

"At the risk of sounding adolescent, I would like to state that I feel the heat right now."

"Yes?"

"And I shouldn't talk about your mother?"

"And I shouldn't talk about your wife."

She adjusted the air intake some more, shutting the bottom wheel completely. She added a few more pieces of hardwood and fiddled with the stove, then shut the door again.

"Okay?" I asked.

"There."

"Okay," I said, standing, finishing the whiskey. "Okay. Listen. Let's talk about everything. Let's be in love." I was blushing, I was drunk on one drink. I shut my eyes. I heard her and then felt her. She stood in front of me. She undid my tie. She unbuttoned my shirt. She pushed at my suitcoat. She kissed my chest in cool pecks in a line going down from my throat. She nipped with her teeth and my eyes opened.

She was smiling, she looked so pleased. She said, "Don't just touch me with your fingertips and make believe I'm a dream. I'm your ancient history, old guy. I'm your ancient history. Grab *hold*."

I did. I smoothed her cheek first, because it was innocent and sweet and so unlikely, what we were doing. I kissed her nose and lips. Her tongue was there, and so was mine, then, and then we did do a great deal of tearing at clothes. She lay down on the rug near the fire. I kissed her breasts, her stomach, her crotch and thighs, and then she turned on me, forcing me back on the cold wooden floor, so that she could bite on my belly while cupping my balls, so she could slide her mouth around my penis. When I arched toward that wonderful blind darkness, she took her mouth away.

"Me," she said, making a terrific distinction. "Inside." And she lay back and pulled me with her. I went there, and in, and I wanted to weep for the sense of home and thrilling foreignness of where I was. She later held me so hard to her breasts and neck that I forced my head away and gulped air. "Oh," she said, "you are still beautiful. You're delicious. And you still hate to drown in tits— remember, you once said that?"

"I was an ungracious pig," I said.

She pulled at the rug, and covered us partway with it. We lay in front of the stove, very quietly, and when

Rhona began to cry with great shuddering gasps, I was pleased—because she was not, I thought and still think now, mourning what of us we'd lost; she was mourning her mother, and she needed to. And I wonder also if I wasn't pleased that she was, however briefly, just a little less competent, and therefore more vulnerable, and thus more available to me, than she had been before we'd made such love. And there I was.

But nothing was static for Rhona, and it didn't take long, sleepy and cold as I was, and eager to be stroked instead of wakened, before she rousted me and drove me up the stairs. In the dark, naked and goosebumpy, I tiptoed while she, behind me, leaned forward to smooch my rear and then bite it, driving me faster. There were three rooms upstairs, and she prodded me into the largest one. The light was on. A brass bed was on the near wall, and on the far one were bookshelves. Aside from a blanket chest and high oak bureau, and a bright braided rug, there were only books in piles on the floor, and a down-filled comforter on the bed, into which we dived. It squeaked each time we moved, and the sound made me think of how the bed would echo lovemaking. I listened to the bed, but Rhona watched me. She knew me, and soon we made more love, simply and slowly and then more slowly, because I wanted to feel what we did as if I listened with my skin. Whether I thought to save sensations to remember—"Yes, first she moved there, then I touched her *there*"—or whether I was as much in love with loving as I now think possible, I don't know. Except for our breathing, which seemed to be effortless, as if we each were an accomplished athlete, there was no sound save the brazen grating of the springs and joints of the bed. Like many a middle-aged man, I was slightly numb this time, and therefore good, I thought, for an hour. She wasn't, but she seemed to know how I felt. I remembered so many isolated hours in the apartment with Lillian, and one or two instances of what I had called impotence, but what I realized here, in the island across the water from my regular life, were moments of failing to concentrate on friction and skin, or moments of acting my age. After some moments of her own, Rhona tightened on me, and held, and then subsided, and I fell asleep.

And when I woke, the room was dark, the comforter was around me, and Rhona was squatting Indian-style, Boy Scout-style, on top of the comforter toward the foot of the bed. She wore a dark kimono. I saw her breasts at the top, I saw the muscled calves and the undersides of her thighs, and I wanted to make love again. "You made me younger, I think."

"That's a bonus," she said. "I just wanted to make you."

"That was—wonderful? Small word."

She said, "We were all right, weren't we? Getting older did me some good, Zimmer."

"Did the poet teach you to finally *enjoy* your fun?"

"Poets don't know about that. Ozal sure didn't."

"Good enough."

"Better than that," she said.

I nodded. She was drinking something fizzy and offered me her glass, but I shook my head. "Just you," I said.

She took the lapels of the kimono and spread them so that more of her breasts showed. She was enjoying herself, and I was enjoying the tease. I hoped that it wouldn't be a tease, though I wondered what was left in me. That didn't seem to be the point, however: I cared less about how to reply to what her body said than I rejoiced in the conversation. I cupped my balls, she watched my hand, her eyes grew pleased, and she sighed. "Tell me if you believe in God, Zimmer."

"Rhona!" I cried. "A bull session? Now? You remind me a little of Rhona Glinsky—I assume it's Rhona Ozal now?"

She nodded her head. "For the credit ratings and so on."

"All the more reason you remind me of Glinsky. She once tried to fuck me into submission. This isn't a metaphysical screw, is it? We couldn't be this happy over *that?*"

She smiled at the clown, the fool, the fucked-out lover, the beanbag lost and found. "No, Zimmer. We made love because we were excited by each other. Because we love each other? It's possible, yes? It's possible. Love. A gorgeous idea. And when you and I were babies, we—"

"For a couple of months?"

"For a *while*, bastard. But this is now, and I am asking. Because I want to know if there is any salvation for you. Because—all right, this too is admitted. I somewhat love you." She closed her eyes. She opened them. "Maybe." She grinned.

"You sound Christian, Rhona. Salvation."

"There is a goodly variety of salvation in the world, Zimmer, and I can assure you that I am not a Christian. There is salvation in going on the Jewish New Year to the nearest body of water and throwing onto it, near the dirty little ducks, your sins. You do it by casting bread on the waters, by reciting psalms. The result is that you have—what?"

"It's a *hell* of a metaphor. I didn't know about that."

"Yes. You think only the Gentiles can use bread for

changing shapes, In church, they get the flesh of a dead man. We get rid of our sins—we deal with *life*. Also, the ducks get fed. It's a service. It is a kind of salvation, an effort at being saved while one breathes. Enough pie in the sky. I'm talking feet on the ground, the gulls and mallards eat, there's bread on the water and some sins, maybe, come out of the heart. You understand? I said this to you once, but a little less clearly. It is possible to worship the practice of the people. The history of the people. God, whatever, can take care of him, or her, or itself. Yes?"

And, of course, I was up on my knees. I was worshipping. I crawled, I kneeled, I pulled the kimono from her and kissed her thighs and pushed her backwards, nearly out of the bed, and tongued her lips there, and licked and prodded deeper with my tongue. I prostrated myself, my hands on her thighs, her hands on my head, pressing it down, and I worshipped what she had told me to—my history.

We slept together under the goosedown, and I thrilled, I swear it, as much to being with Rhona as I did to not being alone.

But I also remembered, waking up with a surge of fear, to realize that I had been thinking of Lillian and Sam— no, not thinking *about* them, but remembering their existence—and then to realize something far more dangerous to the fragile tissue of this safety beginning to grow around me. I recalled how profoundly I had hurt Rhona once, and the memory was a wound to me. It seemed to me a matter of moments, days at best, before I would be moved to speak and make some sleazy verbal reparations —or, more interestingly, before Rhona woke to make some cruel demands. And thus I thought once more of Lefty, in the loft above Varick Street and the egg roll

factory below. I recalled how sourly he'd spoken of love
—a job of work is what he'd made it sound like—and I
thought too of what he'd offered me when Rhona and I
had parted. He had told me that he would, if I needed
him to, come upstairs again and give me consolations
about love—"lies," he had offered. Indeed, Rhona, we
are worshipping history, I thought, alone in the bed beside her. We are praying to the consolations we might
have come to know as lies. "What we have learned,"
Andreoscu had said, making the question an indictment,
and assuring no answer. But it shouldn't *be* that even
this, tonight, now in my life, is also a Jewish joke! I said
this to the pillow and the smell of her skin and hair, to
the dark little room on the island. As usual, in such
matters, nothing replied, and I breathed as she did, and
I fell away into my sleep.

And woke, to stand beside the bed, heart pumping,
naked skin gone hot with fear. Downstairs—it had wakened me, I thought, and then I was sure I heard it again:
the slow rasp of a lock's tongue being, like a lazy lover's,
withdrawn. I didn't know what her former husband
looked like, but I was certain that Sukru Ozal stood inside the house now, *this instant*, gargoyle's face con-
torted, curly hair straight and stiff with the currents of
his madness, the love of pain a kind of liquor in him as
he flexed his fingers in the living room where lately—
had he watched? had he peered with his back hunched
and nose twitching to see us, on his own former floor?—
Rhona and I had rolled around on one another. This
was a crazy poet, I thought; I disliked poets even when
they were alleged to be sane. Poets wore the vests of good
suits over dungarees and dirty white shirts. They wore
gold-rimmed glasses. They were pale, and they looked at
you with little interest because you were neither an idea

nor a crucial circumstance of their life nor someone well connected with a foundation or a private press. Poets played half-court basketball in the winter with their vests flapping. They had catastrophic affairs with suicidal people and wrote long poems with short lines about the ghosts of their fathers smoking lemon pips in broken-down Hudsons that were stranded in cornfields. They translated from the French or Latvian, and they had no courtliness about the pain of others, *Shulamit we are digging a grave in the air there's room for us all.* And this one was a maddened Turkish-Armenian Jew. I knew about Armenians only from William Saroyan, who had led me to think they all grinned and drank copious quantities of booze and left behind a trail of language while suffering with grace on behalf of the lost ethnic peoples of the world. What I knew about Turks was that they'd slaughtered the Armenians. Ozal was a man who beat the woman who had latterly rescued me from adulthood and romantic deprivation. He was the man who had socked her into submission despite her breaking his nose. I thought with admiration of her punch, and then with great pleasure of our lovemaking, but my skin still was lively with fear, my heart still pounded, and in the darkness I was compelled by either inborn domestic protectiveness, or Lillian's fear before a man who had called himself only "Me," or my own sheer terror.

Naked, somewhat paunchy, shriveled of balls and nearly cockless with panic, I stumbled against walls and the upstairs railing until I was on the first step, crouching against the inside railing, blind. I sometimes, at home, when we were happy and good to each other—this was years before, I realized, realizing how much we'd actually lost—sometimes I would walk from the shower, head covered with a towel, and understand that I had left my glasses on some surface or other of the big old steam-filled bathroom, and that I couldn't find them. I would read the surfaces with wet fingers, but still not hit upon them. And then I would have to wail for Lillian, who would matter-of-factly enter the room to find my fogged eyeglasses so that I could see well enough to locate my deodorant and hairbrush and talc. That's how old I've become, I thought, advancing on the Middle-Eastern terrorist. I was blind in the service of love, I also thought; such a locution, even silent, made me smile.

And then I was down the stairs, around the corner from the latest melodrama of my life. I cried out warning, a high shriek such as I had heard in my own recent nightmares, and I leaped, great bulky white shape—I could hear the kid in my tent crying "Bear! Bear! Bear!" —and I slapped at the light switch and assumed the sort of Oriental unarmed combat stance one sees in third-rate films. Unfortunately, I didn't know where the light switch was, so I merely struck the wall. I was in the dark, screaming danger, limbs extended like those of a frightened man about to be beaten by someone ugly and tall in a rage. My chest heaved so hard and breath was so difficult to draw that my voice ran out like a thread of spittle and stopped, and I felt as if a lump of clay were stuck in my breastbone, blocking the passage of everything.

"What?" called Rhona, upstairs. "Zimmer? Who?"

"Shh," I tried to whisper.

"Zimmer," she called again, exasperated.

"It's *him*," I whispered weakly. I started to cough. By the time I found my breath again, and the energy to speak, my hands were over my face in a case he struck in the dark.

Then Rhona turned the lights on. In her open kimono, barefoot and so recently, intimately, mine, she excited me again. "Zimmer," she said, gently, as if I'd gone mad.

And I said, "Me." I said it to her, and the room in disarray—the rug disturbed, a blurry turned-over glass, some fogged pillows out of place—and, except for us two, quite empty. "Just me," I said.

"You expected someone else?" She sounded as if she grinnned, or was beginning to, mildly encouraged about some semblances of sanity in her house.

I had to squint to see her face. "I thought I heard your husband."

"Why aren't you wearing your glasses? You look funny, all squinched up like that. You also look naked."

"I am naked."

"Yes. And Sukru's in Seattle, he teaches there now, he's been there for about four years, Zimmer. Why would he be *here?* Why would you be standing around and screaming, naked, without your glasses, if he *were* here?"

"Defense of territory?" I suggested weakly.

"Who would be defending whose territory?" she asked. "You or Sukru? Because I don't belong to anyone's turf at the moment, except my own, unless I'm mistaken." The smile seemed to have gone. The face of the Jewish avenger had returned.

Naked in all ways, I sat on the sofa and put a little foulard-pattern pillow over my crotch and the fold of my gut. I was a child begging indulgence, not a masterful athlete of the orifices, when I said, "You told me—love? Didn't you! Didn't we say that upstairs? Down here? Someplace. About *love?*"

"Oh, Zimmer," she whispered.

"It's the kind of helpless middle-class middle-aged sort

of shittily pathetic permanence thing you can get caught in," I said, looking at the pillow.

"It's what you need. So don't make fun of it."

"What do you need, Rhona?"

"You, right now."

"How now-ish would that be?"

"As long as we stretch it, Zimmer. Last time it didn't last very long. You were on your way, remember? You were traveling, in a manner of speaking."

"As in leaving you in the lurch, maybe?"

"This time, you seem to require something more definite."

"And you?"

"And me," she said. "I sure did think of you over the early times away, after I left."

"After *I* left."

"Oh, we were both leaving, Zimmer. You just left at a certain unfortunate time."

"As in the lurch."

"As in. And I don't know what my plans are," she said, "or what's going to happen, or kind of *when*. But I would dearly love your company."

"I guess I was acting like a husband when I heard the noise. I don't know what kind of noise it was. You know what's weird? I can see what you're wearing. Not wearing, actually. And I can sort of make out the color of your skin. But without my glasses, I can't see your eyes. I can't really tell your expression, you know? It's really like being blind, Rhona. You have me at a terrific disadvantage right now."

"Your chest isn't jumping around so much now," she said. "You look better. You silly fool, Zimmer. We're safe. We're alone. Come upstairs with me and let's not talk for a while. Come. It's all right. It's safe. And then later, we'll see."

"And then let's see? I don't know. I don't know."

"Come upstairs," she said, "and get into bed and let's go to sleep in the same bed again, and in the morning let's make some coffee and skip work and we'll talk a little. Yes? Or, you want to be industrious, we can ride in together and talk on the way and later in the day we can meet. We did a lot of that in the old days, remember? Old times?"

"Old times," I agreed.

But it was more like being a husband at what once had been called home. Rhona went upstairs, and I, appendages flapping, went around her living room, tidying. "Come on, Zimmer! Don't be embarrassed!" she called. I heard the brass bed gently moan as she shifted her weight, and then, as the bed went silent, I wrapped a sofa blanket around my waist the way you'd wrap a towel after a shower. And, as blind as I usually was after a shower, chilled on top and prickly beneath, I felt and stumbled my way about, making a long drink and sitting on the coffee table to drink it. I tried very hard to think, in clear categories, with some vision of the future. But I was as blind inside as I was out. I knew only that I wanted lots and lots, but I couldn't have named very much of it.

After a while, after something of a long while, I went upstairs, and eventually I slept. Despite the time bomb of Jewish revenge lightly snoring beside me, and despite the biblical nastiness—all that Old Testament cruelty: you asked for this shit, okay, you got it—of what my life seemed to be, I was pleased with the odors and textures about me, and the prospects, however also sad, of what my life could possibly become.

We woke together, and she was so immoderately at ease, I lost the shyness and sense of humiliation I'd so readily accepted the night before. It felt reasonable, and even desirable, that we sat naked in bed together, and brushed our teeth with the same brush, and poured each other's orange juice, and drank instant coffee in the bright winter sunlight off the edge of what Rhona told me was Latourette Park. We were not uneasy; we behaved, quite correctly, as if what we did was familiar to us—being fresh from one another's fingers and mouth, being together, being side by side in our lives. We showered, separately and chastely. Rhona dressed in a plum-colored skirt with a long slit—it looked like a Bloomingdale's ad—and in a pinkish blouse that showed the shape of her nipples to me. I knew that those nipples were there for me, and there to announce that I had been at them—that someone had been at them, that Rhona (Glinsky) Ozal was not alone. Such a state is worth celebrating. We said little as we got into her small car, in which she drove us down back roads. She took us to glints of sea, and then seasmells, the divings of birds, the *whoop-whoop* of a real fireboat crushing water against our ferry to get past off St. George. We didn't kiss farewell at South Ferry slip, but we did grip each other's hand at the terminal and smile a wee bit smugly. We would, like lovers, meet for drinks, we tried to say casually. As she walked off, I watched her. My stare was possessive. Without turning or slowing her stride, she acknowledged my stare by lifting her hand in a comfortable sign that told me she knew I was looking, and we were, at least for a happy while, bewitched into mutual comfort. We had avoided most of the sugar—more work for me than for my realistic huntress friend—and then she'd left by train for 42nd Street, to arrive late for work at the main branch's Berg Collection, while I walked over to Pine Street, toward an office where once I had thought to drop my trousers and humble myself in exchange for permission to come home. I wasn't certain, this time, what I would offer, and what I'd expect. But there were signs and portents: I didn't get lost when I looked for Pine Street; I wasn't as nervous as I was excited; I detected, racing back and forth between the walls of my skull, what the Germans called an "earworm"—a tune you simply can't shake from your brain—which said, over and over, *Rhona Glinsky, puddin' and pie, kissed my ear and made me cry.*

I had forgotten how rumpled my suit must be, and how crazily my eyes must have gleamed, and how cockily I must have worn my tie knotted an inch below the open collar of my dirty ecru shirt. Lillian's receptionist knew, and then Lillian's shared secretary, and then Lillian herself, so tall, so poised, so rich-looking in a heavy black dress made of something like blanket material, with a notch cut in the neck to show a marvelous thin ribbed turtleneck of metallic gray, and a very expensive ivory brooch I remembered.

Her face was almost friendly, surely concerned—I saw lines above the nose, vertical lines I didn't like to see on her—and she acted as if she'd known I was coming. She held her hand up to fix me in place, she dashed into her office on high-heeled shoes that precisely matched her sweater, emerged with a long black alpaca-looking cloak, and of course I thought of Rhona and her immigrant's cape, worn for the night of our confrontation with Andreoscu. I blushed, I know, because she stared at me as she does when I blush.

"You got my message," she said.

"No. I wasn't home, Lil. I haven't checked in with the office. I'm sorry. Something's up? Sam's okay?"

"No. Yes! Stop jumping like that, please, relax. Yes, his health is fine. His mind—well, I don't know: he's worried. He is starting to make dirty jokes, he is starting to sass me, he is beginning to have nightmares. He's troubled. We're producing a troubled boy."

"You should've called me, Lil," I said, as we waited for the elevator. "No, you shouldn't. Well, you should have, yes. But I saw it too. He had to pee—did I tell you this? I forget where this happened. He had to pee three times on the way."

"It was a long while ago. It was when you kidnapped him to go to Hoffritz. It was a whole fucking *day* ago, imagine that. What are you doing? What are you letting happen to you? You took him out of school, you bought him a *knife*. Remember?" Through the long lobby and among pedestrians who didn't exist, into traffic that was only lighted cabs on a dull day in lower Manhattan, Lillian and I, the only ones alive on lower Broadway now because of something she was trying to tell me about Sam: "You bought him a horrible male thing is what you did. A little *machismo* utility device for castrating opponents while picking your teeth and clipping important newspaper items relating to the ebb and flow of power. Remember?"

And in the cab at last, and turning to fight our way uptown, then crosstown, and sitting beside her, smelling her perfume while there seemed, still, to be other smells beneath my fingernails and in my hair, my eyelashes, even, I could think only to say, "Easy, Lil, you're getting distraught. I understand. It sounds to me like you're leading up to something—some kind of behavior problem, am I right? But take it easy. We'll manage this." She snorted.

And in the lobby of her—our—building, and then our elevator, and then outside our door—it had been a while since Lil and I had both stood at the same time on the same side of that door—she said, "I want *you* to take it easy. I just want you to think. Then tell me *what* you think. And then we'll talk. All right?" It sounded so much like Rhona slowing me down the night before as I rushed to sign her to a forty-year personal services contract that I tried to smile; I did twitch.

And then we were inside, and there I was, in Sam's room. His animals were dead. They were minus ears, they had round glass eyes plucked out, some were disemboweled, with stuffing of several colors in scraps and handfuls and heaps around the room. I thought, as I held one of them up, of two kids in a tent: "Bear! Bear! Bear!" For there were murdered bears and maimed rabbits and creatures from books and TV programs in various states of disintegration. A minor frenzy had swept the room, a small kid's awful dervish of breaking because something was breaking in him. I turned around and there was Lil, softly tossing and catching the red-handled Swiss Army Knife I had bought him at Hoffritz for, as I recalled telling him, "You never know." And you never do. He had carved on the foot of his bed and on the newel posts at the head. His bookshelves were scarred, and there were even gouges in the painted plaster of the wall, where he'd stabbed. I winced at the thought of his face, and the risks he'd run of cutting himself. And before I knew I would speak, I said to Lil: "Two things. Is that my voice? Two things. At least he didn't use the knife on himself. You know that's something to think about. He's mad at us—me. *Maybe* not just himself. Maybe we'll be lucky."

Lil's eyes were wet, of course, and her face was twisted. I hugged her. I held her until she wanted to step backward. What was left of us was in trouble, and what we could give to one another we should have given—even if only big dumb chests, wide shoulders, words.

"And the other is words," I said, sniffing as I watched her sniff. "At least he didn't carve awful words about us and him. Because now, anyway, we can hope for the best instead of understanding the worst, and maybe we can do something."

I waited for her rage—something about my selfishness, my insistence on seeing it my way. There was a flash, like a film of a storm taken from a weather satellite and speeded up; it passed across her face and was gone. I wondered if it was gone because she saw no use in expressing such angers anymore. I wondered if I was wasting her time. And I thought that I'd never felt sadder.

"We'll help him," I said.

Jemimah Puddleduck and Peter Rabbit, Oscar the Muppet and Teddy the Bear, the pink bunny with the key you wound up when Sam was one and it played a baby-tune, Ralph the yellow rubber duck that honked when you squeezed him and who dripped water when you pulled him from the tub—slashed, like flesh—and Rocky the Flying Squirrel and Donald Duck with angry eyes, and the big black labrador stuffed so full he grunted when you hugged him, and a pink pig named Porkchop who was made out of velvet, and the curly-tailed sheep made of real Lake District wool and carried home on the plane, and poor dignified Babar, all of them cut and torn, gouged, and wouldn't it have made a dandy metaphor? And shouldn't it have? And it would, and it should, if it hadn't been for the fact of Sam, who was now a good deal less mine, though still half mine, and feeling more pain than the rest of us, and surely more than the animals he'd sawed and ripped, weeping with what terrible noises?

"We have to do something," Lillian said.

"Well, we will. He'll get over it. He'll adjust. There are a lot of kids in the world whose parents get divorced—"

I looked up, and so did Lil: because I had said it first this time.

"What if he does something to himself, I keep wondering," Lil said.

"I'm gonna keep wondering too. We have to take him someplace—no, just stay here. I don't know yet. We have to sit down with him and we have to talk."

"What he's mad at won't change, will it? Us?"

"No," I said. "I guess it won't." She was tossing the knife up and down. "I know this'll sound funny, but what I want to do is, I want to go away from here now and think a little. You know? I realize you've been stuck with it alone since last night. But I really want to do this. I hope you won't mind."

She said, "Do what you want."

"Don't be angry, Lil."

"Will you stop being so fucking *ju*venile?" She was shouting. "Our baby is tearing his life up—this room is the complete story of Sam! And you're talking separated-parents protocol with me?"

I kissed her on the forehead. I took the knife and put it in the pocket of my coat. I seized her by the arms, which felt very thin, then, and kissed her on the mouth. It wasn't like kissing a stranger, it was simply beside the point. Realizing that made me realize that I had wanted something more from the kiss than comfort for her, and the routine proximity of people who had lived together for a long time. "Let's have a cup of coffee," I said. "My place or yours?"

Lillian went into the living room, and I followed her. "Boil the water," she said. "Make us a pot of coffee."

The beans were still in the freezer, the heavy kettle

was still half-filled with stale water, and everything was as it had been. I said, "You kept the kitchen the same."

"It's only been about five weeks, dumb-ass," she called in. From the sound of her voice, I knew that she was sitting on the sofa with her long legs curled beneath her, and with her arms along the back of the sofa, her head tipped back so that she faced the ceiling, and her eyes closed. "Has it felt like longer?"

"Like most of my life, Lil. Extremely long. Infinite."

"You want to move back in?"

"Just like that? You're a failure and pervert, get out, leave your kid in a nightmare about losing his parents and get out—whoops! Come on back for a while until I get crazy from you some more, I'll let you know when, and you can move out again."

I seemed to have thrown the kettle at an adjacent wall, and the pottery mugs were on the floor. I was stepping on one of them, grinding at its fragments. I was breathing so hard, so deep, and still listening so closely to the clatter of the kettle, that I heard only part of what Lil had said: "—the best for everyone. It wasn't, if you remember, a unilateral decision. We don't make unilateral decisions. We discussed it rationally and on a multilateral basis it was decided—"

"I am not a fucking nation-state at a fucking international fucking *conference!*" someone bellowed, apparently me. "I am a middle-aged man who is married to a middle-aged woman who told me I was a failure as a husband and father and who instructed me to leave. Not to mention my failure as a lover."

"I never said that!"

"You sure as jumpin' Jesus did, Lillian."

"Well, I didn't mean to."

"You called me impotent because it was a birdcall you were practicing?"

256

"*You*, Oh cocksman and King of Publishers, now that I remember, *you* called your*self* impotent."

"You're right. I remember that."

"So don't tell me—"

"I remember. You're right."

"Jerk."

"You know, Lillian, we're supposed to be talking about Sam."

"Sure. When you're losing the argument we can shift to Sam."

"Lillian: who can *win* this?"

After only a second or two, she said, "You're right."

"Because we *are* involved with a lit—"

"I said you're right. Goddammit. What?"

"I don't know what. I broke two coffee cups and spilled the beans which I forgot to grind anyway and I can't find the cover to the kettle. If you'd have asked me, I would have moved back in. Never mind."

"Never mind anyway. I did ask and you said no. So *you* never mind. Who are you fucking?"

"Lil! Sam tears his room apart because he's so sad, and you ask me a question like that?"

"I can smell it on you. And you're walking on your toes again, like a jock. You're doing it, Zimmer, goddammit. I'll never forgive you for any of this."

"What about Sam?"

She said, "Ask the man who owns one: big blade, small blade, corkscrew, folding scissors, ivory toothpick in slide-out metal sheath, marlinspike in case you have to —what? splice a rope on a schooner? and then there's the utterly necessary folding fork and spoon which swing out in the event you're struck with hunger in Balducci's, and then there's the collapsible tracheotomy tube, the emergency aluminum splint for broken limbs on high-ways, there's the baked-enamel tongue depressor, there's the two-way radio for when you're beset and you need a crime-fighter, and naturally the ever-popular put-and-call meter so you can check on the rise and fall of your portfolio."

I said, "Goodbye, Lil. I'll call you later. No. Tomorrow. Hang in there. We'll talk later on." To say I flounced out tragically would be to say it accurately. I left her there, and in the cab going downtown, I tried to remember what it was I'd seen as so sad in Sam's room —aside from poor Sam's mind, which the room was, furnished with eight years of us-and-him, and falling apart on him, all over him, and easier to tear at than us or his small sad self. I felt so awful for Lillian, and then I remembered: we had stood, first in the living room and then in our little boy's bedroom, with its baseball posters of Reggie and Graig, with its toys and tools and memories of his whole early life now mutilated—we had stood there with our coats on. Like a couple buying a house or renting an apartment, like a couple on their way in or out, like strangers, that was it, like fugitive inspectors in someone else's residence we had stood in our outer garments and we hadn't removed them because we weren't at home. And then the guy who should have given some comfort, shared a ton or two of psychic load, had taken off. And how many women *have* you fled at the ultimate hour, Mr. Zimmer? No comment, please. No comment.

I was downtown and at the office, and I must have paid the cabbie something, because he'd allowed me to walk into the littered foyer of our small office building in which, for the sake of low rents and the cachet of looking unlike what we called the "uptown" houses, Abromowitz insisted we work. Sally looked at me and looked away. There were small pink slips to tell me that while I was out—how long had it been, I tried to remember, since I did business, did something besides fight to publish Rumanian poems? *He whistles for his Jews, he has them dig a grave in the earth.* A first author had called three times, a slip noted, because he had just realized that we weren't sending him on a nationwide TV- and autograph-session tour. In black felt-tip pen, I scribbled *For a 5-grand advance, he gets letters, sympathy, and one fancy meal. Tell him.* No one would unless I did. I might. His book on the sisters of nineteenth-century poets was in the same league as poems: we published them, we thought in our self-serving way, out of obligation to the language, and to our reputation; the author was secondary, and he ought, I thought, growing angry, to have learned that. There were calls, dated yesterday, from Lillian. I had apparently replied to them with my person, however unsatisfactorily. There was a call from my father in Arizona. There was a call from my mother in Arizona. I smiled. My two old folks, living in a condo we all just managed to afford, were apparently having another one of their fights. I had come to enjoy them. My father would become outraged at an imagined public debasement of his slight, good self by my mother, who had, from some genetic pool, plucked the ability, in her eighties, to grow chunky. My father would lock her out and cry "Fatty!" through the door. My mother would call the police. Eventually, I would be called. And I almost always, unless one of them had acquired a bruise or abrasion during the argument, began to laugh. Once a social worker phoned to complain. I had told him to save it for the drunks and parole jumpers. And I had laughed. I was sitting at my desk in my dingy downtown office and I was crying. I wouldn't understand why. And I couldn't stop. Then I remembered: "Bear! Bear! Bear!" I remembered how I had stood on a country road in a far more rural Staten Island, bleeding on my Boy Scout khaki, and had dialed our number in Brooklyn at night and had said, "Can I come home?" I wished that I could make a call now and, finding where I needed to go, simply go there. That's why you're crying, I told myself. Now you have to stop. I sniffed, and stopped, and started again, and then I slammed the side of my fist into the top of my cheap oak desk. I slammed and I slammed, and soon the knuckles of my little finger, having crawled into the path of my blows, began to throb. The pain made my crying stop. I sat at my desk and sucked my finger and wished that I could lift the phone and get permission—from whoever could give it—to go home.

I wiped my eyes and sniffed. On the back of a pink message slip, in Sally's handwriting, was this note: *We're going to do the poems. S.* A little in-house therapy, and a generous deed, I thought. I smiled with pleasure, because there was so much generosity among us. Under Sally's initial, I printed—I didn't trust my handwriting to assemble itself readably—THINK NOT. VAGARIES ARE BAD BUSINESS. I'LL GROW UP SOME, WHY DON'T I? LOVE. I underlined "love," and I didn't put my name down because, as I remembered doing it later, I had put the marker between my teeth and had shoved the message slip out of the way while already dialing. I had to dial three times before the main office at the Lenox School answered, and then I had to do a considerable bit of evasive maneuvering and speeded-up talk to convince them that I *was* Sam Zimmer's dad and that he should be released to me for a while.

On the way out, I put all the message slips on the receptionist's desk. She was a short, dark-haired, beautiful Colombian kid, too dumb for work, too exquisite for us not to look at each day. I begged her to distribute my answers to people who would do something with them, and she shrugged. It seemed a sufficient response, and I took off. A zonked-out blond man of about my age and build, who wore a raglan overcoat only slightly more wrinkled than my raincoat, raced to hold the door of my cab. His stare reminded me of the plucked glass eyes of Sam's dolls. He was running at the nose, and his skin was like orange peel left out to dry. He needed something, probably drugs, very badly. He tried to bow as I entered the cab. I heard him squeal with pain, and I saw that he wore no shoes, and that I had crushed a couple of toes. I pulled bills from my pocket and tried to hand them to him, but the wind took them at the open window, and they blew up into the air. Through the back window, I saw the blond man wrestling with a ferret-faced high school boy and an old black guy who was punching at them both.

"Merry Christmas," the driver said.

"No conversation, please," I answered, dropping a twenty into the tray of the Plexiglas wall between us. "No talking, please."

He shrugged. And when I was done being embarrassed at how presumptuous I'd been, I became envious of the broad-shouldered man with blue-black skin who had learned someplace not to take people like me too seriously.

He dropped me at 70th and Third, and I walked back to the gray stone buildings, finding the one I wanted by spotting its bright red wooden door. I suppose someone had timed me, or his teacher knew a good deal about his problems, if no specifics, unless Lillian had spoken with her. For the door opened out when I was half a block away. In the doorway, a slender woman with large blue eyes and a big smile in her square, fair Irish face was pulling the lapel of her navy blazer against the December winds off the East River. Sam leaned against her because she held him that way. Tall as he was, and slight as she was, her protectiveness, and her humor, and the wisdom which had caused her to stand there sheltering him, made him look small and very fragile.

Mrs. Noonan and I shook hands. She lifted a strap of Sam's small knapsack to adjust it on his quilted down-filled jacket. I kept a hand on his head, and he didn't squirm away.

"Sam's due for some time off," Mrs. Noonan said.

"A little overwork, old buddy?"

"Maybe a little confusion over domestic matters?"

I looked up from Sam's pale face and said, "There are changes going on in the composition of that cloth." As usual, grown-up code alerted the local kid, who pretended, by erasing all expression from his face, not to listen.

"Whole-cloth alterations?" she said, her face reddening, her wide mouth curving down in sadness or embarrassment.

"Yes," I said. "There are going to be rents in the material. We're all going to have to do a lot of invisible mending, if you know what I mean."

I could feel my head turn, cocking at what I'd said, while Mrs. Noonan lifted her chin and nodded. My damned and infantile eyes flooded again, and my throat was locked. I waited, and pushed with my fingers as if my larynx were jammed. I finally whispered, "Thank you." And still I didn't know why what I'd said had such a disturbing ring to it.

Sam pulled at my fingers which, I realized, were still on top of his thick brown hair. I said thank you again and shook her hand. I wanted to embrace her, to be embraced by her, despite her smallness. I wanted a bit of comfort to take away with me as I sought to comfort Sam. I settled for another shake of the hand, and then a turkey's-dart of the neck as I stepped closer, kissed her on the cheek, and guided Sam away with the hand at which he was tugging. "Thank you," I said.

We went eastward, Sam and I. I said, "You want to see if the guy's selling hot dogs near the river? You hungry?"

Sam shrugged. He said, "When're you coming back, Daddy? I mean, to the apartment. You know."

I knew. I slid my right hand into my raincoat pocket and I felt the knife I'd taken from Lillian. We walked past wallpaper stores and an art gallery that specialized in Haitian paintings, and of course the small pastry shops from which the odors of butter and coffee came like invitations to get fat. I looked down and sideways to see Sam's face. There was a blueness to his pallor, and purple smudges under his eyes. When Sam felt unhappy or sick, his face also got sick. He always looked the way he felt. He looked awful as his big feet in clumsy high work shoes dragged along 74th Street. Usually, he walked on the balls of his feet, long arms moving to bat an imaginary ball, gripping the imaginary bat with his big hands. I always thought of him as a dog, a puppy, say a Golden Retriever, with enormous paws into which he'd slowly grow. Now he looked like a sick kid who'd been indoors for a week, whose legs were heavy, whose hands hung tired at his sides. I tried to hold his hand. It was limp and hot, as if he had a fever. I was pretty sure he didn't. What he had was me and Lil—whom he also didn't have.

We made it across the FDR drive, and we stood at the iron fence above the river, after a while, each of us holding onto the metal. The man who sold the hot dogs wasn't there. I said, "We can go to McDonald's later, if you want. Or—you want to go to a restaurant? Geez. God. I was remembering. When I was a kid, there was a store in town, I forget where—maybe in the Thirties? I don't remember. It had this restaurant called Charleston Gardens where my mother would take me. It was like this old Southern garden, except of course it was inside. But it felt like it was outside, the walls were painted with green vines and everything. She took me there on Saturdays once in a while when she went shopping. And we'd eat these cream cheese on date-nut bread sandwiches, like the ones they serve in Chock Full-o'-Nuts. Would you like to go *there?* Maybe I'm wrong, I don't remember. I remember something about this store, and a restaurant. Maybe Charleston Gardens was someplace else, though. This one, they always gave you balloons. Everybody was so—relaxed. This was not so long after the war. World War II. You want to hear any more about this, Sam?"

He was looking through the bars at the bright river, and at barges slowly moving in it, pushed and pulled by feisty wide tugs. Below us, traffic roared on the East River Drive. We were too far from the river, really. For example, we were too far from the river for me to rear back and wind up and throw the knife into it and see it sink away.

Sam was talking about Mrs. Noonan, whom I'd called delightful. He said, "I wish—I know I'm not supposed to tell you that you make me feel embarrassed."

"No, sweetheart, please. Tell me."

"I wish you wouldn't kiss her!"

"Is that it?"

"Do you have to?"

"Nope. I'll stop now. I'll never kiss her again. Okay?"

"Thanks, Dad. I hope I didn't embarrass you."

"You didn't, Sam. I'm not breakable. You don't have to apologize so much. You don't have to worry so much."

"I didn't want you to get mad at me."

"Sam! Sweetheart, I wouldn't get mad at you for that."

"You know, and go away again."

Thank you, Lord. Thank you, Historical Force. Thank you, God of Abraham and Issac. Zimmer: thank you too. My especial thanks to whoever and whatever and whenever and why. For this. For having to decide whether you *do* take your kid out and have him close his eyes and lie against you in your arms at the sacrifice stone. While you lift the knife up and prepare to hand him over, washed in his own blood, burned at your altar, to the object of the sacrifice. For what should this kid be opened up and bled? And toward what end? For my happiness? Lil's? For the honesty we say we seek in our lives? I'm asking, goddammit! Do we separate, divorce, so as to find our happy endings? To which presumably we're entitled since we're living at the end of the twentieth century? I'm asking: is Sam the kid we kill so our lives take on the desired tone of what we call fulfillment? Or is it in the name of honesty that we divorce and split the kid into parts? Because we'd make him unhappy if we lived together without a perfect well-oiled love? This is what the shrinks say. Of course, they're all divorced. And their kids cut things open with pocket knives.

I looked surreptitiously at my watch. Sam and I were standing side by side at the fence, looking across the water at, probably, Astoria, Queens, where, presumably, at that very moment, men and women were leaving each other to find honest and wholly formed happiness while being fair to their children. Downtown, a woman named

Rhona whom I once had deserted and who last night had been my good friend, at 42nd Street was, as I recalled, helping to prepare a special exhibition of the manuscripts of Wilkie Collins. She was going to meet me for drinks and then dinner and a late ride home and wooden stairs and funny bed and pure, improbable romance.

"You know, and go away again." That was what Sam had said. I actually trembled—with rage? tenderness? I couldn't tell. But I shook, as if I too had a fever, as if a hand around my bones were causing them to move. I gripped the knife in my raincoat pocket, and I thought of that old scared worshipful Jew, Abraham, crazy with obedience and eager to make sacrament with the blood of his baby. He was only obeying orders, he would later explain to Issac. And by the time he reached high school, Isaac would be seeing an analyst three times a week, Rhona.

"No," I said to Sam, still wishing that I could reach the river with a strong throw. I left the knife in my pocket. I squatted down and finally—there are so few occasions for kneeling, so few objects or people worth kneeling to—I got onto the knees of my rumpled slacks and, keeping my arms before me, but not on his shoulders, because I wanted this to be about Sam and not my own emotions, I said, "No. I won't."

He looked at me and all of a sudden his face had stilled. "Okay," he said. "Was there anything else?"

"Excuse me?"

"Was there anything else we wanted to talk about?"

"Oh. No, Sam. That probably does it."

"Because could I get back to school if there wasn't?"

"Oh."

"You know," he said.

"Well, what the hell," I answered.

"Shame on you, Daddy."

"I apologize. I was excited. I've made a unilateral decision."

He nodded as if he understood. He looked at the Timex on his wrist. "Maybe you'll get used to it," he said. He fell onto my shoulder awkwardly and laid his face against my face for kisses. "Thanks for the—what was this, Daddy?"

"I don't know," I told him as I climbed up by pulling on the fenceposts, brushed off my trousers and raincoat, eyed a battered phone booth nearby—"Can I come home?"—and started, with Sam a pace ahead of me, to walk him back to school. I said, "It was an early recess or something. I don't know. Mrs. Noonan can name it for you. She must have seen a hundred like it. It was a sabbatical, maybe."

"Yeah," he said, not listening. We went past pictures of the Tonton Macoute in their reflecting sunglasses, and past pastry made like the pastry doubtless eaten by the Andreoscus long ago, and by sad Mrs. Glinsky. We passed the wallpaper store, and Sam said, "What would you mean by 'inevitable,' Dad?"

"Inevitable? Uhm. Something that has to finally happen I guess. Why?"

"That's what Mom called it."

"Called what?"

"When you moved back in."

"She did?" This is how I was raised, in the gene pool of a people who invented Freud, that voice of inner imagination, not mere fleshly realities—and this is what I have learned: pleasure demands payment, innocence guilt; you're happy because someone's suffering made this moment possible. It is an interestingly Christian point of view, it seems to me. And it explains, perhaps, why just as Sam spoke to me I thought of Rhona at the Loeb, at NYU, taking on the poet and his claque.

"She said it wouldn't be easy."

"No," I said, seeing Rhona's eyeliner and her arms across her chest, as Sam and I approached the school.

When I had seen him inside, I walked, my little earworm—*Rhona Glinsky, puddin' and pie*—chiming in my head to the slow rhythm of my long, banging leathersoled shoes on the spit-slick, shit-dappled sidewalk. *Rhona Glinsky, puddin' and pie*, and soon Lillian would emerge from her taxi at the Lenox School to pick up Sam and ride with him to the West Side where, in our—their?—apartment, the lights would go on, the music would go on, the ritual would go on of Lillian sipping her first Scotch and shuddering while Sam watched cartoons full of exploding ducks and defeated coyotes on TV in what had been our bedroom. Past the Frick Museum, then, and past—what else?—Temple Emanuel, and then St. Patrick's and the corner, then, of 49th and Fifth, where latterly I had been only mildly suicidal and somewhat dazed, and then to 42nd, for the corner saturated with smells—chestnuts, hot dogs, knishes, the bright watered yellow mustard for soft pretzels, the armpits of bums, the loins of bag ladies, the breathings and coughings and hawkings of the corner where the city shifted from east to west and from possibility to despair. The air seemed grayer at the corner across from the library, and so did the people. Scholars, I knew, were sharing Bryant Park, behind the library, with needlefreaks and winos, and inside there were people doing good research, and people writing prose that might change someone's life, and people expressing their love of the word by sitting at the tables of golden oak in the library's parchment-colored light and touching pages with their fingertips. But it looked to me, that fast-fading afternoon, like a palace on whose steps at least betrayal would take place.

I changed directions and walked over to the Record Hunter. I stared at album jackets and their pictures of men holding flutes, women in opera costumes, at people beyond the albums searching in bins. I also saw myself, disheveled in a dead shirt and loosened tie, my suit jacket askew beneath the wrinkled heavy raincoat, my eyes within my glasses hidden by reflections—an essentially faceless man, his jaws clenched to keep himself at bay, who stared but not with longing, who waited but not with ease. I went back to the corner and crossed Fifth Avenue, then crossed 42nd Street, and then went to wait at the right-hand lion, as we'd arranged. And there was a moment, among the tides of people climbing up and climbing down, pausing to light cigarettes or eat sandwiches or simply to look down from the palace of language and see what had once been the great new avenue of the world, when no one climbed or descended, when no one paused, when for only an instant the steps were bare, were nothing but themselves—geometries of granite that in the final burnt-orange light threw mineral dazzles up among the shadows, and a terrible sense of infinitely extended vistas, as if the steps went on forever, so that no rational sense of where things ended and where they began was available to me. I put my forehead on the lion's rough pedestal stone and closed my eyes to make the image disappear. It did, and all I had to do then was button my coat and slick back my hair with my palms and, like a kid on a date, wait for Rhona, my old girl.

She descended in her long blue coat and high boots,

her coat open, the slit in her skirt showing me her thigh —had she intended that?—and the confident stride of someone who knew the size of step it took to get safely down. She didn't smile at first, and then she did, and then she stopped. By the time she'd reached me, as I worked at grinning a welcome to her, she was working her lips. She looked closer, stopped a few steps above me and peered in.

"Oh, Zimmer," she said. "No."

"I went over to see Sam. Hi. Actually, I went over to see everybody. I saw Lil, and she took me over to see the bears and the other creatures. Sam cut the hell out of them."

"What kind of creatures, Zimmer. Slow down for me."

"Toys?"

"All right. Toys. In his school?"

"His room. All his baby toys. He killed the poor little bastards with this knife I gave to him. I gave it to him— I don't remember. Yesterday? The day before? I gave it to him. You know, for a present."

"And he slashed his room up? And your wife was upset."

"Rhona, she was upset, I was upset, I went over and saw Sam and he was upset, his goddam schoolteacher was upset."

"Naturally," she said.

"Naturally. Naturally, he asked me—" But she had taken my hand in hers—large, cold, strong hands—and she was holding it, looking at my face, waiting for me. I said, "He asked me if I was coming home."

"And you didn't say you'd be there on alternate Saturdays and each and every Thanksgiving?"

"I didn't say that, Rhona."

"Zimmer, I don't know how much this means, but I

couldn't feel better about you than I do. You understand? You're a nice man."

"You're—"

"Yes, I am," she said, still holding my hand in both of
hers. "I am. But what I am not, I want you to remember,
is the *rite de passage* lady they give to Jewish boys, if
you'll pardon the expression, for the big moment of their
choice. You'll remember the routine? God sends down
an angel in the shape of an inflated prophylactic, and he
gives you your alternatives: You get the thirty-five-year-
old former piece of ass when you're eighteen, and she
breaks you in. Or you get the neurotic girl with the big
jugs and heavy thighs and growling belly with whom you
spend a short, insane, and ferociously sexy time and
then go on to become a grown-up. *Or*, you meet her
when you're middle-aged and you live together in a
strange place doing exotic activities and *potentially*, this
isn't covered by the maintenance contract, possibly living happily ever after, except she busts it into pieces by
revealing that she's just as crazy now as she ever was,
and so are you. But I don't want to *do* that anymore
anyway, you know? I want to roll around in the sack with
you a while, or a while longer, or a *long* while. *I* don't
know. But I don't want to be anybody's conveyance to
anyplace. Does that make sense? I don't want to be a
cab."

I cleared my throat and said, "I don't know if you're
doing this because you're brilliant and prescient and
kind."

"I'm not brilliant," she said, "just competent and muscular."

"And beautiful and prescient and kind."

"And not a mode of transportation, right?"

I kissed the hands that held my hand. I lifted them to

my face and rubbed them at my mouth and kissed them. She took her hands away. She was crying, and somehow I was relieved to see that I wasn't the only one to have lost control.

I said, "Boy, it would have been so terrific, Rhona."

She said, "Well, you never know, Zimmer."

She took her hands back, she walked past me, down the rest of the steps. I stayed at the lion so that I wouldn't see her wave, as I suspected she might, with a careless assumption that I would be watching her. Then I wanted to see if she did wave, and I jumped down a couple of steps to look at her, but she was around the corner, or screened by pedestrians, and I couldn't see her. I walked to the corner and stood for perhaps a minute. Perhaps I stood longer, obstructing tired strangers and waiting, really, for nothing. It seemed to me that everything in my past—the vigor of my parents, the innocent slow summers of my youth, my son's fragile babyhood, the strength I had admired in my wife—was lost to me with Rhona's disappearance into the city in which she and I had lived, for eighteen years, like people in uncontiguous neighboring countries, she on her island and I on mine. *Rhona Glinsky, puddin' and pie*, my brain was singing to me as I walked uptown and west, not getting lost, *kissed my ear and made me cry.*

It was, I suppose, about two miles from the main branch library to where I—or maybe only they—lived. Add those long filthy streets'-worth of walking to what I'd walked, from the Lenox School to 42nd and Fifth, and you'd expect a man to get some thinking done: I thought nothing. I listened to my brain sing *puddin' and pie*, and I looked at the colors of skin and colors of cloth and lack of familiar expression on everyone I passed, and I looked at windows and doorknobs and various makes of car, I watched the colors of neon light that went on, and the shades of blue available in ice-cold fluorescence, and, hearing *kissed my ear and made me cry*, and hating it, and yet feeling relieved not to hear the dirge of Celan for everyone he loved, *your golden hair Margarete*, I more or less went home.

In the lobby, I nodded at the security man and he studied me a while before he acknowledged, with a nod, that he finally recalled the guy who lived with Mrs. Zimmer. The elevator man looked at me, told me my floor, and forgot I was there until the car stopped. At our characterless door, I thought to knock, or ring the bell. I was sweating from the walk, I noticed, my knees were shaking, as when I'd married Lillian, as when I had listened to her tell me that she wanted a divorce, as when I'd stood with Sam that afternoon. The sweat continued to run, and I felt clammy, unwashed. And I thought not to knock or ring the bell.

For what if she called out, "Who is it?"

And what if I answered, "Me"?

And what if she said, "I heard that one before, you creep"?

And what if she were right?

No. I took my key case out and dropped it. While I picked it up, I grew dizzy, and I went back down to one knee, just resting. "Just resting," I said, staring at the composition of the floor, when I heard the door across the hall open on its safety-chain. "Just resting," I said to the old man who lived across from us in terror that blacks were coming to drool and pee on his collection of first-day covers. His door clicked closed.

I got hold of the doorknob and pulled myself up. It took me a while in the dim light of the hall, with my fingers now shaking as well as my knees—not shaking anymore, really, just offering little tremors of the bones in their sockets—but I did get the key out, and I did guide it into the lock, and I did hope so earnestly that Lillian was careless with her safety, indigenous Huns and Vandals to the contrary notwithstanding, and had left the deadbolt unlocked and the safety chain off. I wanted to get in on my own. I wanted to get in.

Having turned the key and pushed at the door, I took the key from the lock and dropped the keycase into my raincoat pocket, where it rested on lint, scrap paper, and an Indian-given Hoffritz Swiss Army knife. I leaned at the door and heard them shouting. They sounded like kids warming up in the infield—"Hey babe! Come on, kid! Whip it in, babe! *Atta* pickup!" Once I was in our tiny foyer, my hands in my raincoat pockets, my shoulders squared as if I were about to be beaten or scorned, I saw that they were playing ball. Lillian had cleared the living room by pushing at chairs and sofas, kicking heaps of newspapers and tented paperback books, by shoving bridge-lamps and pulling at extension cords. The room blazed with clustered lamps, as if they were playing night baseball and the stadium lights were on. Lillian stood at the far end of the long room, wearing jogging shorts and no socks or shoes, her Property of New York Yankees gray tee-shirt, and her official Yankees hat. She had her mitt on, and was throwing grounders along the W & J Sloane carpeting to Sam. Rhona, listen to this: in a similar tee-shirt, but in dungarees and canoe moccasins, and wearing no hat, his fine dark hair naked to my vision and gleaming in the accumulated light, Sam, my son and Lillian's, was gobbling up the bunts and solid hits. Lillian had switched to her Phil Rizzuto radio-narration, and she was describing their game as Sam threw the ball back to her with the easy lope of Graig Nettles, the Yankees' brilliant middle-aged third baseman. In Scooter

Rizzuto's voice, Lillian called, "Holy Cow! It's a *sharp*ly hit smash along the line! Nettles can't get *that* one! He *did!* Holy *Cow!* Can that guy *play*, or *what?*"

Sam glided with confidence as the ball rolled, he fumbled it, recovered it, plucked it from his big glove, and gently threw it to Lillian, who leaned forward and down, as if from an imaginary first base, to trap the ball while praising herself in the Scooter's voice, "And a *super* catch by the rookie at first!"

Sam still was pale, and his eyes still looked unrested. Each time he caught the ball, his lower jaw dropped. I remembered feeding him oatmeal and watching that jaw. He moved, despite his eyes, as if he were at home in his body and maybe even the apartment, their apartment, our apartment, our apartment. Lillian had been thinking, as usual, and Lillian was doing something intelligent and purposeful, as usual, and Lillian's hair, heaped under her Yankees hat, was shaking down, and her long thin neck looked strong to me, her bare arms muscled, her bare legs long and hard. The shirt was tight on her and I looked at her breasts. I expected to want to do something about them and about her calves and thighs. I didn't, though. I wanted to be safe with her and with Sam in our home. I wanted not to think about Rhona, and I wanted to help Lillian do something for Sam. I wondered if, in her eyes, that would mean my moving out again.

"He's *out!*" she shouted in the Scooter's voice, "did you see that guy *throw?*" She stood still, then, and took her hat off, wiped at her forehead with her forearm, as if she were a jock who wore a sweatband on her wrist for the purpose, and as her hair tumbled, she blew up along her face from her lower lip, crossing her eyes and making Sam laugh.

"I'll get you a Coke," he said. "I'll get us both Cokes."

"Milk," she said.

"Coke," he said. "A treat."

"The treat was the game," she answered. "The milk is an order. You could, of course, go thirsty."

Sam answered with disgust and resignation, "Okay. Milk."

He walked across the living room and around the corner into the kitchen. He didn't see me. Lil did. As he went around, she looked at me and set herself. I thought her mouth wanted to smile, but I didn't want to make the mistake of assuming that. Her chin lifted. From across the room, and in spite of our heights, I felt shorter than she. I shook the metal in my raincoat pocket and waited.

She put her lips together the way women do after they've applied lipstick. Her lips were bare, like much of the rest of her. Then she opened her mouth. She said, "Sam, do you know where Daddy keeps his fielder's mitt?"

He said, "Hall closet. I think the hall closet. Why?"

He came around the corner carrying a speckled blue metal mug of milk. He stopped when he saw me, and then he slowly walked to Lillian. He turned to face me. Seeing the resemblance between their faces, and seeing my face in his, I grew confused and saw my face in Lillian's too. We were all standing in the bright living room, sweaty and looking alike and waiting.

Lil said, "Where did you say his mitt was?" She continued to look across the room at me.

Sam did too. He shrugged derisively, as Lil might, or as I might too. "I told you," he said.

Looking at me, she said, "What?"

I went to the hall closet, which was on the way into our bedroom, near where Sam had been playing third.

276

On the floor, near the front, among unused shoe trees and the galoshes we all refused to wear, was my boyhood fielder's mitt, cracked and dry and small-looking, folded. "It needs breaking in," I said. "It needs oil, and you tie it around a baseball with string for a while," I said.

In my flapping raincoat and in my apartment and on the other side of the room from those alleged by history and law and circumstance to be my wife and child, I stood with my hand in an ill-shaped baseball glove and waited. Sam, his mitt on the floor, holding a tin cup of milk, leaned back against Lillian's legs and watched me. Suddenly, Lillian chucked the ball underhand across the room at me. I caught it. I pounded it at the pocket of my glove a couple of times and tossed it back. Without moving Sam out of the way, she caught it and threw it back across the living room to me, and I caught it with both hands. They watched to see what I would do. I kept it in my glove a while. I stood and let them see me: the old ram, fastened in place. When no one spoke, I lobbed the baseball back to Lillian. But Sam stuck out his bare paw and caught it. There was no expression on his face. He'd spilled some milk on his chin, so he wiped at his face with his wrist the way Lillian had wiped at her brow. There I was, Rhona. Jewboy of the baseball diamond in my dirt-stiffened raincoat and filthy suit, glasses slipping on my nose, an unconditioned fielder's mitt on my hand, I stood and waited. So did they. Then Sam threw the ball back pretty hard. He didn't spill a drop, his eyes became almost merry, and I caught his peg. Lillian watched me. She took her Yankees hat off and then jammed it back on, low over her forehead. She tugged at the bill and watched.

"Not bad," she said, not in the Scooter's voice.

Afterword

1.

I called this novel *The Outlaw Jew* when I first wrote it, probably in late 1982. It was a scrawny little Semite, mostly about the early days of Zimmer, with no Lefty, minimal Lil, not much Rhona, and lots of riffs on the more or less autobiographical stuff—the Lutheran college anti-Semitism, the insane life at American Synopsis (which corporately dithers on under its actual name) and the tension for me in being an Official Jew, someone the cannibals might decide to intern at a *lager* in Idaho, who simultaneously was the product of Christmas eves and Christmas trees and long love with a blonde who was anything but Jewish (as well as anything but what the fictive mother-in-law in this novel wished her to be).

I think I tried hard to avoid writing about these matters with any depth. For I wanted to use them for a book while avoiding any commitment to confronting them with much seriousness: a steady, deep look meant too much pain. So I compromised with my fears. When you do that, you write a lousy book, and that's what I produced. And that's what my editor at Farrar, Straus and Giroux told me. Patricia Strachan was, though young, legendary among serious writers. She read brilliantly, and she worked herself to exhaustion for the writers to whom she was committed, and for the publisher she always called Mister Giroux. Her editing was rarely wrong, and when she described the manuscript as unpublishable, she was right, and I knew it.

I went back to the manuscript, and I went into its material. I saw that I was writing about two forces at once. There was my grandfather, Sam Buschlowitz, whose name was shortened on these shores by his children, who feared persecution. He remembered the cossacks who rode through Russian streets, scything down Jews with their swords. He remembered how, when he was a boy, he tried to take refuge in a synagogue during a cossack raid; the frightened rabbi refused to open its doors to admit him. He never forgave the rabbi, or any rabbi. He was the keeper of the pistol, that mild, small man, for his Anarchist cell in Minsk. He came to America and hated it here, and then went home. When he returned with Dorothy, my grandmother, he raised my father and uncle and aunts without marrying her. He forbade a bar mitzvah for my father or Jack, his younger brother. While Sam was at work, Dorothy sneaked a rabbi into the apartment to tutor my father. Sam was a master carpenter in Russia, but in America pushed a wheelbarrow filled with cement for bricklayers, and on the day of the furtive bar mitzvah lesson, he came home with a sore back. The back was sore, but it was also up: spitting, he chased the rabbi out. Sam's skepticism and anger had come directly to me and through the doubts of my parents, and through my mother's revulsion against the faith of her poverty-crushed, uneducated mother and father. Education, as is so often the case with first-generation parents, was the key for their children, and doubt was the tonic chord.

And yet my parents knew, as I knew, what it was to be reviled for a Jew. I knew to take the Holocaust personally, not only because I felt that the deaths of strangers did diminish me, and not only because a number of my Russian and Austrian relatives were killed because they were Jews. I knew because the hatred was available here, and during my boyhood and young manhood (and, alas, during this my middle age).

And I was a man who was not unconscious of the desirability of belief. However, the belief I saw, in much modern Judaism, as in much modern Christianity, was about death. One prayed to a dead god, or one prayed to six million dead, I thought, and I wished to do neither. And focusing only on the sacred self, in those days and these, led one to another religion: the cult of self-fulfillment. I watched families torn up by the need of one or another parent to fulfill him- or herself. I had witnessed this slow-motion convulsion in my parents' home, and in the homes of friends and colleagues, and I suspected my own every move: writers are always selfish; that is how the work gets done.

Yet what I wanted more than the making of world-class art was the happiness of my wife and children.

Liar! I wanted to write great books, and the family would have to fend for themselves.

Not so! You can write *and* put others before yourself.

Oh, really? Try it.

And so the unspoken dialogue went. And so the fictive Sam, a boy with equal parts of my sons Nick and Ben, was tied to the altar like Isaac, soon to be sacrificed, perhaps. And that was why Zimmer carried a knife in his raincoat pocket. He, like Abraham, was going, perhaps, to kill his son to please his god. In the case of Zimmer, the god was his need for what he might bleat about as happiness. It was during this time—as I rewrote my *Jew* while confronting myself and my history—that I reread in Reynolds Price's *Things Themselves* of 1972 the meditation "Four Abrahams, Four Isaacs by Rembrandt." I had waited almost a dozen years to contend with the writer who had been my older brother in fiction, my long-distance teacher, my literary hero; I wanted to rescue him, and to rescue me, and to rescue mine, from

Reynolds's stunning, bleak last line which says that, in spite of the angel's announcement that God would not seek the life of his child, he might set down his knife, "The man is going to kill the boy."

So: a novel of tensions—the Jew who wasn't much of a Jew but who was one nevertheless, and the husband and father who was maybe seduced away by his love for his own flabby heart. Rhona was the name of a girl on my block in Flatbush in the late '40s and early '50s whom I adored; she was leggy and long-armed, and a better athlete than I, rosy with health and always merry. Rhona was modeled, physically, on a woman at Muhlenberg after whom I secretly lusted for several years. Intellectually, she was the community of Jewish intellectuals I both feared and admired, disliked and was drawn to. Nothing in this novel, I have come to think, was not born of contesting forces.

Pat Strachan liked the new *Outlaw Jew*, and Farrar, Straus would issue it. I was once again about to publish a novel—to go naked in public, Zimmer might have said.

2.

I received and spent my advance, which was not terribly large, but which Judy and I, with two young sons, very much needed. Pat Strachan had written the catalogue copy, and I was looking forward, though without much joy, to the novel's publication.

My apprehension was in part the usual: the writer's fear that he has failed to serve his characters, that he hasn't found the structure or honed the language or mastered the material. In part, too, I was worried because the title was brash, the material touchy—you are not supposed to trifle with the Holocaust—and I was afraid that my book would be received as trifling, or as failing to respond with the few acceptable notes a writer is allowed to sound (without a public flaying) when confronted with the hideous grief and God-damning pain and boundless evil of the war against the Jews. I had in mind the treatment accorded my friend Leslie Epstein, whose fiction is among the smartest and most moving work I know, and whose 1979 novel *King of the Jews* ranks with André Schwarz-Bart's *The Last of the Just*; they are the two finest novels of the Holocaust—which Leslie Epstein had been accused of trivializing, I believe, because he understood and employed irony. One either sings with the chorus or shuts up. I could and would do neither. But I knew that I might well take a beating.

I knew too that I had written a love story. I knew that I had written a story about marriage and about a man who attempts to revisit, to defeat, his past. Such contentions with history are the concerns of writers, and surely of this writer; and I liked the idea of wrestling with the domestic and the historically immense, and both at once.

I write facing only the keyboard and monitor (or sometimes the inky legal pad). On the wall behind my desk, I keep no pictures and I see no window. I want my vision to concern only what the characters see, or the context in which they are seen. But I broke my custom while I re-imagined, then rewrote this novel. I typed out Michael Hamburger's translation of the Paul Celan "Death Fugue" —

> Black milk of daybreak we drink it at
>   sundown
> we drink it at noon in the morning we drink
>   it at night

we drink and we drink it
we dig a grave in the breezes there one lies
    unconfined
A man lives in the house he plays with the
    serpents he writes
he writes when dusk falls to Germany your
    golden hair Margarete
he writes it and steps out of doors and the
    stars are flashing he whistles his pack out
he whistles his Jews out in earth has them dig
    for a grave

—so that I would see the words of the Romanian whose parents were killed in a camp and who himself survived a camp only, like so many survivors, to later commit suicide. I asked the poem to help me stay honest about the dreadful background of my novel. And I found myself, months into the writing, fastening Celan's poetry to the consciousness of my protagonist, then weaving it into the story itself.

Despite my admiration for Celan's work, and my responsiveness to his pain and despair, the novel contains a kind of cruel peasant's joke about a man who survived the Holocaust. It inveighs against a kind of worship of death which sanctimony can engender—or so I see it, and so, in so many words, I said.

Mr. Roger Straus, who has been a major publisher of major authors far longer than I have been a writer, had been very gracious to me when Farrar, Straus was publishing the 1979 novel *Rounds*. Although I saw or heard little from him after 1979 (FS&G also published my 1983 novel, *Take This Man*) what exchanges we had were cordial, and I felt, and said aloud that I felt, honored to be published by his house. In late 1982 or early 1983,

I was telephoned by my agent, Elaine Markson, who told me that Roger Straus had finally read *The Outlaw Jew* and wanted Pat Strachan to stop its publication. The book, he said, would somehow be bad for the Jews — whether because it spoke differently about the Holocaust or for other reasons, I never knew. You should not publish a book with someone who disapproves of it. Pat had therefore called Elaine, and Elaine arranged at once with David Godine, the president and editorial director of David Godine, Publisher, of Boston, for his house to take over the book. Godine was to pay off Farrar, Straus's advance in installments, as I recall, and *The Outlaw Jew* would no longer be the novel's name. At its new publisher's request, I changed the title; I believe, now, that the original title was my idea of *me* as much as of the novel, and to call it *Invisible Mending* seemed to properly address the wounds with which the novel was concerned.

Bill Goodman was my new editor, and we used Pat Strachan's careful, insightful editing as our guide in preparing the manuscript. The book duly appeared, a little late, the source of some considerable concern to its author and, perhaps, its publisher — though David Godine was nothing less than hospitable and encouraging.

The Jewish Book Council gave its William and Janice Epstein National Jewish Book Award in Fiction to *Invisible Mending*. On a hot and humid early June night in Manhattan, in the Judaica department of the New York Public Library, down in the basement, far from the lions on the steps, among the thousands and thousands of yellow, brittle index cards fingered by generations of scholars, in distinguished company, I sweated through a shirt and then a suit, and not only because of the heat. I was certain that at any moment I would be denounced as a spy for wrongful thinking, as a traitor, insufficiently Jewish, unreligious, the child and then father with presents under a Christmas tree! But I was treated with cordial grace, and at last I stood on the platform.

I knew at once that I was a character in a curious novel I inhabited, a book improbably plotted by its clumsy writer, architected with an affection for coincidence that canny readers tend to reject. For there, in the first row of the audience, directly before me, sat Roger Straus. I am afraid that I assumed a pious expression, a kind of nauseous self-renunciation, in an effort to clear any hint of victory from my face—although, I have to confess, I wanted to crow and flap my arms. There were the tensions that for me are this novel's emblems. It was my principle, then as now, that just as one should never believe the praises or calumnies in reviews of one's books, one ought to read no sign of diminution when not given awards, nor assume that he matters more when awards come his way. So I let the tensions vie within my belly and my brain, as they do today, and I tried then— as I do today—to speak without rancor. Publishers publish as best they can, and writers do their best to write.

And, happily for me, thanks to the SMU Press, Zimmer sallies forth again, unwilling, at last, to sacrifice his child on the altar of self. Lil, a smart woman and a pretty fair umpire, sees the world as it is, and I continue to hope that she is describing Zimmer, as well as our life, and maybe even the novel that he is condemned to inhabit—as you are yours, as I am mine—when she looks him in the eye and makes her call: "Not bad."

Sherburne, New York
October 28, 1996

About the Author

Frederick Busch is Fairchild Professor of Literature at Colgate University, where he teaches fiction and creative writing and conducts the Living Writers course. In 1991 he received the PEN/Malamud Award for short fiction. A well-known critic and reviewer, he is the author of twenty books, eighteen of them fiction —  most recently a novel, *Girls,* published by Harmony Books. He has been acting director of the Writers' Workshop at the University of Iowa and has held Woodrow Wilson, National Endowment for the Arts, James Merrill, and Guggenheim Fellowships. He lives with his wife, Judy, in Sherburne, New York, in a rambling nineteenth-century farmhouse. The Busches have two grown sons.

John Hubbard